CRAWFIELD FOOTBALL CLUB

The Underdog

BOOK ONE

KATE LAUREN

First paperback edition April 2024

This book contains coarse language, erotic scenes, and mature subject matter. It is intended for those who are 18+.

Cover Illustration by Jessica Lynn Draws www.jessicalynndraws.com

Editing by Cassidy Hudspeth

www.cassidyhudspetheditingandproofreading.com

Interior Formatting by Grace Elena

Graceelenaauthor.com

ISBN 979-8-8611-3824-6

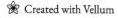 Created with Vellum

The Lineup

CRAWFIELD FC

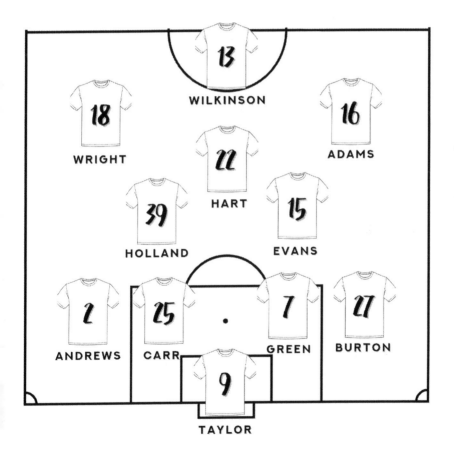

13 WILKINSON

18 WRIGHT

16 ADAMS

22 HART

39 HOLLAND

15 EVANS

2 ANDREWS

25 CARR

7 GREEN

27 BURTON

9 TAYLOR

HEAD COACH: WARREN PARK
ASSISTANT COACH: ALFIE LEWIS

The Warm-Up PLAYLIST

TUBTHUMBING	**CHUMBAWAMBA**
LONDON BOY	**TAYLOR SWIFT**
TRULY MADLY DEEPLY	**ONE DIRECTION**
FRIDAY I'M IN LOVE	**THE CURE**
SHOULD I STAY OR SHOULD I GO	**THE CLASH**
GOLDEN	**HARRY STYLES**
IF I COULD FLY	**ONE DIRECTION**
BREATHLESS	**THE CORRS**
KING OF MY HEART	**TAYLOR SWIFT**
ROCK DJ	**ROBBIE WILLIAMS**
ONE WAY OR ANOTHER	**BLONDIE**
(I CAN'T GET NO) SATISFACTION	**THE ROLLING STONES**
BALLROOM BLITZ	**SWEET**
HUNGRY LIKE THE WOLF	**DURAN DURAN**
LONDON CALLING	**THE CLASH**
DO I WANNA KNOW?	**ARCTIC MONKEYS**

This book is dedicated to the inner child that this story helped to heal.
You can create your own family.
Remember that.

#One

WARREN

FIVE YEARS AGO

"WARREN, GET STUCK IN THERE!" *My teammate shouts as the sweat drips down my forehead, and my chest rises as quickly as it falls. I turn my head swiftly in the direction of his voice, ridden with urgency as he points across the field.*

"Warren!" he yells again, causing me to divert my attention to where it should've been all along—the ball headed in my direction.

It's midway through the season, and the pressure intensifies with every game that passes. Tonight's game is the culmination of years of relentless training and dedication. It's not just about beating the best team in the league; it's about being the best player in it.

It's always been about that.

I laser in on the ball, locking myself into the game the way I've done so many times before. As I rush towards the player in front of me, I'm reminded that it's not just my team I'm playing for. It's my shot at proving that I deserve to be competing at the highest level. Playing amongst, against, and becoming one of the greats.

It only takes me a moment to gain possession of the ball, though the brunt of my opponent's elbow collides with my shoulder as he grazes my chin.

He's simple to think that I'd give it up that easily. It would take a bulldozer to knock me over right now. I push back against his frame in an attempt to break away.

"Give it up, Park." He spits. "You're not the only one they're watching tonight."

His words ignite a flame inside of me, but I suppress the urge to fire back as I give him a shove to create space.

I know I'm not the only one they're watching tonight, but I intend to be the only one that they remember.

I huff out in frustration, given that he's filled the gap and managed to kick the ball out of play. I turn to face him as the ref makes the call in our favor.

"You're not as good as you think you are, mate." I shrug as I push past him. "Remember that."

Robby Clarke is no different than most guys in the league. I'm certain he only got into the sport for the reputation that comes with it, though I can't judge too much. The life of a footballer in England is the life of the rich and famous. You're treated like a king because football is royalty.

"Fuck off, Park. That's not what your mum said when I was in bed with her last night," he snaps in response, trailing me up the sidelines.

His words hardly phase me, a fact that I know will surely ruin his night. Saying you've slept with someone's Mum is universally the laziest attempt at an insult one could muster up. Although, I'm not sure what else I expected from Clarke. I'm surprised he was even able to get his head out from under his arse long enough to think of a remotely entertaining response.

"She always did have a thing for guys with micro dicks," I mutter under my breath, loud enough so that he can still hear. (Thankfully, that trait wasn't hereditary.)

As I throw the ball back into play, I don't have to look back at Clarke to know he won't say anything else for a while.

"Pick it up, boys!" Coach yells from the sidelines, indicating that we're about to begin three minutes of extra time. We're drawing nil,

thanks to the beauty of a play I set up in the second half of the match after Higgins gave away an easy goal thanks to an open net. But I know that's not enough. As the seconds tick by, I realize there's one thing that will set me apart from everyone else: being the reason we win tonight's game.

A surge of adrenaline rushes through me as I dart across the pitch, inserting my way into the gameplay as I see my shot.

"Pass the ball," I cry out as my teammate continues to dribble towards the net. "Pass it!" I plead even louder until he finally lifts his head, wasting no time in making the seamless pass over to my direction.

The ball naturally fits into the curve of my cleat as if it's always belonged there. I'm confident I've never had such a clear shot on target in my life. My heart thumps against my chest as it all comes down to one final shot.

And it's not just the shot on net.

It's the shot I've dreamt about since I was three years old, after watching my first football match.

It's the shot at making my dreams a reality and proving that the sport that has encapsulated decades of my life has all been for something.

"Shoot it!"

The crowd hushes in anticipation as I gear up to make the shot, feeling the weight of my future on my shoulders.

I set my eyes on the net, the goalkeeper bracing himself from side to side. I narrow in on my target for a final time before glancing back down at the ball and striking it with all my strength.

A hush falls over the stadium as thousands of eyes follow the ball in anticipation. I hold my breath as it soars toward the net, watching it graze past the keeper's outstretched arms and into the upper right corner. It takes less than a split second for the crowd to erupt into deafening roars, my teammates sprinting towards me in delight—but none of it happens fast enough. As I let out a shaky breath, I buckle to the ground as the weight of my right leg gives way, a sudden unbearable pain searing through my body.

"*Fuck,*" *I groan, but I can barely hear myself speak. My voice is overshadowed by the popping of my knee that replays on a loop in my mind, drowning out the cheers of the crowd.*

"*Warren, you legend!*" *one of my teammates belts out as he finally reaches me. Yet, his wide grin fades as he pauses in his tracks and processes the visible pain I'm in.* "*Are you alright, mate?*"

"*It's my knee,*" *I muster out, my chest tightening as waves of pain radiate throughout my leg.* "*It's my fucking knee.*"

He immediately drops down to my side along with some of the other players as the word "*medic*" *is called out repeatedly. My vision blurs as each plea becomes more frantic than the last.*

The crowd slows to a stop, an eerie silence flooding through a once-enthused stadium.

And that's when it hits me. Reality—coming down on me like the bitch it is.

They say that in moments when you least expect it, life can flash before your eyes. A series of images, memories, and regrets that remind you that you're only on this earth for a short period of time. And that one day, you'll be nothing but a distant memory.

I'd like to think that on the real day I leave this earth, I will be remembered as nothing more than a simple man with simple wants, but big dreams. Dreams that have landed me in these life-flashing moments more times than I can count. Only this time, it feels too real. It feels like my life is actually over.

Before I know it, I'm stretchered off the pitch. As I close my eyes in absolution, I catch sight of the England scouts who'd been eyeing me all game, doing what I can only assume to be crossing my name off of their list.

"WARREN?" A gentle voice breaks me out of my hazed thoughts. "Can you hear me, Warren?"

I briefly glance up at the nurse that's been seeing to me for the past few hours—although I can't say for sure how long I've been lying in this hospital bed. It's been test after test, accompanied by the dreaded feeling that everyone's avoiding telling me the truth.

Although, I don't need them to. After I overheard my doctor say the harrowing words, "It looks like a torn ACL," I refused to process anything else.

"Warren?" she says once more in an attempt to grab my attention. I make eye contact with her this time, imploring her to continue. "Someone's here to see you."

My brows furrow in confusion. "What?" I finally speak, my voice hoarse. How would my mum have been able to reach the hospital so quickly? We had an away game today, meaning we were up in Blackpool, more than four hours north of her home in London.

"Can I let him in?"

Him? I pause and stare at her for a moment. I have no idea who "he" could be—but at this point, I've been stuck in a hospital bed for hours, surrounded by unfamiliar faces who know nothing about me and what I've just lost. I could use some comfort. "Sure, let him in."

"Will do." She smiles at me and turns to leave the room. Within a few moments, the last face I expect is walking through the door.

"What have you managed to do to yourself now, my boy?"

My eyes widen in surprise, a grin spreading across my face as I take in the familiar figure entering the room. "Ira? What the hell are you doing here?"

He plants himself into the armchair across from my bed. "You didn't think I'd miss the big game, did you?"

My heart sinks at not only the mention of tonight's game but the fact that Ira had a front-row seat to everything that went down on the pitch in those final seconds.

I've known Ira Matthews for over a decade. I was first introduced to him as a cocky 16-year-old boy who had just been asked to join in on his first-ever professional practice with Crawfield Football Club.

At that age, I thought I was the shit, mostly because everyone around me had always told me I was. All except for Ira. Ira laid it on thick. After finishing that first practice, I paraded my way off the field, relishing in all of the praise I was receiving along the way.

"You're good." A voice called out as I made it to the changing room to take off my boots. "But if you really want to make it far, you're going to need an attitude adjustment."

Instantly, I was caught off guard by the American accent and the Southern twang that came with it. I glanced up to see a stocky man with thinning gray hair and a pot belly that hung over his belt. He was dressed in a washed-out pair of jeans and a plain button-down shirt that looked like it had been a little bit too loved.

"And you are, Grandpa?" I responded, like the smart-ass I was.

The old man chuckled to himself. "Yeah, definitely an attitude adjustment needed here."

"Listen," I began. "I don't know who you are, but you should mind your own business. I don't need advice from someone who calls this sport 'soccer.'"

His eyes widened, "Oh, boy," he groaned as he took a seat across from me. "Let's just say when you get to be a 'grandpa' like me, you learn a thing or two about impressions."

I snorted. "Impressions don't matter when you're the best at what you do."

"See, that's where you're wrong," he retorted. "How do you think you even got here, huh?"

"I got here because I deserve it. Because I prove myself on the pitch." My response was smug, assured.

The old man's eyes crinkled in amusement, a smile spreading across his face. "And who do you think you're proving yourself to exactly?"

I paused, contemplating the answer to that question. Did I even really know? I was too busy enjoying the cheers from the crowd and the constant praise from Coach to think about who was even really watching.

"How about the owner of the club?" He beat me to a response. "Would they be important to impress?"

I raised my eyebrows at that. "Of course, yeah," I responded, shrugging nonchalantly.

"And if the owner of the club was here right now, what would you say to them?" He lit a cigar from his back pocket, examining me as he awaited my response.

I toyed with the bag on my shoulder, an unfamiliar feeling of anxiety taking over. "Well, I'd thank them for this opportunity and tell them that I have a lot to offer. More than they've already seen, if you could believe it. I'm one hundred percent in this. Nothing else is more important to me."

He let out a puff of smoke, tapping some ash off to the side. "Hmm..." He pursed his lips as we locked eyes, and I had an overwhelming feeling that I'd just majorly fucked up.

"Remember what I said about impressions?" he asked, standing up. "Lucky for you, Warren, I'm giving you a second one."

I looked up at him, face full of confusion. "And why would I need a second chance from you?" I challenged, trying to reignite that courage that had seemingly dissipated from me entirely.

"Well, because you said it yourself." He shrugged. "It's important to impress me, right?" He brought the cigar back up to his lips.

I stared at him slack-jawed for a moment, each piece of our conversation fitting together like a puzzle in my mind. "You're...Ira Matthews?" I questioned, thinking back to all of the Crawfield history I'd read up on prior to showing up to the first practice. The reason I was so good on the pitch wasn't just because of my knack for the game—it's because I did my research.

His silence confirmed my thoughts to be true, and instantly, I felt ashamed.

"Mr. Matthews," I began, adjusting my tone. "I'm sorry. I didn't mean to speak to you like that. I shouldn't have talked to you like—"

"I'll tell you what," he cut me off, taking another puff of his cigar and inching closer to me. "I see something in you, Warren.

Something that I don't see in every player that walks onto my pitch. I meant what I said earlier. You're good, and I want to help you be great. But before I can, you need to remember that you're an underdog, Warren. Always remember that."

I watch as Ira places his walking cane against my bed. He's no longer the pot-bellied grandpa I grew up with. His body and face have narrowed as the years have passed—partly because of age and partly because he's had to put up with me for so many years. As he's gotten older, Ira has chosen to spend less time in England and more time back home in Houston, where his family lives, while he manages the club from a distance.

As I look at him, all I can see is wasted time. All the time that Ira has spent mentoring me to get me where I wanted to go. Time that we'll never be able to get back.

"Did you hear?" I mumble, laying my head back on the pillow and staring up at the ceiling. "It's over."

"What's over?" he asks, leaning forward and resting his arms on his knees, concern furrowing his brows.

"All of it," I respond blankly. "It's done. I'm done for."

"Don't say that," Ira counters with. "You don't know yet what exactly it could be—"

"It's an ACL tear," I admit quietly. "I heard the doctor."

Ira stares at me for a moment before he sinks back into his chair, clearly attempting to process the news in the same way I was. "Are you sure?" he asks finally. "Maybe you misheard. Maybe they're misdiagnosing it. It's only been a few hours."

I shake my head, feeling a lump forming in my throat. I can't tell who he's trying to convince—me or himself. The conversation I'd overheard, the nurses tiptoeing around me, the pitiful glances they'd been sending my way any time they got the chance. It all adds up.

"I'm sorry," I choke out after a moment, my voice wavering. "This wasn't how I wanted things to end. Getting this close, all for it to fall apart."

"Don't do that." Ira grows visibly frustrated, yet his voice remains calm. "Don't talk like that, and don't you dare apologize to me."

"Why not?" I ask. "Everything's been ruined. All the work we put in together. All the time that you've spent getting me these opportunities. It's been for nothing. It's all been for God damn—"

"Enough," Ira finally raises his voice. "This is not the boy I raised."

"And who is that boy?" I snap, emotion threatening to take over. "He's a grown man with a busted knee and no other prospects. I'm no good for anything else. I never have been. This was it, Ira. This was it."

Ira pauses for a moment, seemingly taking in what I just said. I turn my head back to the ceiling as the two of us sit in silence, the weight of the situation slowly dawning on us. With a defeated sigh, Ira stands up from his chair, reaches for his cane as he makes his way to the bed and sits beside me.

"Look at me," he commands my attention, yet I know if I look into his eyes, I won't be able to hold my emotions back any longer. "God dammit, Warren, look at me!" He places his hand on my shoulder.

My tearful eyes eventually peer up. "Don't count yourself out so soon, my boy," he whispers with reassurance. "When one journey ends, that can only mean another one is about to begin."

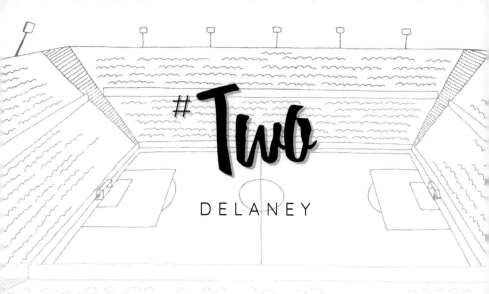

#Two

DELANEY

PRESENT DAY

"HELLO, everyone. Thank you all for being here today. I know how busy each of your schedules are, so we'll make this as brief as possible. With that said, let's commence the official reading of the will of Ira Matthews."

It's been six months since the passing of our beloved grandpa, or as I always called him—Gramps. Gramps never loved my nickname for him, but he loved me, so I guess that's why he put up with it for twenty-five years. He was always good to people like that.

Gramps was the peace amidst all the chaos of our family. He was the voice of reason, supportive, and most of all, humble.

Gramps started from nothing, and throughout his eighty-four years of life, he went on to create an unrivaled legacy. By the time he was my age, he had a net worth of over five million dollars as a result of his serial entrepreneurship. Eventually, he went on to make his mark in the realm of real estate. At the time of his death, he had acquired over 12 properties throughout the United States and England—his second home.

My dad joined Gramps' real estate empire as soon as he was

out of college—which means we're now one of Houston's wealthiest yet greediest families.

The way everyone was debating about what they were entitled to before our family lawyer, Mr. Cunningham walked in the room, proved that to be true.

"Grandpa said he was leaving the Mercedes for me," Mabel, my cousin, boasts proudly.

"Nuh-uh! He told me to my face that I was the one getting the Benz *and* the Caddy!" Her sister, Connie, folds her arms in a huff.

I can't help but roll my eyes at their little display, but they aren't the only ones debating which of Gramps' riches are soon to be theirs.

Aunt Maggie wants our late Grandma's 22-karat diamond engagement ring. Uncle Roger has been eyeing Gramps' limited-edition golf kit from Belgium and my parents? Well, they're most concerned about who Gramps left his properties to—the greatest assets of all.

It's all too overwhelming. It's as if everyone's forgotten one simple thing—that Gramps had to pass away for us to have even inherited half of this stuff. Have we all just moved on already?

I seem to be the only one in this room with a heart—and a desire to spend one more day with him. Something that would've surmounted any material items he could've left behind.

We may have been generations apart, but Gramps was genuinely my best friend. He was the only person in this family who actually kept me sane. Gramps knew me like no one else did, and I fear now that he's gone, no one else ever will.

"We'll start with the estate," Mr. Cunningham speaks as he stands at the front of the room, commanding everyone's attention.

I never thought that the culmination of one's most prized possessions—and a lifetime of hard work—could be easily divided, pawned, and charted off in the span of 20 minutes. Nor do I think I've ever heard so many technical words in my life. *Bequeathed, appendix, trustee?*

I have no idea what a single one of them means. All I know is that everyone around me is absolutely thrilled.

Aunt Maggie got not only the diamond ring she wanted but Grandma's entire jewelry collection that dates back to the 30s. I fear Aunt Maggie isn't the collector type. She sees these precious gems as an easy cash grab to funnel her real passion: Saturday nights at the roulette table.

Much to his dismay, Uncle Roger doesn't get the golf clubs. He started to kick up a fuss about that one until it was revealed that he was about to inherit Gramp's entire collection of boats and yachts (yes, *collection*). That sure beats a couple of sticks, if you ask me.

Tweedle-dee and tweedle dumb—Mabel and Connie, don't get their dream cars, but with the cash allowance that Gramps left them both, they'll be able to buy those cars ten times over.

And to top it all off, I don't think I'd ever seen my parent's eyes light up more than they did when Dad got appointed the sole beneficiary of all of Gramps' U.S. and U.K. properties.

As everyone celebrates amongst themselves, I'm left to wonder...what about me? The only one who didn't show up today with selfish intentions?

The lawyers say there was apparently an oversight in processing my inheritance—one that's going to take at least a few more weeks to resolve.

I don't care.

Truthfully, there isn't a single thing that I desire more than to leave this room full of disturbingly satisfied people ready to take their cheques to the bank.

"Wait," Mr. Cunningham chimes in once more. "There is one more thing. Ira has left a few additional assets that may come as a surprise."

Everyone's eyes shoot up from admiring their new treasures as they glance back toward the front of the room.

"Additional assets?" Dad narrows his eyes with curiosity. "What does that mean exactly?"

"Well, Mr. Matthews..." Mr. Cunningham pushes his glasses back up the bridge of his bulky nose. "It appears that Ira purchased a football team in England about two decades ago. Crawfield Football Club, to be exact. Were you aware of this?"

Crawfield.

I haven't heard that in a while.

As much as Gramps was a true businessman at heart, he also had a profound, all-consuming love for one other thing in his life —soccer... I mean, *football.*

Some of my fondest memories with Gramps consist of watching football on his couch—in fact, it's what we used to do every Saturday morning, from when I was old enough to sit through a game all the way up to the months before his passing.

Truthfully, I never did know what exactly I was watching. I was always more concerned with rating the players by their looks versus their actual skill level. I think Gramps knew that, too, deep down.

"You know, Delaney." Gramps re-adjusted himself on the couch. "You should get yourself a guy who plays football." His request caused his eyes to crinkle in a smile.

It wasn't the first time Gramps had put his two cents in when it came to my love life. I shot him a playful glare in response. "Don't you remember, Gramps? I did."

"What?" He looked at me in surprise. "You never said."

"Yes, I did, Gramps," I protested. In his later years, Gramps wasn't known to have the strongest memory. "We were dating for a while, but then he got drafted into the NFL and moved to Wisconsin. Wisconsin. Do I look like someone who wants to live in Milwaukee? Especially during the winter?"

Gramps shook his head. "First of all, different football, darling, different football." He chuckled. "Second of all, Delaney, it wouldn't have mattered if you went to Wisconsin or the Moon...you bring sunshine with you anywhere you go."

Gramps always had a way with words. He'd always been a real charmer—the only person in the world who could pick me up when I was down and put a smile on my face.

I settled in beside him, releasing a sigh. "Who are we even watching, anyway?" I asked, seeing a familiar group of players on the screen and a score of four-nil in favor of the other team.

It had only been 15 minutes.

"Not to be rude, Gramps, but they kind of suck."

"Delaney!" Gramps scolded me, although I noticed the corners of his mouth lifting in a subtle smile. He could never be mad at me.

"Sorry, Gramps." I raised my hands in defense. "But weren't you the one that said always tell the truth, even if it hurts?"

"You always seem to have a point." He grinned, sipping on his sweet tea before pointing the glass at the television screen. "This is Crawfield FC, darling, these are my boys."

I assessed the players before a repressed memory came to mind. "You know, I dated someone once with the last name Crawfield."

"Did you, now?" Gramps always tried his best to be as interested as possible in my stories—even if they were mostly about sappy romance and celebrity gossip.

"Yep, I think you met him, actually. He was my prom date, remember?"

Gramps nodded his head, pulling his eyes away from the screen and meeting mine. "How could I forget your prom? You looked beautiful."

"I did, didn't I?" I beamed, accepting his compliment. "But get this. He ran off with Caroline while I was on stage being crowned as prom queen! Can you believe it, Gramps? I was the queen, and he still ran off with a peasant."

"Oh, Delaney..." Gramps seemed to have lost his way with my story as he placed his head into his hands. "I love you, my darling, but I have no idea what you're talking about anymore."

"That's okay, Gramps." I leaned against his shoulder, the way I'd done since the very first time we watched a match together over 20 years ago. "Not many people do."

"That'll change," he reassured me, placing a tender hand on my cheek. *"I know you'll find someone, sunshine. But when you do...I have one condition."*

I looked up at him curiously. *"And that is?"*

"That they need to be a Crawfield fan."

I'm brought out of my memory at the sound of my dad's voice. "Oh, Crawfield, okay." He nods. "That team. The terrible one, right?"

Mr. Cunningham looks back down at the paper. "Well, it doesn't indicate their skill set here, Sir, but it does say that the team is valued at just over two million."

"Hmm." My dad juts out his bottom lip in thought as he turns to my mom "Not too shabby. Not too shabby at all."

My mom joins him in his delight as Mr. Cunningham continues. "There is some urgency to act on the team's future, given the fact that they have been without an owner for quite some time."

"The decision is simple," my mom chimes in. "Sell it and wipe our hands clean."

It's not only my mother's words that take me by surprise—it's everyone's reaction to this hasty decision.

I watch in shock as the rest of our family absentmindedly agrees just so that they don't have to wait a second longer to grab their things and file out of the room.

Now, all that remains is me, my parents, and Mr. Cunningham to sign off on the final proceedings.

This is crazy. How is this so simple for everyone? How come no one remembers just how important Crawfield was to Gramps?

The look of anticipation as he'd watch the players line the field.

How he'd rub his chin in thought when they were in the heat of a play.

The way his eyes would light up the (very few) times they scored a goal.

These are memories I'll hold onto for the rest of my life, and sitting here watching everyone willingly let this go feels like I'm losing an important piece of Gramps—one that I'm not ready to say goodbye to yet.

"So, it's settled!" My dad claps loudly, cutting through my thoughts. "Mr. Cunningham, how do we move forward?"

"Well, the first step is to find a buyer and then—"

"Wait!" I catch myself by surprise at my sudden outburst, everyone turning their attention to me. "We can't sell it."

#Three

WARREN

IT WAS the hardest phone call I'd ever received.

"Ira passed away last night."

That was it. Five words that have haunted me for the last six months, and the worst part? I didn't even get a chance to say goodbye.

Goodbye. The simplest thing I could have said to the one person who gave me hope when I felt like I had none left.

I still remember the last conversation we had like it was yesterday. It was stupid, really. It's not the type of conversation I imagined or hoped would've been our final one.

"My boy, tell me how we've managed to lose every single game this season. Do I need to start looking for a new coach already?" Ira *teased as he stepped down from the stands and onto the field, making me glance up from my clipboard.*

We'd just wrapped up a late practice, and the field was silent as all the lads had rushed back into the changing room.

"Ira?" I stepped back in surprise. "I thought you weren't coming down here 'til next week?"

"Well, given the scores I've been seeing, an emergency intervention seemed appropriate." He let out a laugh that turned into a raspy cough. *"So, tell me, what's going on?"*

I shook my head and looked back down at my clipboard, a smile playing on my lips. Ira had a way of brightening my mood—he always had.

"The team has just been in a daze." I shrugged, unsure how else I could best describe it. *"We're trying new moves, different strategies, but nothing's been clicking. The lads held a players-only meeting the other night, only to come out and lose three-nothing the next day. Even the captain can't seem to get through to them."*

Ira looked up in thought, assessing my words, until I saw his eyes suddenly light up. *"You should promote Wilkinson instead,"* he suggested. *"I think he'd really be able to motivate the boys and give the team some positive encouragement. What do you think?"*

"Wilkinson?" I repeated hesitantly. *"Are you kidding? He's fresh meat. He hasn't even gotten his toes wet."*

Gary Wilkinson, or as we call him, *"Wilks,"* was our striker—only in his second season. A total goof at heart, a solid player on the field, and an even more solid friend off. The team trusted him, listened to him, and, without a doubt, respected him. It wasn't a bad suggestion; truthfully, the only thing I disliked about it was that I hadn't thought of it myself.

"Sounds a lot like you," Ira smirked, gesturing towards one of the chairs strewn along the sidelines of the field. *"Mind grabbing me a chair, my boy?"*

Ira's frame settled as I carried a chair over. He sat down in his seat, placing his walking stick off to the side and letting out a long sigh.

"You alright?" I asked, noticing a sense of exhaustion wash over his eyes. It worried me to see him get older by the day.

"I'm just old, Warren." He sunk into his chair. *"That's all."*

"You're not that old." I tried to give him the benefit of the doubt with a small smile.

"Oh yeah?" he began. *"Do you remember World War II?"*

I shook my head.

"Exactly." He let out a gruntled sigh. *"Exactly."*

I pulled up a seat beside him. "Hey, you're not too old to tell me how to coach this team, though, right?"

He chuckled at that. "Never...I am your boss, after all."

We'd spent that entire night sitting under the open top-roof field, shooting the shit, laughing, joking, and bonding as if we were father and son because deep down, it felt that way.

Was Ira my father? No, definitely not. But did he take me on as a son? Yes. A million times, yes. He'd always called me his "problem child," "my boy," the person he trusted so much that he gave him—a young retired footballer with no experience—a chance to coach his team.

It was five years ago, just a few weeks after I'd found out that my ACL tear was a career-ending injury. At first, I rebutted the thought. Crawfield Football Club already wasn't doing great, and frankly, they didn't need some rookie coach coming along and making them any worse. But Ira had insisted, and I'd wanted nothing more than to be back on the field in any way possible.

So, Crawfield FC began their new season with an inexperienced, passionate, and very good-looking new coach, might I add.

As it turns out, that first season was one of the best the team had seen in years. We weren't good, by any means—but were we the worst? Almost, but not quite.

I've grown more comfortable in my role as a coach than I'd expected. At first, I let the players call me by my name.

Warren.

Park.

Sometimes Parker.

But now, it's Coach. It's strictly Coach.

After all this time, I think I finally understand how Ira felt about me. He saw something in me, something that I now see in my team, in my boys. I want nothing more than for them to achieve everything they've hoped for. Everything that they work towards each day on that field and everything that I promised Ira that they would accomplish in those final few words we shared.

"You won't let me down, right?"

"Have I so far?" I questioned, raising an eyebrow.

Ira smiled over at me. "Not once...not ever."

I had no idea that that would be the last memory I'd make with him.

I'd spent the first 16 years of my life without Ira and the next 16 being completely inseparable from him. The latter years created a completely new version of myself—one that has since disappeared.

Ira completed a piece of me, and since he's been gone, I've been left searching for what else will fit in his place.

The first few weeks after that phone call were rough. I did absolutely nothing but mope around and feel sorry for myself. I couldn't even build up the courage to attend his funeral, for God's sake.

It was in Houston, halfway across the world, and in the middle of the football season, which I selfishly used to rationalize my decision not to go. I told myself I couldn't possibly leave my team. Not when they needed me most. I'd told myself Ira would understand, that he'd assure me I made the right decision...and maybe he would've.

But a part of me believes that the real reason why I chose not to go was because I wasn't ready to say goodbye. Just like I hadn't done that last night.

Because of that, I've learned that you never know when a goodbye will actually be the last.

A few weeks ago, I ordered a memorial picture of Ira. It was a photo I'd carefully selected, considering he "stopped aging" at forty. The photo finally arrived on my desk last night. It brought some emotion to my eyes, but thankfully, I was alone, and no one could see just how impactful it was.

"Where do you want to put it?" my assistant coach, Alfie Lewis, also known as Alf, asks me, holding the photo up at different angles around the team's tunnel.

Alf is a vet when it comes to football. He played professionally for many years before retiring *(un-injured)* and opting to jump back into the game from the sidelines. We're more alike than I'll admit. That's why I like to push his buttons most days.

"Try a little higher," I call out, watching as Alf, a mere five-foot-seven, fully extends his arms up higher along the wall.

"Higher," I add, waving my hand upward and watching as he stands up on his tiptoes, trying to push the photo up along the wall. "Higher, higher, higher, c'mon Alf!" I have to bite back a laugh as he loses his footing and stumbles slightly.

"Alright, Park." He pulls back, the old grump side of him finding its way out. "Now you're just taking the piss."

I cross my arms in delight, a playful grin taking over my face. This is why we work so well together.

"What? Do you need a step stool or something?"

Alf grumbles to himself for a second before he reaches to the side and grabs a chair to stand on.

"Remember, I'm doing you a favor, Park." He grimaces. "It's not like you know how to turn a screwdriver."

I see this as the perfect opportunity to take things one step further. "Yeah, but I do know how to screw your wife."

Alf shoots me a glare, ready to step down from the chair. "I swear to God, Warren—"

"That's it! Place it right there," I shout, and Alf freezes in his tracks as he holds the picture in place.

"Don't move!" I demand. "Put it right there."

Despite our banter, Alf secures it against the wall and hops down from the chair.

We both take a step back, intently admiring it for a moment. "Do you think he'd like it?" Alf asks, peering up at me.

"Probably not," I joke. "That's too bad, though. I like it," I admit. "Besides, now he'll always be with us—before we start a match and after. In approval or not..."

"Heyo, Coach!" The now team captain, Wilks, runs down the tunnel, patting me on the back as the team follows suit. "Are we starting practice any time soon, or are you and Alf too busy playing home makeover?"

Wilks is a total smart ass, true-and-true—I'm Alf in his eyes. It's a vicious cycle. Wilks irks me, and I irk Alf.

What can you do?

"You know what, Wilks?" I throw my arm across his shoulder as the rest of the team joins us. "We *are* about to start practice. And because of you, the whole team can warm up with ten laps around the pitch."

His face falls flat. "Oh c'mon, Coach—"

"Go on." I shoo them away, nodding in the direction of the field. "Alf and I have to decide what color we're painting the walls. Don't we, Alf?"

A smirk is plastered across Alf's lips as he shakes his head, and the lads drag themselves onto the field, groaning in annoyance. "You're a real dick, you know that?" He laughs.

"I know." I place my whistle between my lips. "And I wouldn't have it any other way."

#Four

DELANEY

"DELANEY." My dad cocks an eyebrow, unamused at my outburst. "This doesn't involve you. You heard what Mr. Cunningham said. You'll receive your portion of the inheritance soon enough," he adds, dismissing me with a wave of his hand.

It's a small gesture that he and my mom have directed toward me throughout my entire life, but the sting never quite goes away when it happens.

Sure, I've had it easy—I'll be the first to admit it. My parents' money has pretty much been my saving grace my entire life. But that doesn't mean that my voice, my opinion, and my involvement aren't important—especially not when it comes to Gramps.

I feel my cheeks burn with a mixture of embarrassment and sudden determination. I can't back down. Not now. Not when there is so much at stake here.

"But Dad!" I rise to my feet. "We can't just give the team up! You know how much Gramps loved them, don't you?"

"Delaney, honey," Mom speaks up gently, brushing her hand through my hair. "Don't you have...something else to do? A little business meeting to host, perhaps?"

I have to fight not to roll my eyes. My parents have never taken any of my endeavors seriously. To be fair, they last just about as long as all of my relationships—which isn't very long at all. I suppose I have myself to blame in part for that.

Since I was a kid, I've never stuck to an activity for longer than a few weeks. The same went with going to college. I switched majors three times in my first year...and then another five times after that.

"It's okay, Shirley," Dad reassures Mom as he walks over to me, placing a hand on my shoulder and meeting my eyes. "Of course, I know how much he loved the team, Delaney. But things don't always work out. Crawfield was important to your Pops, but to us..." He looks back at Mom. "It's of no value. You wouldn't understand."

You wouldn't understand.

I think making backhanded comments about me is my dad's favorite pastime.

"If only there were a degree that required you to be on your phone all day...then maybe, just maybe, you'd actually finish a semester."

Unlike his other snide comments, this one made something click inside me. As it turns out, the thing I am best at *is* being on my phone. But not for me. For others.

I like to say I have a gift: the ability to know what consumers want. When you spend every moment of every day consuming things online, you learn something or two about what sells. Even the worst brands can come back to life after the right makeover.

Makeover. Perceived value. That's what sells.

"I got it!" I exclaim, confusion falling across Mom and Dad's faces as a grin spreads across mine. "What if I could make the team of value to us?"

"Oh, Delaney." My dad immediately starts shaking his head. "No, no, I don't think that's a good idea."

"Dad, give me a chance to explain," I plead, clasping my hands together. I've never been one to beg, but right now, I need to pull out all the stops.

My dad flashes me a stare but stays silent, which tells me that this is my chance to say whatever it is I have to say to get him to change his mind.

"How about this?" I propose, theatrically spreading my hands out in front of me. "I could re-shift everything. Give them the PR that they need. I could make people care...make the world see what Gramps saw. Then you'll see. You'll see that they can and *will be* worth something!"

My dad's hardly as receptive to my pitch as I'd hoped he'd be. "Delaney." He frowns. "You could hardly get through four years of schooling, and the only reason you stayed in college that long is because I had to meet with the Dean himself to convince him not to kick you out for your poor attendance."

My poor attendance was only the result of being in all the wrong classes. I'm sure you'd skip if you had to attend a three-hour lecture on mathematics and statistics when you barely know your times tables.

If that wasn't enough, Dad sinks the knife in that much deeper. "Let's not forget the fact that your PR firm has one client, and that's your best friend."

Another unnecessary remark. You have to start somewhere, am I right? At least my best friend was willing to give me a chance, and you know what? The 150% increase in followers on her social media accounts tells me that this PR rep knows a bit more than just a thing or two.

"Is there a point you're trying to get to here?" I fold my arms across my chest, partially in a huff but also to shield myself from another one of these impending strikes.

"Yes, Delaney. The point is that you're expecting us to trust you with a multi-million-dollar team. It's just not happening. I'm sorry, sweetheart, but it's not."

I feel tears forming in my eyes—partly because of the way my parents clearly feel not an ounce of shame when it comes to embarrassing me in front of Mr. Cunningham, but also because my dad's words, as blunt as they are, have some truth to them.

I'm not perfect; I know that, but does that mean I'm incapable of change? Do I have to go the rest of my life without being allowed to make mistakes and try something different?

Gramps always told me I could do anything if I put my mind to it. He was the first person who believed in me when no one else did. So, when I did eventually walk across the stage at graduation, even if it did take me an extra two years, Gramps was right in the front row cheering me on. I still remember him whispering "congratulations" in my ear after I stepped off the stage, telling me he'd always known I could do it. It's as if I can hear him telling me that exact same thing now.

I need to fight.

Fighting in the book of Delaney means that this somber, scolded act is no longer going to cut it. I need to crank up the tears here. Although all of my classes might've been wrong for my first semester at university, the Dramatic Arts class sure taught me a thing or two about a *spectacle*.

"You know what? Maybe you're right..." I sniffle through the tears, putting my head in my hands. "You and Mom did say that I'd never amount to anything." I kick my foot out in front of me. "You both totally warned me about starting my own company. You said I'm not driven enough, not passionate enough..." I break my voice with a false sense of hurt, meeting their eyes and subtly glancing at Mr. Cunningham as I finish my sentence. "*Smart enough...*"

My parents exchange worried glances, and I immediately know it's working. This isn't my first time pulling out the waterworks on command. There's a reason why I'm an only child.

I continue to dramatically wipe my tears away with the back of my hand before glancing over at Mr. Cunningham's suit pocket. "Sorry, do you mind?" I ask tearfully, nodding towards his silk handkerchief.

He hands it over to me, looking equally alarmed and shocked at the situation unfolding in his office. This is a hell of a lot more than he is getting paid for.

"I guess I'll just...wait to hear from you, Mr. Cunningham," I mumble, handing the handkerchief back to him, but it's not before I notice the glare he shoots at my parents before I leave.

"Delaney, wait!" I hear my dad's exasperated voice behind me, making me stop in my tracks. Of course, it's my dad who stops me. He's always been the pushover of the two.

A smirk falls over my face for a moment, but I let it drop back down to a frown before turning my body in his direction. "Yes?" I sigh, with slumped shoulders. "What is it?"

He straightens his spine before reaching for his jacket that hangs over the back of one of the armchairs. "You have three months, Delaney."

My mouth falls open in surprise before I hear Mom's voice pipe up. "What?" she jolts her head in his direction. "Hank!" she says with conviction. "Are you sure that is a good idea? We could have this sold within the next week or—"

He puts up a hand, stopping her mid-sentence as he makes his way towards me.

I gulp as we stand face-to-face. I think he knows that it's not a surprise that my tears have conveniently stopped. "Three months, Delaney," he repeats a second time. "Double the team's value, and we'll keep them," he instructs, slipping his arm inside either sleeve of his jacket. "But," he lingers, and I fear for what's about to come next. "If you don't, they're gone. No ifs, ands, buts...or *tears* about it."

I take a moment to take in his words. There's no way he just agreed to this—no way they're giving me this opportunity.

My feeble attempts at suppressing a squeal are surmounted. I can't hold back any longer as I run over to my parents and pull them in for a hug, jumping up and down. "Thank you *so* much, guys! I won't let you down. I promise."

Silence now falls over the room, but the buzz of excitement in the air is inevitable as Mr. Cunningham looks my way, placing a careful hand on my arm. "Well, Delaney," he smiles. "Looks like you're going to Crawley."

#Five

WARREN

"PICK IT UP, BOYS," I cup my hands around my mouth, shouting across the field. It's Monday morning, and as usual, it's clear that the boys have somehow completely lost sight of what it means to show some aggression in their step. "What EPL are you trying to play in here? The English Premier League or the English Princess League? This is pitiful, lads!"

"Coach..." a few players groan out in exhaustion, but it's our lead defender, Daniel Green, whose voice trumps the group. "It's been three hours. Can we take a break?" He cranes his neck from side to side before stretching his hands out in front of him, cracking his knuckles. "My whole body is sore. Even my hands hurt."

"Green, let me be the first to tell you that that's not a result of this practice. It's because you probably never stop wanking off!" I blow the whistle loudly, catching everyone by surprise. "I've had enough!" I prompt everyone to come in and take a knee. "What's going on with you lot?" I ask, glancing around at their weary faces. "We only have a few weeks until the start of the season. Now it is more important than ever to start training, not be acting like a bunch of mard-arse's out there. What's gotten into you?"

"But, Coach—"

"You know what? I don't want to hear anything else come out of your mouths." I cut their explanation short. I don't need to hear their justification. I just need to see that they're going to do something about it. "You want this practice to end? Then stop prancing about and show me that you're ready to play. Then, and only then, I'll call it, alright?"

They don't seem convinced, exchanging skeptical glances amongst one another—some of the lads have even taken the liberty to lie down on their backs.

It's infuriating.

Growing up, I used to hate it when my mum would say things like, "Your generation has it easy," while I listened to her explain the treacherous walk to and from school she'd embark on every day, but now, I'm finding myself falling guilty of that same habit.

I'm not the most "laid-back" coach around. I know that. But these boys have had it easy compared to me. Back when I was making my mark, I worked my arse off. I didn't have time to complain because I knew it would get me nowhere. I had a vision from the start and knew that if I wanted to make it big, I had to push. I had to motivate myself, even on the days when I was completely and utterly exhausted.

But nowadays, it seems like the only two motivators the lads have are women and booze.

Winning hasn't been a luxury to this group, and I can't expect them to want to practice like winners when they don't know the feeling. But they can...and I have full faith that one day, they will.

My mum always told me you've got to meet people where they're at.

"Not everyone can work like you, Warren."

"Alright." I let out a huff, knowing exactly what I need to dangle in front of them to get this practice back on track. "Here's the deal." I rub my hands together. "The first team to score in the scrimmage today will get drinks on me tonight at Tenner's. Sounds good?"

Their eyes light up one by one at the mention of the local

pub, conveniently located down the road from our football grounds.

Wilks shoots up with a sudden renewed motivation. "You guys heard Coach." He gestures for the lads to follow. "Get your bloody arses up! I want a free pint."

I worried about making Wilks the captain despite knowing he was perfect for it. Wilks is young, freshly eighteen—it's a lot of responsibility taking onus of the entire group. I know this because I was team captain at one point, too. I know the pressure that comes with it, and I'd never want to incite that on someone, especially at the start of their career.

But like the day I met him many years ago, Wilks has always taken everything in stride. I see a lot of myself in him, although I'm pretty sure he sees me as some sort of annoying Dad figure.

For the record, I'm hardly old enough to be his father.

I'm hard on all the lads, but I know deep down I'm the hardest on him—and it's not because I want to be a pain in his arse, but it's because I know what Wilks is capable of. He has what it takes to make it big. He just needs that push. The push that Ira gave to me.

I break free from my thoughts and direct my attention towards the field at the sound of Green calling out. "Can we start?"

I don't respond. Instead, I simply blow into the whistle yet again to prompt them to kick off the match.

"Hey, Park," Alf's voice is the next to command my attention as he sprints out of the tunnel toward me, causing me to turn my head in his direction.

"What's up?" I question his urgency, considering the only place I've ever seen Alf sprint to is the local chippy during their buy-one-get-one-for-a-pound special.

"I just...I just got a call from Houston," he says, huffing in and out as he finally reaches me.

"Houston?" I repeat. "As in Houston, Texas?"

He nods his head. "It's about Ira," he explains. "His will was released. The new owners have been announced."

My heart begins to pound as the words leave his mouth. Although I'd known it was inevitable, I'd been dreading the day that this news would come out. I've never had to operate with another owner before. It's only ever been Ira, who had always been so trusting in me to lead the team's decisions.

How would things change now?

"So, are you just going to stand there? Or are you going to tell me who it is?" I ask impatiently, glancing back out at the field and trying to ignore the nerves coursing through me.

"It's the Matthews family," Alf finally reveals. "I believe Ira left it to his son."

Ira's son.

The prestigious multi-millionaire whose only job is to boss others around as he ponces about in his real-estate firm. I mean, I can't shame him too much—I am a coach, after all. But there's a key difference. Ira's son has hardly had to work for anything in his life. Everything's been handed to him, just like this team has been now. Whereas me? I've never stopped working.

Not to mention, the guy couldn't care less about Crawfield. I'd only ever met him once, a few years ago, when Ira begged him to come down to the club and "watch" a game. He ended up leaving at halftime. I'll never forget the disappointment in Ira's eyes when he joined me for our usual post-match debrief.

I think Ira always loved that he and I could bond over the sport, whereas he and Hank could only bond over their assets. Though Ira was never one to gloat, I knew he was wealthy. Yet, the greatest riches he ever gave to me were his unwavering loyalty and friendship.

Alf's news has me stressed. And right now is not a good time to be stressed. We're just weeks out of a new season, one that I plan to make better than ever. I don't need changes and distractions swerving us off track. We have a system that works. A system that doesn't need disrupting.

"So, what does this mean, exactly?" The question comes to mind. "What did they say are the next steps?" I ask, redirecting my attention back to the match, though I can't help but clench my jaw as I wait for his response.

"Nothing seems to be changing except for the fact that they're sending their girl down to join us," Alf responds.

"Their girl? What girl?" I raise an eyebrow in his direction.

"Hank Matthews's daughter," he clarifies.

I close my eyes and pinch the bridge of my nose in annoyance. "For what reason, exactly?" I ask. "Does she even know anything about Crawfield? About football?"

Alf shrugs, clearly not privy to the answers of a single one of my questions. "She's supposedly a PR manager." He shrugs. "I think they're sending her to give our team some more status. Build up our reputation."

"Status?" I debate the ludicrous thought. "Reputation? We don't need either of those things, nor do we need some girl thobbing about here. The guys are hardly focused as it is." I let out an exasperated groan as my attention was diverted to the lads over on the field. "These Americans...they're always trying to glamorize everything. We're running a simple operation here— kicking footballs around the field. There's nothing *tantalizing* about it. Tell them no! It's not happening—"

"Warren!" Alf interjects my rant with annoyance. "This isn't a question of whether or not she's coming. She *is* coming, and she'll be here within the next few days. So, get over yourself."

I suck in a prolonged breath in and release it out slowly. "Fucking hell," I grumble, shaking my head as I chew on the inside of my cheek. "I'm not letting some rich girl come down here and tell me how to run my team, club, and boys." I point in their direction, dropping my voice slightly so that they don't hear. "Ira might not have left the team to me, Alf, but he sure as hell left it in my hands, and there's no chance...*no way*, I am letting him down!"

Alf places a hand on my shoulder to settle me. "First of all," he begins, his voice soft. "She's not just some 'rich girl,' Parker. She's Ira's granddaughter."

Ira's granddaughter.

I shut my mouth and take a deep breath—diverting my eyes back over to the field where, although I'm watching the scrimmage take place, I'm hardly paying attention. Instead, I'm focusing on my almost immediate regret for my harsh words—forcing me to chew on my bottom lip as I ruminate.

In the rare instances that Ira talked about his family, his eyes would light up at the mention of his granddaughter. His *sunshine*, he used to call her. I'll admit, I never asked much about her. I'd always just allow Ira to take the lead, but without any follow-up questioning, I knew that he loved her with his entire being. It was clear all over his face.

"And second," Alf's increasingly bothered tone snaps me out of my thoughts. "She's just coming to do some PR, social media... some shit like that. So relax, lad." I look over at him. "It's not like she's coming here to take your job. In reality, that'll be me if you don't snap yourself out of this rut." He playfully nudges my shoulder.

I release a breath, the tension of the conversation slowly feeling as though it's subsiding—but now I'm internalizing it, and instead of getting mad, I'm bottling it all within. "Listen, Warren," Alf's voice picks back up. "I know this isn't ideal, trust me, but this is the best-case scenario for us. We're pleasing both parties here."

I'm silent as I take in his response. Some days, I'm certain I have a thing or two to learn from Mr. Wise Guy to my right. I'd never admit it, though.

"You said she'll be here soon?" I change the subject and focus on another, more pressing one instead. "When's soon?" I hope to clarify.

"Three days," Alf reveals point-blank. "So, we'd better start preparing and letting the boys—"

"That's fucking right, lads!" My attention is drawn away from

Alf as I watch the ball soar into the net. "That's what I'm talking about." I crack a faint smile as Wilks rejoices with his group.

"You see that, Coach?" He calls out to me with a cocky grin, followed by a wink. "'Cause all I see is free pints tonight!"

I roll my eyes as I blow my whistle a final time, officially calling it a day. "Alright, alright." I attempt to settle the group's enthused state. "As promised, we're done for the day. Now, hit the showers. We'll meet up at Tenner's in an hour."

Despite the long-hauled practice, the boys find energy to sprint their way down the tunnel, hooting in delight. "We're going to meet some birdies tonight, boys!" I hear Green's voice echo down the tunnel as Alf and I follow closely behind.

"Three days," I tell him with assurance, though my gaze is fixed upon Ira's photo atop the tunnel as we walk. "Tell the family we'll see her then."

#Six

DELANEY

"PEOPLE OF INSTAGRAM, you'll never guess where I am!" I speak cheerily into my phone camera as I strut out of the airport, an assistant trailing behind me with my six suitcases in tow.

Okay...he's not really my assistant. He's just an airport employee who I convinced to help me load my bags into my cab. But he's cute and buff and clearly knows how to manage things in his hands.

I love it here already.

"I'm in London town!" I squeal excitedly. "Not for long, though. This country girl is headed to the town of Crawley!" I say with amusement. "Never heard of it? Well, that's all about to change. Swipe up to follow my new dedicated soccer page, where you'll get all the inside scoop on my new life here in the U.K."

I flip the camera onto the airport worker, who's now stacked my bags into the trunk of the cab. "Do you want a shoutout?" I ask him, playing with the filters on the screen.

He drops my suitcases in the trunk before he flashes a blank look. "Piss off," he tells me before walking away.

Piss off? I run the phrase through my mind but come to no conclusion, instead, I shrug off his comment and end the video.

"Call me?" My voice weakly lingers before he's out of sight, and I step into the cab out front.

"Right, where to, love?" He asks, peering at me through his rearview mirror.

Love. God, I *love* how the guys talk here. "Love" is the equivalent of "darling." Only, it sounds ten times hotter when it comes out of the mouth of someone with a British accent—even if he's a good 20 years older than me.

"Crawley," I tell him—frankly, I only really know just the name of the town, not much else.

"Where in Crawley?" he asks, glancing up at me through his rearview mirror.

"Um..." I peer down at my phone, reading out the address Dad had given me before I boarded the flight.

"Ah, I see," he enters the address into his GPS. "Right near the Football Club, is it?"

"Oh my God!" my voice rises in delight. "You know them? Ah, I'm meeting the team this week! I'm *working* with them, actually!" I excitedly pull myself forward between the seats. "Do you watch them?"

He pauses, scanning my face before letting out a chuckle. "Of course not. They're shite."

His blunt response leaves me taken aback for a split second before I nervously laugh with him, tucking myself back into the seat and fastening my seatbelt. "Well, that's all about to change," I announce optimistically.

"Are you a miracle worker or something?"

"No, I'm not." I rest my purse on my lap. "But I believe in them."

AN HOUR LATER, the taxi driver shifts the car into park, and I scoot my way to the side, peering out of the window. "Um, are you sure this is the address I gave you?" I ask reluctantly, glancing around at the street he's pulled into.

My dad had said he'd found the nicest place in Crawley for me to stay. At first, I debated why I couldn't just stay at Gramps' place nearby, but Dad insisted that if I was going to Crawley, I had to abide by his rules. In other words, I'm certain he's already in talks with an estate agent over here to get the house sold as soon as possible. Dad doesn't like residential real estate. It's commercial that makes his eyes light up.

Because of that, I'm surrounded by narrow roads, smaller cars than I've ever seen in my life and brick. A crap ton of brick.

The driver reads the address back to me word for word. "Yep, this is it." He looks back over at me. "Good luck with your miracle."

"Wait..." I'm caught off guard by the fact that he hasn't gotten out of the car. "You're not going to help me with my bags?"

He scoffs. "I'm a taxi driver, not a bellhop. You figure it out."

He doesn't sound quite as hot anymore as I step out of the car.

As he pops the trunk open, I've hardly had the chance to pull out my bags and place them on the side of the road before he automatically closes the trunk and pulls away, leaving me standing in the middle of the street.

I turn around to face the building that lies ahead. "No elevator?" I say out loud in resignation, fearing that the only way up this three-story building is the dreaded word...*stairs*.

"Oi!" I hear someone call out, causing me to squint across the street to where the voice came from. "Over here, babe!" The voice attempts once more, leading my eyes to find three teenage boys leaning against the building across the street.

"Hey," I call over to them with a wave of my hand. "My name's Delaney! And you are?"

Mom and Dad never did have the "don't talk to strangers" talk with me; now, I can't seem to help it.

They exchange glances with one another as if they'd just

struck big in the lottery. "American?" one speaks up. "You've got to be kidding me."

I stand up a little straighter, my signature smile coming across my face. "Sure am," I respond as patriotically as possible.

To be honest, I'm accustomed to getting this reaction out of men when they hear me speak. My accent *is* pretty adorable. It's the perfect combination of Southern hospitality mixed with a city-girl twist.

"Aren't you a little far from home?" The same guy remarks, his friends eyeing me up and down with smirks on their faces.

"That I am," I agree. "But I'm here on a mission. I'm going to work for Crawfield FC."

Their reaction is the same as the cab driver. "Crawfield FC?" They burst out into a menacing kind of laughter. "As what? Their water girl? Cheerleader?" They playfully push against one another, evidently finding their humor hilarious.

I frown. There's no way I'm letting some teenagers make a mockery of me right now. Besides, it's ten in the morning on a Wednesday. Shouldn't they be in school?

"No, not as their water girl. I'm going to be their PR Manager."

Confusion falls across their faces. "PR?" One repeats. "What does that stand for? Personal Referee? What are you gonna do? Call it when they get a little too rough?" He raises his eyebrows suggestively, causing the other boys to burst back into laughter.

I suck in a breath, finding some confidence to march my way across the street. "Oh, Jerry..." I sigh, shaking my head. "Can I call you Jerry? You look like a Jerry."

"It's James," he calls back matter-of-factly.

"Close enough." I take a small step closer. "Can I ask you a question?"

He gulps back some reluctance before nodding his head.

"Tell me." I fold my arms across my chest in question. "Do you get laid often?"

His face turns redder than my cousin's at her thirteenth

birthday party when she got her period for the first time. Not quite the birthday surprise she'd been hoping for.

"Hmm, that's what I thought. You see, Jerry, I'll let you in on a little secret." I lower my voice to a whisper as I lean into the group. "In order to make calls, you actually have to be on the field. And by the sound of it, you're still on the bench, sweetie."

I pull back at the sound of James' friends uproaring in laughter, smacking against his chest as he purses his lips.

"Oh, and word of advice," I add, spinning on my heel to face them again. "Most girls like it a little rough."

I smirk, flipping my hair over my shoulder and turning to grab my bags as they remain in place, clearly taken aback by my comment.

"Now, if you're all done with this little parade, these bags aren't going to carry themselves."

James folds his arms across his chest. "What makes you think we're going to help you after that?"

"Hmm, let's see." I pull out my phone, typing in "schools in Crawley" into my search engine. "I wonder what school you guys go to? I bet they'd be quite disappointed to know that you're skipping class. What did you say your name was again? *James—*"

"We'll help!" James rushes his way to my side, his voice much more sheepish than it had been a moment before.

I can't help but grin as the rest of the boys make their way over, reaching for my suitcases. "Good decision!" I clap my hands. "Now, chop, chop. I don't have all day. I haven't updated my followers in, like, an hour. That cab ride was a total drag."

"THANKS, GUYS! YOU'RE THE BEST!" I call out after the boys as they head out the door one by one an hour later.

"See you, Delaney," they respond—we're on a first-name basis now. "You give us a ring if anyone gives you trouble, alright? We'll be sure to sort them out."

I playfully roll my eyes. It's nice to know that there's someone here already in my corner, but truthfully, I'm not sure if this group is capable of a whole lot of damage, so to speak. "I will." I nod, waving my phone in the air to get their attention. "But remind me, how do I add that little plus sign before I call?"

They chuckle, and instead of showing me how to do it, they playfully save a number in my contacts as "Jerry James" before they leave my apartment, which, apparently, I need to start calling a flat.

Not only had I convinced them to help me carry my bags upstairs, I'd also convinced them to help me unpack. I'm on quite a roll with this persuasiveness lately.

I flop down onto my bed with my phone in hand, attempting to catch up on everything I'd missed on the flight, reminding me that I haven't eaten anything since that disgusting mid-flight meal I was offered.

Opening up my web browser, I search for the closest quick-service food spot, rushing out of the building once I've found a place that sounds promising and doesn't require too much walking.

It's August and 50 degrees Fahrenheit outside. It was 88 in Houston when I left. Needless to say, I'm absolutely freezing. I wrap my coat around myself tightly and follow my phone's GPS down the street.

After a whole five minutes of walking, I stop when I notice a building with a bright blue poster plastered on the side facing the street.

I'm compelled to get a closer look as I travel slightly off course, realizing that the text on the poster says "Crawfield Football Club."

My eyes light up in excitement. So, *this* is where I'll be spending my time for the next three months. Had I found it? Or, had it found me? Or, is this town so small that it would virtually be impossible for it to have gone unnoticed? The fateful part of my identity wants to believe the earlier—but the logical part finds sense in the latter.

I cross the road and rush towards the front entrance of what I can now tell is a soccer stadium. *Stadium* is a generous word, given some of the venues I've had the pleasure of watching shows in, but still, around here, this feels huge.

It's crazy, isn't it? That the smallest of towns will allocate such a considerable amount of real estate towards kicking a ball around.

Gosh...now I'm starting to sound like my dad.

The parking lot to the stadium is pretty empty, with the occasional car occupying some spots. It's also eerily quiet around here, so much so that it's almost peaceful.

When you grow up in the most populated city in Texas, the sound of dense city noise becomes customary.

But here, besides the occasional car that rolls down the street and the wind that sways through the trees, it's quiet. All I can hear right now if I really listen closely, is the repeated sound of a whistle being blown and muffled voices.

I follow the noise to what appears to be the front gates to the field, which are sealed behind turnstiles and four unmanned "ticket" booths.

Curiosity gets the best of me as I lean my head through the gap of the gates, craning my neck to get a peek inside.

It's smaller than I'd anticipated, even though the only visual I've ever had of the stadium was what I saw on TV with Gramps. I'm pretty sure the venue for my 16th birthday party was bigger than the space the field occupies. But Gramps always said, "Crawley is a small town that becomes a big part of your heart." Maybe that just means that there is only room for this place to grow on me.

Another sound of the whistle is followed by a voice calling out, "lads, you're absolutely smashing it. I'd better see this same energy on game day."

Smashing it?

"Keep it up," they encourage as I glance toward the voice that commands not only my attention but all of the players.

There's roughly about 14 to 16 guys in total, but only one seems to draw in my gaze, and it's not a player at all. It's the man who stands along the side of the pitch, with one hand perched against his stubbled cheek as he surveys the field in deep thought.

Unlike the players, who appear to be wearing a mixture of Crawley uniforms, this man is dressed a step up in a form-fitting white button-down top. But it's not the way the shirt clings to his chest that keeps my attention. No, it's the way he's got the sleeves tensed up around his vascular forearms.

"Coach, can we take a quick water break?" One of the players turns to ask him, catching his attention.

Coach.

He's the coach. *Good Lord.*

I'd always envisioned a coach being someone much older. A person who's been through their own fair share of years in the industry and opted to return because the sport is all they've ever known.

The older gentleman who joins the guys on the field, setting up what appears to be a drill, is exactly what I had in mind.

But no, the Coach of Crawfield looks as though we could be the same age. Yet, he's got a look in his eyes that tells me he is, in fact, older, more experienced, wiser. There's something profoundly unsettling about that—I just can't put my finger on exactly why.

The players sense his approval as he subtly tilts his chin upwards, granting permission.

As each player starts to make their way off the field and over to the bench, I sneak a quick glance back at him, only to be completely caught off guard when I realize his gaze has now fallen onto me.

"Oi!" he shouts, his face falling flat. His outburst causes the players to shift their attention back at him before they follow his intense gaze over to me.

I freeze in place. What should I do? Should I run? No, I don't do running. But I also don't do awkward first impressions. Ugh, think Delaney, think.

"Hey, love," one of the players shouts, nodding in my direction with a playful smirk. "We don't usually let fans in early, but if you want a tour, I'd be happy to take you around—"

"Wilks!" Coach calls out in a sharp, assertive tone. "Water break's over. Get back out there."

The boys groan out in annoyance, playfully punching "Wilks" in the chest as they head back onto the field. "You knobhead, you always manage to ruin it for the rest of us."

Knobhead?

What does that mean?

And why am I still standing here?

I attempt to answer the lingering questions in my mind before Coach straightens his spine, his posture tall as he begins to head in my direction. It's clear that he's got a purpose in mind—that purpose probably being to tell me off. Let's just say I don't do well with being told off. My high school gym teacher, Mr. Barnes, yelled at me once for giving up halfway through my morning laps. Let's just say I cried so much that I was hospitalized for dehydration.

And it's at that moment that I realize, much to my dismay, that running might be my only viable option. I bet this is my payback for complaining about Mr. Barnes' excessive volume levels and getting him suspended for a week. It's all coming back to bite me in the ass.

I hate that it's come to this.

Without wasting another moment, I quickly tuck myself around the corner of the building, just in time for Coach to meet the gates.

"Hello?" I hear him call out in question. "Is someone there?"

His accent is thick, so thick. It's way thicker than anyone else I've met today—but so irresistibly smooth. Now, I'm partially regretting not giving him something to yell at me for because, as sickening as it is, I think I would've liked it.

My heart pounds in anticipation that he's going to come out of the gate—but he doesn't. Instead, I hear him grumble something under his breath before his footsteps travel away and make their way back onto the field. "Right, from the top," he announces, blowing the whistle.

Briskly, I break free from the wall and make my way back onto the main street, pulling my phone back out only to realize that my GPS has given up on redirecting me.

I huff out in frustration and open up my contacts app, dialing the one and only U.K. contact to save me from this distress.

"You calling already, Delaney?" James picks up after a few rings. "It's only been an hour."

"Listen," I bring my voice to a whisper, even though I'm far enough from the stadium that no one can hear me. "I'm, like, *miles* away from home. And I'm starving. I need you to come get me."

"Drop your address," James responds.

As I share my location with him, it prompts a long pause on the other end of the call.

"Hello?!" I snap impatiently. "Are you coming to get me or not? Do you even have Uber out here?"

"Delaney," he speaks up after a moment. "You're literally just up the street."

"I guess that means I'll see you soon then," I end the call before diverting my eyes back to the stadium.

Day one has *not* gone the way I expected so far.

#Seven

WARREN

"RIGHT, boys, she'll be here any minute. Shape up." I clap my hands together and gather the team in a line on the side of the pitch.

"Coach, this is ridiculous," Christoper Hart, our center-fielder, calls out.

"Yeah, it's not like we're meeting the Queen," Wilks scoffs, prompting the rest of the team to groan in agreement.

"Well, you wouldn't be, 'cause she's dead," I remark point-blank, forcing some redness to rise to Wilks's face. "Besides..." I run a hand along my forehead. "Do you lot ever stop complaining?"

Some days, I wonder if I'm a football coach or a primary school teacher. Seriously, all they've been asked to do is wait civilly for a few brief minutes to meet Ira's granddaughter after practice —then they're free to sod off and do Lord knows what.

I've spent the last 72 hours since Alf broke the news of her impending arrival going back and forth between how I feel about welcoming an entirely new person into our club.

It's a terrible idea. We don't need anyone new coming in here and changing our team dynamic—end of story. But then there's that looming reminder....*she's Ira's granddaughter.*

Regardless, she could turn out to be nothing but a distraction to the boys. Is that what we want? What we need?

But she's Ira's granddaughter.

This is ridiculous. The season's just around the corner, and we need to focus on strategizing and practicing more than anything. That should be our only priority.

But she's Ira's granddaughter.

This is infuriating, I don't even know this God damn girl, and she's already clouding my judgment. Who is she, anyway? Is she a charismatic, passionate football fan like Ira? Or is she the money-grabbing, prideful spawn of her father?

Who knows?

The only thing I know for a fact is that she is, Ira's grand-daughter, and for now, that's what will warrant me being on my best behavior.

Still, it doesn't change that at the end of the day, she's on our grounds, and I'm in charge around here. I call the shots. These are my boys and this—

"Must be the team!" I hear an overly excited high-pitched squeal come from a few feet behind me, the lads and I turning our heads in the direction of the voice.

The team goes silent as they lay eyes on the girl who's skipping across the field toward us. I'm certain it's not her hair flowing behind her that they're looking at. It's the way she's ridiculously styled a Crawfield jersey by tying it in the front much too tightly, exposing most of her midriff and toned abdomen while pairing it with some skinny jeans and heels.

"Aw, were you guys all lined up to meet me?" She places her hands on her chest adoringly. "That's adorable, I'm so...*woah!*"

She doesn't get the chance to finish her sentence as she stumbles over her feet, face-planting into the green—and I'm not just talking about the grass. Within a moment, the whole team rushes to her side, and Daniel Green is the first to reach her.

"You alright, love?" the boys all ask one by one, leaving me with an unfamiliar sense of discomfort, not because of their concern but because of their desire to get their hands on her.

Her cheeks are slightly flushed, but she flashes an effortlessly brilliant smile as she takes Green's hand and thanks him, bringing herself to her feet. Clearly, she doesn't mind the attention as she laughs in response and tucks her hair back into place. "Whoops. Gramps always did say that I was a bit of a klutz."

It's *her*.

I clear my throat loudly, ending the conversation abruptly as the lads turn around to face me. All the while, the girl looks up and directly into my eyes for the very first time.

"Hi!" She confidently struts her way over to me despite the fact that I'd basically just witnessed her make out with the ground. The rest of the team trails behind, likely making sure she looks just as good from the back as she does from the front. I don't need to. I'm already convinced she does. "I'm Delaney Matthews." She reaches her perfectly manicured hand out to shake mine. "And you are?"

I analyze her for a moment. God, this girl has the biggest eyes I've ever seen. The most delicate of features. Soft lips, rounded cheeks, and a faint layer of freckles along the bridge of her nose.

Holy shit.

She's definitely nothing like Ira or Hank.

She's her own.

"You'll have to excuse Coach." Wilks walks over, slinging an arm around Delaney before I can reciprocate her handshake. "He's hardly ever around women."

Delaney giggles while I scowl.

"Back in line, Wilks," I say between ground teeth, prompting him to shoot me a mischievous grin.

As he removes his arm along Delaney's shoulder, she takes a moment to brush the remaining green off of her hands and onto her skinny jeans. "And do you have a name, *Coach*?" she asks, and I almost don't want to give her the answer just so that I can hear her call me that over and over.

I'd never been a fan of the American accent—it was always too peppy-spirited, but her voice is sweet—a forbidden nectar that I know I shouldn't be enjoying the sound of as much as I am at this moment.

"Warren." I have to swallow in order to resolve this massive lump that's formed in my throat. "It's Warren Park."

A stint of silence falls between us until she flashes me another doe-eyed gaze. "Well, *Warren Park*," she says my full name back to me like a symphony humming through my mind. "It's nice to meet you."

I nod in response, letting the silence settle between the two of us before the team eventually chimes back in.

"You going to introduce us or what?" a few of the boys call out, causing an uproar from the rest of them.

"Yeah, introduce us, Coach! Don't be shy."

Delaney bites down on her bottom lip as she turns back towards the team. "Don't worry, boys, there's enough of me to go around," she teases, causing a few glances and not-so-subtle obscene gestures amongst the lads—she doesn't take notice of it, but I do. Something inside me prompts me to shut it down, and it's almost so instantaneous that I don't have time to question it.

"Delaney," I say her name for the first time out loud, noticing how smoothly it rolls off my tongue. "This is the team. Team, this is Delaney Matthews, joining us from Houston, Texas. She's going to be your new..."

Shit, what the hell is she here to do again?

"Public relations manager," she finishes my sentence for me, saving me the trouble yet leaving me to wonder what in the world that is. I left school at sixteen to play football full-time. Life outside of the stadium might as well be a foreign language to me —let alone career titles.

"And uh—what exactly is that?" Wilks asks the question I can tell that everyone is wondering. I'll thank him for that one later.

"Well..." Delaney places her hands on her hips, looking up in thought. "I'm here because I want to make you guys the most popular soccer team in all of England!"

I have to fight the urge not to roll my eyes while the team bursts into laughter for a number of reasons. First, because of Delaney's absurd enthusiasm, and second, because of her use of the forbidden word "soccer." She really doesn't know a single thing about us. Just like I'd told Alf—this is going to be a joke.

"Listen, babe," Green is the first to put his two cents in. "The reality is, we may get two hundred and fifty people *max* at a game, and that's when the tickets are free, and our extended families are in town. So explain, how on Earth are you going to convince a country of over fifty-five million people that we're the best?"

It's a great question. Such a great question that I can tell that Delaney doesn't quite seem to know how to answer it.

"Well..." She starts, shifting her weight from one leg to the other as she rubs the back of her neck. "That, I'm not quite sure about yet! But what I do know is that I have a ton of experience when it comes to getting eyes on you and building *intimate* connections!"

Oh no, here it comes.

"Are you looking to expand your resume?" Wilks snickers in response, causing the team to explode into laughter.

And there it is.

"Wilks!" Alf joins me by my side, a frown of disapproval on his face. "All of you!" He scolds as the laughter comes to an almost immediate halt. "We're done with introductions today. Get in the showers. Now."

The team sighs in defeat as they trudge their way off the pitch, but that doesn't stop the lads from suggestively glancing over at Delaney one last time before they disappear into the tunnel.

"You know where to find us to build more *intimate connections*." Hart flashes her a wink, prompting Alf to slap him on the back as he walks by.

Christ, I can only imagine what the topic of conversation in the changing room is about to be.

"I'm sorry about them." Alf takes the liberty to apologize on behalf of the group. "They're just excited, that's all." He brushes aside the guys' sexual enthusiasm as genuine enthusiasm before as he shoots me a stare. "In fact, we're *all* excited to have you join us, aren't we, Parker?" Alf asks rhetorically, nudging me as he speaks.

I do my best to nod, even though the only value I can see Delaney bringing to this team so far is an opportunity for an easy punch-line amongst the group and a rest for the eyes.

Wilks wasn't completely unhinged with his remark earlier about my involvement with women. How can I find the time to secure a relationship when this team takes up far too much of it? I wouldn't have it any other way, though, but the truth is, I already know that Delaney is unlike any girl I've seen before. She's unique, bold, and a ray of...*sunshine.*

"Right." Alf disrupts my thought, clearing his throat. "Well, I've got some work to do..." He gestures back. "But how about I catch up with you two tomorrow? Sound good?" Alf proposes, giving Delaney one last reassuring smile before heading off through the tunnel and toward his office.

Once he's out of sight, Delaney beams in my direction. "I think that went really well!" She cheers as I close my eyes, rubbing my hand against my eyebrows. "I think they already really like me," she adds proudly. "What do you think, Warren?"

"Oh, they liked you, alright," I mutter under my breath. "But maybe not for the *public relations* work you're hoping to accomplish."

Within an instant, the bright smile on her face is replaced by a frown as her brows furrow in deep thought. I hate that I'm the clouds in contrast to her.

"Really?" she mumbles in response, playing with the knot in the front of her jersey. "Why do you say that?"

Rather than rhyming off the plethora of innuendos she'd just set up for herself, I opt for something much simpler instead. "You want a word of advice?" I ask her solemnly, crossing my arms and finally meeting her gaze as she delicately nods.

I swallow the dryness in my throat before speaking. "Remember that at the end of the day, you're talking to a bunch of grown men who kick footballs—*footballs*, not *soccer* balls—around for a living. It's going to take a whole lot more than you stumbling your way in here to earn your place on this team."

Silence washes between us for a couple of moments as I look past her and out onto the field. A part of me is hoping that she'll take that and walk away. But she doesn't. Instead, she stands in front of me as if waiting for me to continue.

"Is that your 'word of advice'?" she retorts, impatiently to mimic my stature.

I can't ignore the annoyance I feel from her shift in attitude—the expression she's portraying that's making me feel like I should've held her hand the whole way through the introduction—figuratively, of course. What does she expect from me? For God's sake, I'm a football coach, not a life coach.

Maybe I should just tell her that she's not cut out for this, send her on her way, and continue with the team the way I had initially planned on doing.

It all sounds so easy, forgetting that this introduction ever happened, though I know the task will be much harder when I try to fall asleep tonight.

But then again, before I go to open my gob, I'm reminded for a final time: she's Ira's granddaughter. I'd have done anything for Ira, I would've—because I know he would've done the same for me.

I let out a sigh of resignation as I met her gaze. She's got a look, as the saying would have it, that sugar doesn't melt in her mouth—whereas I know sugar wouldn't stand a chance in mine.

Because of that, I give out my one, only, and final real piece of advice to her before both her claim to Ira and this innocent stare hold me back any longer.

"You want some real advice, Delaney? Here it is. If you really want to be a part of this team, you've got to earn it, just like everyone else. And once you do, only then can you start whatever it is you're here to do."

I attempt to walk away, but her voice brings me to a halt. "And who made you in charge?" She stands her ground, her face unwavering. "Huh?"

I purse my lips as one. "Your grandfather," I tell her without a slither of doubt, as the words fall from my lips, her face softens ever so slightly. "And I made him a promise I'd take care of his team—one that I don't refuse to renege on."

Delaney's arms fall to her side as she straightens her spine—seemingly giving up on this back-and-forth between the two of us.

"How exactly do you expect me to earn my way onto this team then, *Coach*?" she raises her brows. "I don't know a thing about soccer...sorry, I meant to say *football*."

A smirk plays on her lips and now, I have to look away. I know she didn't "accidentally" say soccer. I don't think anything Delaney says isn't calculated.

Good thing she's met her match.

"Well, guess what, love?" I take a step towards her, unwilling to entertain her little games.

She hones in on my movements as she swallows, but I don't let up.

"Tomorrow's your lucky day. You wanna be a part of this team?" I speak. "Well then, your trial starts at six AM. Don't be late."

#Eight

WARREN

"I WONDER if Delaney has been to London before. If not, I'd happily give her a tour of my Big Ben instead!" I hear Green's remark, followed by an abundance of laughter coming from the team's changing room, drawing my attention away from my beeline to my office as I halt in place.

"Yeah, right, as if she'd want to end up with you, Green," a voice shouts above the noise. "You're only five-foot-nine."

"So? What the fuck does that matter?" Green says with resignation. Since day one, the guys have always opted to use his height as a weapon against him. But Daniel Green is the only one who can get some air when it comes to getting the ball—the rest of these tall tossers are too busy with their heads stuck up in the clouds.

"It matters because when she face-planted into the ground, she was finally at your eye level."

As another round of laughter erupts, I decide to make a quick U-turn and head in their direction, my feet guiding me toward the changing room before I have a chance to rationalize and determine why their remarks are irking me so deeply.

I knew this would happen. Not only is Delaney the topic of

today's conversation, but I'm certain she'll continue to be for the foreseeable future. The boys are losing sight, and so am I.

As I storm into the changing room in a fit, I'm faced with the sight of Green charging towards the space in front of him, headed straight towards Hart.

"Oi, knock it off!" I shout, yet they can't hear me. They're too busy spitting pitiful jabs at one another. Green and Hart are the epitome of "frenemies", if such a pathetic term exists. I've never seen two people work so in sync on the field but butt heads the second they come off.

If my memory serves me right, I'm pretty sure their mutual distaste for one another was a result of liking the same girl. I try not to get involved in the team's drama, but this...this I can't stand or watch a second longer.

"I'm five-fucking-ten, you idiot. Stop spreading rumors to boost your ego," Green protests, slamming a fist into Hart's gut. "Besides, if we want to talk about rumors, your girl told me last night that you don't pack a punch. Had to show her what she was missing out on."

"I'll pack a punch in your face!" Hart goes to retaliate, but right before his fist connects with Green, Wilks jumps in between, accepting a punch in the jaw that clearly wasn't intended for him.

"Wilks!" Hart pulls back, visibly frustrated. "You're a complete idiot. What the fuck is wrong with you?"

"What's wrong with me?!" Wilks rubs along his red face. "What's wrong with you two? Fighting over some—"

"Oi!" I shout out, unwilling to see where the remainder of that sentence leads him, halting them all in place. "What's going on in here?"

"Nothing, Coach," Green responds, unaware I'd just watched their entire sprawl unfold. "Just talking, that's all."

"Just talking, huh?" I repeat, crossing my arms as I stand ahead of them. "Talking about what, then?" I play dumb to the fact that I'd just overheard the ridiculous remarks they'd been making.

The room is silent. It was so silent that you could hear a pin drop until someone finally caved, pointing directly toward Green. "Green was talking about how he's going to show Delaney the *southern* parts of him," one of the lads calls out, prompting the team to burst into cheers, smirking amongst themselves as if that comment didn't just trigger a chain reaction of flying fists— surprisingly, mine not being one of them.

My face stays firm. I'm not immune to the changing room talk. I was a part of it for many years. It's different when you're on the outside, though, and it's especially different when the subject matter is about the one person you can't shake free of your mind.

"Hey, do you think Delaney owns a ranch?" Hart remarks, prompting everyone to shoot him an unsuspecting stare. "'Cause you know what they say, right? Save a horse, ride a cowboy?" He mockfully does a gallop around the changing room, prompting everyone, Green included, to stifle a laugh.

"That was a good one, I'll give you that." Green shakes his head in amusement as the two of them clasp hands.

Yep, back to being friends again.

"Or how about I tell her 'Houston, we have a problem'...in my pants!" Wilks suggestively boasts his way forward, and now, the remaining boys are howling with laughter, some crutched over themselves, while others are practically on the ground.

My blood boils, and before I know it, I shout, "Enough!"

The room turns silent as my voice echoes on, but that doesn't appease me one bit.

"I don't want to hear you talking about Delaney like that, you hear me? Not another word."

The boys stare at each other in mutual confusion, visibly weighing up the ulterior meaning behind my words—at the same time as I am.

"Why? What's wrong, Coach?" Wilks is the first to push his luck as the sides of his mouth lift up in a grin. "You want her all to yourself, or what?"

The sheer weight of his words falls onto my shoulders as

quickly as I brush them off. They're meaningless, change-room talk. The boys will do anything to taunt and push my buttons. I'm convinced that testing just how far they can push me is one of their favorite pastimes.

I take a firm step forward, prompting Wilks to cower back subtly. "What I want," I begin, "is for you lot to stop fawning over every bird that walks in here and start worrying about the fact that your season opener is in two weeks. And if you don't get your heads out of your arses, the only thing that's going south is our ranking in the league. Understood?"

This time, the silence remains as slowly, but surely, they all give me an agreeable nod—clearly afraid to push the boundaries any more than they already have.

"Right then." I turn to walk out of the room—this time, too emotionally drained to wonder what's going to transpire amidst my exit. All I can do is seek refuge in my office, close the blinds, and remind myself that this is only day one.

There is still so much left to come.

DELANEY

Soccer for dummies.

Football* for dummies.

I let out a sigh as I stare down at my laptop screen. It's the only source of light illuminating my dark room. Since leaving the stadium earlier today, all I've done is go on an internet deep-dive in an attempt to learn anything and everything about football. That, and replay Warren's "word of advice" on loop in my mind right before he'd left me alone on the field.

The search has proved to be somewhat beneficial. I've learned a few things.

1. Offside is when the player is ahead of the ball when they aren't supposed to be.
2. Eleven players are allowed to be on the field at once.

3. Crawfield FC is in serious need of help.

Today's a bit *too* warming of an introduction has left me wondering exactly what that "help" looks like.

Warren said that in order to earn my way onto the team, I need to pass the "tryout." The word "tryout" scares me. *Immensely.* Delaney Matthews doesn't "try out" for teams. Why? Because Delaney Matthews doesn't play on any teams. *Duh.*

I tried once—yes, just once. It was when I attempted to try out for our high school's volleyball team. With full transparency, I only did it to get closer to the captain of the boy's team, but when it came to the actual volleying part of the game, I seemed to have missed the memo, and the ball ended up hitting me square in my face.

I can choke back tears, trust me, I can. But when pools of blood, followed by the words "ew" and "gross" come out of the mouth of the so-called "love of your life," let's just say it's humbling.

I never spoke to the captain of the boy's team again. After that, I decided that tryouts just aren't my thing.

But the reality is, right now, I don't have all that much of a choice unless I want to pack up after the first few days and head back to Houston.

I'd rather sell my left kidney than hear the words "We knew this wasn't cut out for you" fall from my parent's disapproving faces.

It's already 2:30 AM., and I have to be back on that field in less than four hours at Warren's request. I can thrive on a lack of sleep, but I can't thrive on a lack of reassurance. And if my brief interaction with Warren left me with anything, it's a lack thereof.

I'm not sure what exactly I was expecting. Warren's the leader of the pack, and I'm an outsider coming into his tight-knit circle. But would a little bit of encouragement kill him? Or even just a compliment on my jersey? I mean, after all, without me, his team and his job would've been sold, gone, *sayonara*. Really, he should be grateful he has me, but can I truly fault him when he doesn't know the truth of it all?

Gramps always said two things when it came to confronting a challenge.

1. Be confident, and 2) Be willing to fail.

The motto always seemed to work since confidence has always come naturally, and failure has been no mystery to me throughout my life. Both, I seem to be good at, but as with anything, it's out with the old and in with the new. That's why I'm revamping the motto.

1. Be confident, 2) Be ready to succeed, and 3) (an additional bonus) Do it *Delaney* style.

I close my laptop and notebook, where I've carefully compiled and color-categorized my list of football vocabulary.

Tomorrow is a new day, and watch out, Crawfield. I'm going to make you love me.

#Nine

DELANEY

EAT. Sleep. Football. Repeat.

Which, in Warren's world, means waking up at the crack of dawn every single morning, freezing my ass off during the walk down to the stadium, and watching the team train for hours on end.

Every. Single. Day.

I don't think I've ever seen so many sunrises in my life, nor have I ever fallen asleep before sunset. Sleep deprivation certainly makes you re-adjust to a new time zone—I hardly even had an opportunity to use "jet lag" as an excuse.

When Warren and I officially met last week, I thought that this "tryout" thing was a joke. Now, I know that Warren might not have a comedic bone in his body.

It wasn't a joke. Until I prove whatever it is I have to prove to him, my role as the public relations manager for Crawfield FC is tentatively on hold.

At first, I was pretty on top of doing everything possible to earn my stripes. I'd be at the field at six AM sharp, looking as cute as ever, might I add. Hair, makeup, coffee, and adorable outfits. What more could you ask for? But when I learned that fashion doesn't earn you much respect around here, a trip to the local bakery seemed to do the trick. They say that the way to a man's heart is through his stomach, and that sure seems to be the case for the boys on the team.

Warren, on the other hand, is harder to crack than I'd expected. Seriously, I don't think I've even seen him crack a smile all week. I have no idea what I can do to make him happy...to make him trust me.

This lack of progression between the two of us has led to a regression on my part.

I've slept in and showed up late to practice for the last three days in a row. The first time was genuinely a mistake. I forgot to set my alarm, but the other two times were because I dreaded coming down to the field. It's hard to continually show up to a place where you feel you're not welcome. Warren is the minority when it comes to the team's fondness of me, but that doesn't matter. He takes up a majority of my thoughts—I want him to like me. I don't think I've ever wanted someone to like me so much before. But I think my desire for him to like me only makes him like me less.

Take this morning, for example. The team started to run some new drills, and in an attempt to better understand what was going on, I started to ask questions.

Gramps always told me, "Curiosity killed the cat." As a child, I never understood exactly what he meant by that. But I understood perfectly as I unloaded a series of questions onto Warren, starting with the drill.

What's this drill called?

"It doesn't have a name. It's just a drill."

How do you think of these drills?

"With my brain."

"Do you like making drills?"

"It's the highlight of my life."

His short, to-the-point, and sarcastic responses left me even more uncertain of myself than I already was—and when I feel unsure, I start to talk...a lot. It's like I can't help it. My mind is so consumed with the idea of not sounding stupid that I end up sounding even stupider. In this case, Warren's wearing patience only grew thinner as I diverted my focus to what I believe to be a much more pressing point of conversation:

Does the team have a TikTok account?

"Tic, tac, toe? Why would the team play that?"

Who would you say is your favorite player?

"Me."

How would you feel about a uniform rebrand?

The last question wasn't relevant, I'll admit. But maybe if the jerseys were cuter, I'd be more inclined to show up on time every day.

Now, although Warren's responses were minimal when it came to my questions, his facial expressions? *Maximal.* Warren has the type of face that hints at a thousand words but won't say a single one of them.

You know that feeling when you write a test, and you automatically know that it's off to a bad start? Warren is the test, and I'm flunking. I'm flunking hard.

But then, sometimes, you have a breakthrough. You see the first question you actually might know the answer to, and a light-bulb goes off in your mind.

"Hey, Warren?" My voice comes off as a question as I watch the boys on the field, all of whom have been playing in this "scrimmage" for over an hour and have yet to score a single goal.

Warren stands next to me on the side of the pitch, his eyes narrowed as he watches them intently. This has been my station for the past week—right by his side, and frankly, it's not a bad place to be. I'll admit: it's interesting watching the way his mind works. The way he's able to see a play run through once and understand exactly what needs to change.

Rarely do you see a passion so evident within a person, but with Warren, it's as if he doesn't have to try. He was made for this sport. I'm positive about it.

I only wish I knew what I was made for.

He hums, not breaking his gaze away from the field as if to tell me to go on.

I take the less-than-inviting response because it's better than nothing. "I was thinking, don't you think maybe the team should try something...I don't know, *different?*"

My words seem to irk him as he turns his intense gaze directly to mine for what feels like the first time all week. I'd almost forgotten how intimidating he really is...or at least, how intimidated he makes me feel as I immediately regret my words.

Yet, at the same time, I don't want him to look away. I kind of like that he's focusing on me right now. I've never felt lonelier than I do here in Crawley, but at the same time, seeing him look down at me makes me feel seen. He sees me, but not for how I wish he would.

"Great insight, Delaney. What do you think we've been doing this entire week? Or have you been too busy trying to stay awake?" he sarcastically remarks.

I snap out of my haze and fold my arms over my chest defiantly. Every conversation feels like one step forward and three steps back. Whenever we speak civilly, it always seems to end up this way. In disagreement.

"I *know* you've been trying different plays." I try to mitigate my comment. "But maybe I can provide a new perspective? You know...as someone who's bringing a fresh set of eyes to the team."

He swiftly turns his head away, kissing his teeth in annoyance. "You're the public relations manager, Delaney," he reminds me. "Not the coach."

"I agree, but...you're only partially right." I choke down my voice after seeing the way he carefully bites down on his lip.

He tilts his head to the side. "Go on."

"Well...it's been a week of your so-called "tryout" for me, and you haven't actually let me do my job, have you? All I've done is watch the team play and spend my nights learning everything I possibly can about this sport. So, technically, I'm not the PR manager yet, am I?"

He places his hands inside his pocket. "And what did the internet tell you, huh?" he bypasses my point with a shrug. "What did you learn?" His voice is low and almost analytical as he questions me, causing my heart to skip a beat.

I need to get it together.

For a moment, I question whether or not I should reach for the journal full of notes that I have in my bag, but opt against it. I'm sure his question was rhetorical—nor do I want to make a fool of myself because on one of those pages is a complete logo rebranding idea. I'm certain that will be the straw that breaks the camel's back.

He continues to look at me impatiently as I twiddle with my fingers in front of me. "I'll be honest, the internet wasn't *that* helpful, but it's not what I've searched that's told me what I need to know. It's what I've seen."

He cocks an eyebrow. "Which is?"

"Maybe some things that you've overlooked," I persist, looking up at him, yet he's not convinced. "Aw, c'mon, Warren, just give me a chance." I shoot him a desperate plea with my eyes. "Please!"

He purses his lips in thought, and his eyebrows furrowed as he studies me again for a moment. I recognize that look—I see it every day when he looks out at the field. It's as if I'm a play, a drill, something he needs to figure out, but he doesn't know how.

And as desperately as I try to pull away from his gaze, I can't bring myself to do it. There's something enchanting to Warren. He can be a real hard-ass, but I know the stubbornest of men can have the biggest heart. Warren's just not one to wear it on his sleeve.

He, however, has no problem stirring the pot as he turns back to the team and slowly brings his whistle to his lips, my gaze lingering on them for a moment too long. "Lads," he calls out, the whistle falling free of his mouth as he signals them all to come over with a wave of his hand.

"What are you doing?" I question, freezing as I watch the boys run in our direction.

"You wanna take over?" he mutters, glancing back over at the team as they gather around us. "Do it."

The team reaches the space in front of us one by one as my heartbeat intensifies. "What's up, Coach?" they ask, prompting Warren to simply nod his head in my direction.

"Well, lads, it seems as though Delaney's got some *new perspective* for you all. Don't you, Delaney?"

I have a hard time reading the looks on their faces. Are they shocked, surprised, confused? Or is that just the way that I'm feeling right now?

Their eyes blaze through me as I stay silent. "Well, go on then," Warren prompts me once more. "You seemed to have a lot to say a second ago."

I grit my teeth for a moment to avoid biting back before I muster up some confidence. Warren's going to give me a chance to speak?

Perfect.

I'll give him something to listen to.

"Coach is right," I begin, finally addressing the team with conviction. "I do have some things I want to share with you all."

"And that is?" They don't seem to take me seriously, causing me to straighten my stance the way I've had to do so many times in front of my parents.

"Well..." I clear my throat. "After standing here and—"

"Standing?" Hart cuts me short. "Don't you mean sleeping?" His comment prompts a few chuckles throughout the group.

I pause and glance over at Warren, waiting for him to scold them the way he had earlier in the week, but instead, he remains silent. Perhaps he really is giving me the reigns.

I place my hands on my hips. I can't contain this fire any longer. "Listen, Hart." I swallow hard. "You know, I'd really appreciate it if you'd let me finish. I'm sure your lovers don't get that luxury with you very often, but please...let a girl speak.

Besides, that was one time, okay? And can you blame me? The way you play puts me to sleep."

The laughter from earlier is now replaced by a chorus of amused "oohs" as Hart's cheeks turn bright pink in shame, and for the first time, I'm convinced the group actually heard me.

Is this how I can get through to them?

I feel a rush of adrenaline course through my body as I gather my thoughts, putting together all of the puzzle pieces I'd picked up while watching the team and figuring out the best way to articulate it to them.

"Green," my voice commands the attention of one of the two main defensemen of the group as everyone goes silent once more. "Remind me again, when did you and Burton get married?"

The boys look at each other in confusion, much to my amusement. "Married?" they repeat. "We're definitely not married," Green stammers.

"Oh..." I pout. "My mistake, I guess. I just assumed you were, considering the way you two can't seem to move away from each other on the field."

This time, I actually see a brief smirk appear on the edges of Warren's lips. I don't think I've ever seen him smile before. Not only is it a relief to see, it feels even nicer to be the reason for it.

His agreeable head nod only prompts me further. "You two need a divorce, and you need it ASAP!" I clap my hands at them, prompting them to move away from one another. Ironically enough, even in the huddle, they'd been right next to each other.

"Yeah, split up, lovebirds," Wilks eggs them on.

"Hey, Wilks!" I seek this as a perfect opportunity to get to him next.

He nods in my direction, confidence radiating off of him through that cocky smile he's always got on.

"Coach here tells me you're the captain, the big shot," I say, meeting his gaze as I speak. "Is that right?"

He egotistically smirks in response. "Yeah, *big* sounds like the right word to describe me." He puffs his shoulders, causing a few muffled laughs and cursing throughout the group.

"Hmm," I ponder. "Then tell me, why can't you make a single *shot* on net lately? I mean, is your aim really that bad? Gosh, I don't want to envision what your bathroom looks like at home, or worse—how your girlfriend feels about your lack of direction... that's if you even have one, of course."

Warren, who was taking a sip of water beside me, chokes back a laugh at my comment before quickly turning in the other direction.

He's not the only one who can't seem to contain themselves. The rest of the team erupts into shouts and laughter, falling over one another as I smirk proudly.

By now, Alf has joined the huddle, and I'm almost sure that I hear him say to Warren, "Look who finally came out of their shell." A comment that, this time, doesn't solicit a frown but instead an intrigued nod.

"Coach!" Wilks urges like a whiny baby. "Are you really gonna let her talk to us like this?"

Warren shrugs in response. "Why not?" he asks. "It's all very true. Anything else you'd like to add, Delaney?"

Not only am I surprised by his sheer willingness to let me continue, but I'm also taken aback by the way hearing him say my name makes butterflies unleash in my stomach. I'd never been a fan of my own name, but now I've never wanted to hear it more, especially when, for the first time, I feel like he actually wants to hear what I have to say.

"That was pretty much all of it," I finish, partially because I think I've made my point and partially because I genuinely don't have another area of feedback. I'd really laid it all on the line just now. "But the rest of you, don't think I'm not watching," I warn them. "I've been doing my research on you guys, and from what I've read and what I've seen, you need a shake-up. You know, there's this ride back home at the state fair called the cranium cracker. God, I'd love to toss you all into it. This past week has been painful, and the reason why is because I know each of you are better than this. So, get your heads out of the gutter and fix it up; otherwise, I'll have to crank the heat up even more. Understood?"

After my lengthy rant, I let out a breath, leaving the team glancing at each other, their expressions almost impressed.

A moment of silence passes by before Warren finally blows his whistle one last time. "And with that, practice is over," he announces. "Come back tomorrow and get on the field with that feedback in mind, will ya?"

I smile at each player as they exit the pitch and head into the tunnel, murmuring amongst themselves about my little display.

"Now!" I clasp my hands together eagerly as I turn towards Warren and Alf. "Can I actually start to do my job now?"

They look at each other in unison, although I know it's been Warren who's been the one holding me back the entire time and not Alf, who waits for his approval.

Warren tilts his chin slightly in the direction of the tunnel, an action that prompts Alf to place a careful hand on my shoulder— one I catch Warren's eyes falling onto before he quickly pulls them away.

"Well then," Alf instructs as I look up at him. "Let me show you your office, Miss PR."

I can't help but squeal in excitement. "Office? Are you serious? I've been waiting for this day for, like...a week!" I grin happily, causing Alf to chuckle. "Are you sure?" I smile over at Warren.

"Go on," I hear Warren's final two words as Alf leads me down a side hallway in the tunnel, the darkness suddenly contrasted by bright sunlight as he leads me into a small office overlooking the field.

"Oh, my gosh! This is mine?!" I run into the middle of the room, glancing around at the walls, the desk, and the shelves just waiting to be decorated with pictures of me...and family, of course.

The large window on the wall, situated right behind the side-lines where I stand next to Warren each day, offers a perfect view of the field.

"It's all yours," Alf confirms. "I'll leave you to settle in." He flashes a warm smile before closing the door on his way out.

I hop into a swivel chair that lingers by a glass desk, twirling in a circle before I stop myself at the sight of Warren cleaning up the field after the practice.

As he picks up the pylons, I can't help but notice the way he's found a ball and is dribbling it effortlessly between his feet, the ball moving from his right foot to his left almost magically.

Even in dress pants and shoes, he takes a shot on the net with a sheer force that I haven't seen one of the players exert.

He runs his hand through his hair roughly as he heads back to mid-field, gathering the last of the pylons and stray footballs.

It takes everything in me to tear my gaze away as I notice a fresh notebook lying on the desk next to a permanent marker, prompting an idea.

I grab the marker and rip a page out of the notebook, quickly scribbling a message on the paper.

Once it's written, I tap on the glass loudly and hold the paper up against it, causing Warren to glance up in my direction. His eyes meet mine, and for a brief moment, it's as if I can see them soften before he looks down at the paper in my hands.

Thanks for giving me a chance, Coach.

It's as subtle as ever, but I notice him toy with the collar of his dress shirt subconsciously as he reads the message. Rather than responding, he flashes me a brief nod as if to say, "You're welcome," turning away as quickly as he'd looked up.

As he walks off the field and towards the tunnel, I could have sworn I saw a smile on his lips.

#Ten

WARREN

"IT'S CALLED A 'THIRST TRAP,'" Delaney explains matter-of-factly as she holds her phone in front of my face, forcing me to watch a slow-motion video of Wilks taking off his shirt while making his way into the change room.

"What the hell was that?" is all I can muster out in response as the video continues to play on a loop with a sultry song in the background.

"It's going to attract a new kind of crowd, don't you think?" Delaney beams from ear to ear, dimples forming on her cheeks—seeking out a sense of approval in my firm face. "It's hot, right?" She looks at me expectantly, her hopeful voice inflating at the end.

I refuse to put the word *hot* in a sentence describing anything Wilks is doing. Frankly, this whole ordeal is painful. I'm already stuck in mounds of paperwork ahead of the season opener next week, and the last thing I need right now is to be bogged down with this image of Wilks and any player on our team who Delaney has decided to make Mr. Hotshot of the week.

She's full of ideas, I'll give her that—and since allowing her to officially start her PR role last week, her constant need for my approval on everything has been excruciating.

I'll admit I like that she comes to me before publishing

anything that is a representation of the team. It's important for me to know what's going on around here at all times, but it'd be nice if it weren't every 15 minutes...

"Delaney..." I take a deep breath in and a slow, pained breath out as I massage my temples. "I'm up to my knees in shit to do right now. How about you go and ask Alf instead? Alright?"

I wish she were that easy to dismiss. Hell, I've been tasked with finding unique ways to get her out of my office all week.

"I already did, and he told me to ask you!" She places her hands on her hips, tilting her head to the side in a pout. It's a cynical face that's been the only reason I haven't put a lock on my office door to keep her out. She has a tormenting way of endearing you. "So, can I post it or what?" She continues to push. "The last one of Green got, like, twenty thousand views!"

I sink back into my chair, grazing my hand along my forehead in thought. "Explain to me how this is going to help us?" I can't help but question how "thirst trapping" the internet is going to make any sort of impact.

"I'm so glad you asked!" She skips into the spare chair adjacent to me.

Note to self: *remove desk chair.*

Anytime she sits, she does this thing where she crosses one leg over the other—and just my luck, today, she's opted to wear a skirt. A skirt that so subtly rides up the smooth skin of her thigh before she gently tugs it back down, but it's hardly enough.

"We need to make the audience *care*. Leave them with something to long for. Here's my formula." Her excessive use of hand gestures barely distracts me away from her exposed skin until she snaps her fingers in front of me, pulling me back in. "Are you listening, Warren?" She frowns. "I'm trying to tell you the plan."

I gulp down a lump in my throat, reaching for the coffee on my desk. It's cold now, but I don't care. I'll do anything to resolve this emotion she's evoking...and everything to make sure she doesn't see.

"I'm trying," I tell her, swallowing the liquid and placing the mug back onto my desk. "I swear, I'm trying."

She lets out a huff in frustration before she continues, switching the position of her legs now from one side to the other.

And here we are again, skirt riding high.

Great.

"What I'm trying to say is if we can rope people in online, we can make them start caring. If they start to care, they'll attend our games. To root for us. To become *fans*. See where I'm going with this?" Her eyes sparkle in delight as she seeks out my approval.

Even with her face like heaven, mine remains stoic. It has to. No amount of adorable smiles and eyelash-batting will make me agree to the absurdity of Delaney's business plan.

This time, I'm the one who shifts in my seat, leaning forward across the desk, my hands interlaced. The way I gravitate forward prompts her to sink back. She's staring at my lips. I know she is. She knows exactly what I'm about to say. I've said the same thing all week. Yet, she's back here, groveling, shooting her shot, consuming my ability to do anything remotely productive.

"Delaney, I don't care if we get twenty views or twenty thousand views. We're not selling this team with sex. It's ridiculous."

She picks up on the unamusement in my tone, causing her shoulders to drop and her eyes to narrow in on me. I know this look. She's not giving up. She's got another plan.

"You know what?" Her eyes dart back down to the phone as her delicately manicured finger swipes over the screen. "Let's compromise. How about this one instead?"

She turns her phone back in my direction, and instead of seeing one of my players shirtless, I'm greeted with some montage footage of the stadium at sunset. It's a surprise, to say the least. Not only is sunset my absolute favorite time of day, but it's what I believe to be one of the most beautiful views of all time.

Believed.

I question my internal use of the past tense as an eerie silence fills the room. Yet, it's the way Delaney's face lights up in delight that makes me drop the thought altogether. Clearly, my eyes have just given it all away.

"I thought you'd like this." She's awfully amused with herself as she peels the phone back, and a playful smirk cascades along her face. "So?" She subtly bites down on her lower lip. "Does that mean I can post this?"

I narrow my eyes, fold my arms across my chest and lean back into my armchair. I hadn't noticed I was leaning across the desk this whole time. "Have you ever taken no for an answer?"

Delaney follows my movements, honing in on my biceps. It's a sad attempt at an anatomy class, the way we're both intricately assessing one another—the worst part is we both know we're doing it. It's the elephant in the room, one I refuse to acknowledge.

I see her swallow before her eyes meet mine. This time, as she leans across the desk, I'm compelled to move forward but remain frozen, still. She's the one making me cower.

"One thing you should know about me is that I'm persistent. I wouldn't be here if I weren't. I want to help, I do. I just...need you to trust me."

Trust.

A simple word with a big ask. How can I place trust in anyone but the person who reflects back at me in the mirror? Trust, when it comes to Crawfield, is obsolete. Hell, I can hardly trust anyone to complete the administrative duties for the team—that's why I've been glued to this desk chair for the past few days.

Although the task is mundane, tedious, and every other adjective in the book that describes tortuous repetition, I know that if I don't do it, or if I leave someone else to, all of my time in turn will be spent worrying.

Worrying if a mistake was made.

Worrying about what's going on without my knowledge.

Worrying that the utmost standards aren't being upheld.

Trust.

I trust that no one can operate this team better than me, and I'm unwilling to take my chances.

"Trust...trust is asking a lot, Delaney." I close the notebook that rests in front of me, finding enough strength to step away from my desk and work my way toward the door.

"Where are you going?" She turns around in her seat, her hair whipping across her shoulder. "I have other things I need to show you!"

"To get some fresh air," I mutter, my hand colliding with the door handle as I swing it open, leaving both my troubles and her frustrated expression behind.

I WAS RIGHT.

I always am.

Sunset over the stadium really is the most beautiful view ever to exist. There's nothing quite like watching as the sky absorbs the sun and feeling the anticipation of the night sky that's to come.

I've traveled to almost every major city in the heart of Britain, and after living in most of them for an extended period of time, you almost forget what the stars look like. How they sparkle, shine, and light up the darkness of night. But out here in the countryside, you're reminded how hard this kind of view is to forget.

On nights like these, I'm reminded that we're only here for a moment. A blink of an eye, and just how quickly life can flash by. That's what keeps me up at night—not the fear of death, but the fear that when that time comes, I'll look back and regret it. Regret that I didn't do everything possible to make a difference here.

In this stadium.

With this team.

With my boys.

"What are you doing sitting out here all alone, Coach?" I hear

Wilks call out before he runs up the stands, weaving his way through the seats and planting himself by my side.

Wilks somehow always manages to bring the energy no matter the time of day or how melancholy my mood may be.

"Just taking it all in," I speak point-blankly when in reality, I'm trying to distract my mind away from the madness ahead of the new season.

The madness of a certain someone.

Wilks softly bobs his head in agreement as we sit in silence, both of us now staring out at the sight that lies ahead.

"How'd you know I was here, anyway?" I can't help but speak up, shifting my body to the right.

Wilks scoffs, leaning back into the chair and placing his arms behind his head proudly. "It wasn't that hard, Coach. You're always one of two places. On the field or in the stands—most specifically, *this seat.*"

His words cause my heart to palpitate. I never knew Wilks could be so observant.

"We miss him too, you know." He toys with his thumbs in front of him, referring not only to Ira's passing but the fact that the seat that I always find myself in used to be Ira's.

As the owner of a multi-million dollar football team, you'd think you'd have a luxury seat along the field or a booth that you'd occupy from the top. But nope, that was never Ira's style.

Ira always told me that the fan's point of view is the best point of view. So, naturally, the back row, on the right side of the pitch, is always where you'd find Ira.

He was right, and now, as I sit here, I can't help but wonder if he also chose this spot to be in perfect alignment with the sunsets in the West. A part of me thinks he did.

"So, is that why you're here? To tell me to stop sulking and get on with it?" I cock an eyebrow in his direction. "Don't you have somewhere else or *someone* else you could be doing right now? Oh, wait...that would require you to have some game."

Wilks playfully rolls his eyes at my jab. Humor is the only

way to combat the somberness within, and thankfully, I have over sixteen lads who aren't shy about exhibiting it. Without them, I'm not sure how I would've been able to handle this grief...this loss. The stadium and everything in it is a constant reminder—but the boys are the motivator that keeps me on track.

"Yeah, yeah, I'm meeting up with that *someone* later," he admits, suggestively wiggling his eyebrows. "Which actually leads me to the reason why I wanted to talk to you."

Oh no.

"Don't be asking me for advice on your bird, and especially not your sex life," I immediately rebut the thought. "I've known you since you were sixteen, Wilks. Besides, you have no idea what Delaney showed me today. My image of you is already scorned enough, so please, spare me the details."

Wilks scoffs, his face full of confusion as his forehead creases. "It's not about my newfound, *very* active sex life." His words prompt me to roll my eyes. "It's about the reason why it suddenly exists."

I can hardly keep up with him. I'm always to the point. Have a thought? Say it clearly and directly. Don't beat around the bush. Wilks always likes to make me work for information. "What are you going on about now?"

Wilks plants a firm hand on my shoulder. "It's Delaney, Coach. It's all the social media stuff she's been doing."

I adjust my seat before sitting up. "This is precisely the reason I'm out here." I slip my jacket on. "And right now, it's the last thing I want to talk about."

"It's working, Coach!" Wilks stops me in my tracks before I can make it very far. "People...they're starting to care. I mean, I've never seen so many girls in my DMs in my life!"

I kiss my teeth, hands in either pocket. "Well, good for you, but that is not what this is about." I start to inch my way back down the stairs before he darts after me.

"Listen." He stops me yet again. "I know that some of her

approaches might not be conventional, but Delaney has some really good ideas. You'll be surprised!"

"The only ideas I've heard from her involve one of you doing a choreographed dance, singing some stupid song, or strip teasing everyone. So please, if those are the ideas you think are *really good*, you need to get checked out." I brush past him and glide my way down the stairs.

We reach the pitch now as Wilks runs ahead, stopping in front of me. "Have you seen the ticket sales for the home opener?" he pulls out his phone. "Look at this, Alf showed me earlier today. We're almost sold out, Coach! When has that ever happened?"

"Let me see that!" I snatch the phone from his hand. "There's no way. I checked these numbers last week, and we only had fifteen percent of the tickets sold. How could this be?"

"Delaney." He recircles the conversation back to her. Everything always seems to come back to her. "She's responsible for this! She put out some challenge online, where people had to show us their best football trick using the hashtag 'Crawfield opener.' The response was wild, Coach. We had kids and even grandparents doing the challenge. People were really getting into it!"

Regardless of the interaction, I jump back into the facts. Let's stick to that. "But how does that sell tickets?"

"Well, Delaney reached out to the people online that used the hashtag and gave them a buy one get one free ticket voucher—"

"She did what, now?" my voice inflates with disbelief.

"She did the numbers, Coach. At most, we've only ever sold twenty-five percent capacity at a game. Now, even if the whole stadium filled up with buy-one-get one's, that's still twenty-five percent more sales than we usually ever get! Plus, Delaney figures that if we hook them in now, we can also offer some sort of season ticket exclusively to those at the opener—keeping our numbers up all season."

For the first time since she arrived, I'm actually taken aback.

Frankly, I had no idea any of this was going on. I suppose some-where along the lines, she'd taken matters into her own hands. I'm not sure whether or not to be angry or happy. I settle on a little bit of both as Wilks carries out the remainder of his thought.

"To top it all off, the first hundred people at the gate on game day are going to get free merch."

My brows furrow in question. "Free merch? What kind of merch? We don't have free merch to just give out."

"But we do," Wilks corrects me, raising a finger up. "Laney said she was digging through the storage closet and found some old scarves and hats. She said the box was labeled misprint, but after we took a further look at things, we noticed that it was just the coloring that was slightly off. Remember? Ira said just scrap it."

I'm not sure what shocks me more, Wilk's use of *Laney* or the fact that Delaney actually went into the storage closet.

Wilks phone goes off before I can debate the thought. "And there's that *someone* now." He smirks, patting my shoulder. "Gotta run, Coach. See you tomorrow!"

As Wilks darts out of my line of view, my dumbfounded thoughts guide me back into my office, even though it's half past nine, and the only place I should be right now is back at my flat.

I swear I spend more time here than anyone else.

"Goodnight, Warren!" I hear a familiar voice shout out from outside my door.

It's Delaney.

"You're still here?" I lean over in my chair to catch a glimpse of her as she wraps her coat around herself.

"Persistence, *Coach*," she reminds me of our conversation from earlier. "Persistence."

#Eleven

DELANEY

"HI, Miss Matthews. This is Mr. Cunningham. I've tried to reach you a few times, but I suppose the time difference is working against us. Can you give me a callback? It's regarding your share of your grandfather's will—"

"Are you ever not on that thing?" Alf makes me jump back in my seat as he creeps up from behind me, planting himself in one of the chairs to my right as I pull my phone away from my ear and close the voicemail.

I break into a smile. "That's like me asking if you ever stop coaching," I respond cheekily. "My phone and my laptop..." I gesture to the device on my lap, "are a part of me. Without them, I wouldn't be able to work, nor would I have gotten five thousand followers on Instagram in the span of a few weeks!" I squeal, prompting the boys on the field to turn their heads in my direction at my outburst, Warren included.

"Can we have some quiet from the sidelines?" Warren coldly bites back.

"Sorry," I mouth, sinking into my chair as he blows the whistle, forcing everyone back on track.

We're days away from the season opener, and with a sold-out

crowd, I'm working full steam ahead at making this start of the season the best one yet.

Not only have I spent the last 48 hours bundling together these merch giveaways I so diligently promised, but I've also taken the liberty to plan a series of events outside of the stadium before the game even begins.

I've learned that Crawley is a small family town and that when the word gets out that an event is happening, let's just say you need to put your money where your mouth is.

Thankfully, money has never been something I've been short of. I'm learning that more and more as I secretly dip into my own allowance to cover the costs for the vendors that I've gone slightly overboard in booking. I can't allow Warren to see the bill I've accumulated.

We've got a couple of food trucks, face painting, a live DJ, tons of pre-game activities, and much more—things are really starting to shape up, which means I need to work at twice the speed.

The sound of Alf chuckling to himself prompts me to break free from the tornado in my mind. "If no one's told you yet, Laney." He pats my shoulder. "You're doing a great job. Really, you are."

Alf is totally the dad of the team. He knows exactly how to lift you up in moments where you hadn't known you needed it. His introduction of "Laney," a nickname that seems to have stuck amongst everyone in the group but Warren, is just another indicator of that.

"I appreciate it." I softly smile over at him, watching as he carefully analyzes the players on the field whilst Warren directs them on the pitch. "But is there a reason why you're not down there?" I can't help but wonder why Alf is sitting on the sidelines with me.

"Ah, Warren is in one of those moods today." He waves his hand in front of him.

Wow, I didn't notice. I internally roll my eyes.

"Besides, I have a feeling that Parker's about to jump into the drill any second now and show the lads how it's actually done. And that...*that* I want to see."

"What makes you say that?" He spikes my curiosity with that pending proposition. The visual of Warren dribbling with the ball replays through my mind.

Alf leans in close, lowering his voice as he speaks. "See how he's tapping his foot in a repetitive motion?" he slyly points ahead. "Chewing on the corner of his pen, staring at the boys in sheer disarray?"

Frankly, how could I not have noticed? Warren has a way of manipulating his body that makes mine wallow in a fit of anguish. He's ridiculously hot. The kind of hot where he doesn't even know it, only making him that much hotter. I'd never admit it to anyone, though. I hardly want to admit it to myself.

"Mhm?" I realize that Alf still awaits my response, dissecting what I can only imagine to be the look of lust that I'm desperately trying to wash off my face.

"Careful, Delaney," he scorns me like an unimpressed father. "From that look alone, I can only imagine what's going on in that little mind of yours." His words prompt the heat to rise to my cheeks, only he doesn't notice and carries on anyway. "The look on Warren's face means that at any second, he's about to flip off and jump into the—"

The whistle goes off, interrupting Alf mid-sentence and scaring me half to death.

"Alright, enough!" Warren shouts, trudging his way onto the field. "I've seen enough!"

Alf shoots me a look that is ridden with the words "I told you so" all over it. I can only playfully nudge him in return as Warren's voice commands my attention back onto the field.

"Pass me the ball," he demands in Hart's direction. Hart fiddles with the ball beneath his feet for a moment before sending it Warren's way.

Warren accepts the ball, kicking it up into his hand the second it makes contact with his shoe. "Here's how this drill works." He walks the ball over to a series of pylons that line the green ahead of the net. "You lot need to be sharp with your movements. Picture the cones as players. You want to be able to go quickly around them. Keep the ball tight to you, then, once you've got a clear shot on net, take it! Put your keeper to work!"

"Yeah, show 'em' how it's done!" Alf stands up, cupping his hands around his mouth and shouting onto the field. "Dust off those shoes, Parker!"

Warren shoots him a daunting glare, and it sends tingles through my spine. As to be expected, Alf's request hypes up the team in response, each egging Warren on one by one.

"Let's see it, Coach!"

"Yeah, show us how the professionals do it!"

"No," he tells them firmly, but I could've sworn I heard a faltering tone in the way he said it. "I'm your coach, not your circus monkey!"

"Oh, he's just afraid that the keeper will save his shot, that's all." I somehow find myself joining in on the action, and now, the entire team erupts in laughter.

Warren's stare is all over me. If it was making me tingle before, it's absolutely making me tremble now. He has no idea the sheer power he holds with those eyes.

"You've got to do it now, Coach!" Wilks cries out, making Warren look away. "C'mon, even Delaney's asking!"

Warren purses his lips together, internally debating his next move before dropping the ball to his feet and sliding his jacket off.

"*Woah!*" the boys cheer, hyping him up. "Yeah, strip it down for us, Coach. Let's see it!"

I can't help but blush at their sexual remarks as I carefully watch Warren throw his coat off to the side. Still, he's wearing a white button-down, but it's enough to see that beneath those layers is an abundance of muscle that's aching to break free.

Fuck, if I thought the chewing on the pen thing was hot, there is nothing quite like watching this man walk with the ball between his feet as he reaches the top of the drill. Perhaps I'm starting to understand why the thirst traps of the boys went so viral after all.

I could only imagine what the response to a video of Warren would be like—but I know I'd never post one. Not because he'd probably kill me, but because editing a video of him would likely do that anyway.

As Warren narrows his eyes, I can tell he's focused and unlike in a way I've seen him before. I've seen Warren deep in the trenches of his work. He has an ability to tune out the world around him, myself included, when I pester him with ideas.

"Go!" Alf pierces my ears when he blows into the whistle around his neck, seemingly giving Warren a taste of his own medicine.

Without skipping a beat, magic happens. Unlike the players, Warren dribbles between the pylons at record speed. As I hone in on each intricate movement he seems to make, I'm reminded that Warren was made for this. It's apparent all over him. As he approaches the end of the drill, the team's keeper sways from side to side. Arms out wide, bracing himself for the shot.

I can see it in his eyes. He knows he's got no chance of saving it. Warren lines up his shot on net, and without wasting a moment, there it goes. The ball soars past the keeper as he leaps to his side, his fingertips hardly grazing the material as it whips into the upper-hand corner of the net.

Immediately, the boys cheer in delight, jumping around with one another as they race over to Warren, welcoming him in an embrace.

"That's my coach!" I hear the tail end of Wilks cheer as Alf plants himself back down beside me, visibly amused by how that play just turned out.

"He's really good." I nod over to Alf, eyes wide, still trying to take in the complete show Warren unknowingly put on. "I've never actually seen him play before," I admit.

Alf nods in agreement, placing a hand behind his neck in a

soothing motion. "You don't get into the EPL unless you can really play, Laney," he tells me. "Warren's a stud. Always has been."

I peel my eyes away from Alf and redirect them back onto the field, where I see Warren reach back for his jacket, giving the two of us a playful wink in the process.

Jesus.

Guess his mood has passed.

"Wait!" Alf's words start to register. "Warren played in the premier league?" I question, noticing that I've subconsciously come to learn much more about this beloved sport than I'd even realized.

"Of course," Alf speaks as if my question was a no-brainer. "Parker played in the EPL for years, all up until his injury."

Before I can question the thought further, Alf's interrupted by the buzzing in his pocket, which he reaches for as he raises a finger in front of me. "Gotta take this." He pulls his phone in close. "I'll be right back."

I nod affirmingly, watching as Alf makes his way back down the tunnel and out of sight. Only, even though he's out of vision, his words remain fresh in my mind.

How hadn't I known that Warren played professionally? I suppose somewhere along the way, I assumed that Warren had always just been a coach. But now that I think about it, any coach I've ever seen has got at least a decade on him or more.

How was this such an oversight on my part?

And did Alf say injury?

What kind of injury happened that took him out?

How long ago was this?

With the racing questions in my mind, I watch Warren sideline the pitch, back to shouting at the boys—taunting them with his flawless execution as he watches their feeble attempts.

"Do it like I just did it," I hear him command with urgency before a guiding thought leads me to peer back down at my computer screen.

Opening up a new tab on my web browser, I simply type "Warren Park" into the search engine, unaware of just what I'm about to walk into.

As the first result appears on my screen, a deep lump forms in the back of my throat.

Warren Park—Game-winning goal, career-ending shot.

"No, you guys!" Warren's loud voice prompts me to peel my eyes back up. "This is how you do it!" he re-joins the drill once more.

I let out a breath, debating with my thoughts as they each pass through my mind, the most prominent being the voice that tells me that I shouldn't be looking at this. Especially when Warren's only a few yards away.

Yet, I can't seem to listen to the logic in my brain as I peer back down at the monitor, desperate to open up the news article and find out exactly what happened.

As I skim through, keywords seem to stand out as they're displayed across the screen.

Career high.

The most important game of his career.

Prospective recruit for team England.

The final shot.

The winning goal.

The career-ending move.

ACL tear.

My hand finds coverage over my mouth as the reality that this article seems to possess sinks in. A truth I never knew existed. Does everyone else know about this? I look back down at the screen.

Warren Park was rushed out of Emirates stadium earlier this week after facing what appears to be a career-ending injury. A spokesperson for Park outlined that the EPL star is currently in hospital seeking treatment for what appears to be an ACL tear in his right knee. Is this the final straw for Park, who was in line for making Team England ahead of the World Cup? He may have won the game, but at what cost?

The words alone haunt me, leading me to believe that the real story itself is far more chilling. When was this released?

I seek out the publication date at the top of the webpage, when suddenly an extensive groan prompts me to dart my attention back up.

"Shit, Coach, are you okay?" I watch as Green rushes to Warren's side—who's on the ground wincing in pain.

"What the hell happened?" I don't realize that I've tossed my laptop to the side and rushed onto the field before it's too late.

"Coach... he just dropped to the ground after passing me the ball," Hart explains as I make my way across the field.

"Get Alf!" I hear Warren call out, demanding of Wilks. "Get him now!"

"Fuck, I'm on it, Coach." Wilks scurries to get up, only stopping when he sees me fall to Warren's side.

"Oh my gosh, are you okay? What did you do? Do you need me to call you an ambulance?" I throw an abundance of questions in Warren's direction as he sits up on his elbows, brows furrowed while shooting me a glare.

"I'm fine!" he's short with me. "Now, can someone please get Alf. I need him to help me," his demand is asserted back over to Wilks, who stumbles back and onto his feet. Only before he can take a few steps away, my next question seems to halt him and everyone else in place.

"Is it your knee?"

A simple question that somehow elicits a disturbingly eerie level of silence amongst the players—one I can't quite wrap my head around.

"Did she really just ask that?" I hear a player whisper from behind me, prompting a series of "shut ups" to follow.

Yet, it's not the universal gossip that fazes me the most. It's the way I watch Warren's face fall flat, and I'm struck with the realization that perhaps everyone knows about Warren's past, and the reason why I've never heard of it is because no one speaks about it. The look on Warren's face confirms that that thought is right on the money.

Shit.

"Can someone help me up, please?" Warren lets out a pained sigh, reaching his hand out. Wilks is the first to help lift him up, followed by Hart, who joins in from behind.

"I'm sorry, Warren," I can't help but apologize as I find myself standing up alongside him, unsure exactly what I'm apologizing for but seeing this as an ample opportunity to do so. "What can I do to help?" I eagerly offer. "How about I get you some ice? Oh, I know. I'll go get Alf. You wanted Alf, right?"

My endless array of offers only prompts an even icier look as he limps off the field with the boys. "No," he tells me, giving me no indication of exactly what that response was directed to.

"Well, what can I do then?" I kick myself for continually asking as Wilks and Hart both shoot me a look that says, "Stop talking." "I just want to help, Warren."

"If you wanna help...leave me alone." He shakes his head, nearly through the tunnel.

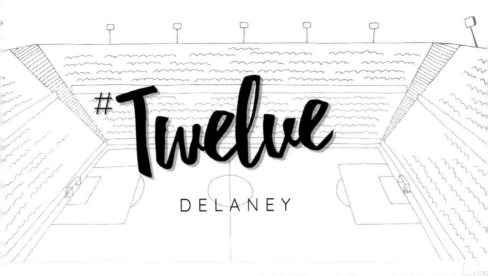

#Twelve

DELANEY

GROWING UP AS AN ONLY CHILD, I quickly realized that entertaining myself was the only real way to save myself from dying of complete and utter boredom.

Mom and Dad worked extensively. Dad more than Mom—but Mom always found herself wrapped up in something that consumed her time. Shopping, wine nights, gossip. You name it, she was involved in it.

Mom and Dad never spent much time together when I was a kid, and come to think of it, they never do much now, either. Frankly, I'm surprised the two of them were able to come together long enough to produce me, and even then, I sometimes wonder where the hell I came from.

I'm nothing like them.

I'm convinced their marriage was one of convenience. Dad knew he was coming into money. I mean, he grew up wealthy, but the reality was, he'd always known that the day Gramps passed away, he'd become an even wealthier man.

Why do I mention this?

Because it's no coincidence that he found the *love of his life* in my mom. The daughter of a joint venture stock broker that made it big in the nineties and hasn't stopped since.

I think Dad knew he needed to marry rich to stay rich. It's a terrible ideology, really.

But this is all besides the point. What am I trying to really get at here? If I'm being honest, these thoughts seemingly weigh on me now because the words "leave me alone" continue to linger through my mind.

I remember being told that time and time again growing up. Not as coldly as Warren told me a few days ago, and I've followed his request ever since, but it didn't matter. No matter how you say those three words, the meaning doesn't change, and that's what hurts the most—the thought that no matter where I go, I'm always a burden to someone.

"Why do you look so sad?" Wilks finds his way to my side, propping his arm around my shoulder. "Today's the big day, Laney!" he announces as if I've forgotten.

I'd been at the stadium since seven AM, setting up, organizing the vendors, and, most importantly, making sure things go to plan, which, thankfully, they had.

The pre-game festivities were an absolute hit. I could've sworn the entire town came out—even those who didn't have tickets. Which, in my eyes, is a win. Tease them on the outside so that they want to make their way in.

Now, with a full stadium and an arrangement of those wearing partially manufacturer-errored Crawfield merchandise, we're ten minutes away from the kick-off to the new season.

"I don't look sad," I lie, tucking a strand of hair out of my face, but Wilks doesn't buy it.

"Is this about Coach?" he brings up the last person and situation I want to talk about right now.

My diverting eyes seemingly answer his prying question as he pulls me to take a seat beside him. "Listen, Delaney. Don't beat yourself up. You didn't know it's something we don't talk about, so don't sweat it, okay?"

I let out a breath. "Oh, I'm sweating it, Wilks! These past few days, I've felt terrible! I didn't mean to embarrass him or bring up his dirty laundry. I was just worried, that's all."

"He's not mad at you," Wilks attempts to reassure me. "He's just a grump. You should know that by now."

"A grump who's refused to look in my direction these past few days," I rebut.

"Okay, fine, he's a *stubborn* grump," Wilks attempts once more, nudging me playfully, his comment prompting a smirk to fall onto my lips. "There's that southern smile," he teases. "We all missed it, you know."

I look up at him. "And whose *we*?" I curiously ask.

"The team..." He gestures back, where each of the boys line the pitch, working through some stretches and pre-game warm-ups being led by Alf. "Don't think we haven't noticed what you've done for us so far." His voice is full of sincerity. "This..." He now points to the stadium around him. "This is beyond what any of us thought would happen on game day. You made this happen, and for that, we're grateful, we really are—"

"Wilks!" it's none other than Warren who shouts from afar. "Keep warming up!"

My face drops as Warren and I make eye contact for the first time in days—I'd somehow forgotten just how nerve-racking it is to look into his eyes.

Wilks picks up on my change in tune, prompting me away with his final words. "And when I say *we* this time." He stands back up. "That means Coach, too."

I toy with the cuffs of my sweater, shifting in my seat as Wilks rushes back onto the field.

"Wait, Wilks!" I call out to him as he's about to walk about onto the pitch. "Thank you." I smile. "I really appreciate it, I do."

He shoots me a faint nod as I see Warren watch our entire interaction in my peripherals.

"Break a leg," I add on, halting Wilks in place as I process the complete ludicrousy of my words.

What is wrong with me?

"I'll try not to," Wilks jokes as he bursts into laughter.

"Ugh, you know what I mean," I stumble in my words as I attempt to backtrack on the thought. "Do good, play hard, score a goal—"

Warren blows the whistle, cutting me off mid-speech, calling the boys in for a huddle. "C'mon in, lads," he shouts, taking me by surprise as he waves for me to join in too. "We've got a game to play."

WARREN

90 minutes.

That's 5,400 seconds of extreme nail-biting, whistle-blowing, and the opportunity where I seek out to use my profound list of cuss words that only make an appearance on game day.

We're approaching the last five minutes of the match.

The score is 2-1 in our favor.

Wilks hammered in an absolute beauty of a shot shortly after the second half, followed by a free-kick play, set up by yours truly, that prompted Hart to sneak in a quick shot on net, one that barely passed the goalie's grasp, but low and behold, went in.

Unfortunately, the peace of mind that two-nil gives a person can get easily lost, especially after our keeper let in a lucky shot on net—one I can't blame him for.

Ira always had an interesting saying to me. One that reminded me that in order for the ball to pass the keeper, it must pass every single person on the field. Now, I see opposing goals scored as an opportunity to learn what went wrong and how we can fix it rather than a means of pointing the finger. Something my younger self most definitely fell victim to.

As not only a season debut win looms ahead of us but the end to a curse of a ten-game losing streak—I'm confident that there are two reasons why we've done so well today, and as much as I hate to admit it, they both draw me back to Delaney.

The first is Ira. Knowing that this is the first season we're going into without him. He has to be looking down on us right now, making sure we're doing alright. And even if he wasn't, I sure as hell had the lads believe he was.

But with Ira always comes her.

Delaney.

The girl who made today a possibility by bringing in this crowd to cheer on the lads and, even better, believe in them, something I aspire to do every single day.

It pains me to know that until now, some of the boys have never experienced quite what it's like to have a crowd of people cheer in your favor. Honestly, I'd almost forgotten what it was like myself. It's been years since I was in their shoes, yet the flare-up of my knee earlier in the week reminds me that the past always has a pleasant way of making its way into the present.

I'll admit. I've been a complete twat to Delaney since then. Ignoring and avoiding her any chance I get. Really, it's not her fault—it's no one's but my own. I should've known not to overdo it, yet when I have those moments where I get back into the game, it's so hard to break myself free from it. Truthfully, nothing has surmounted the feeling of the sport, and with full transparency, I'm not sure anything else ever will.

When it comes to this formidable use of the word "knee" that seems to exist within the group, I want to set the record straight to say that I've never explicitly told anyone not to talk about my injury. That would be ridiculous.

I'd always thought that I'm not *that* emotionally fragile, but I suppose my actions the other day say otherwise, proving to the group why they've chosen not to mention it.

But I think they've got it all wrong. You see, rehashing my injury isn't what stings, nor is it the reminder that I'll never be able to play the way I used to. I've come to peace with that—I have.

It's the pity that comes with it. The look on people's faces as they stare down at me and see this version of Warren Park I'm trying to learn, as much as I've grown to despise. Before the injury, no one looked at me that way. People saw me as a threat, a sheer powerhouse in the sport. Now they see me as this fragile damaged good from the past, and you can say it's all in my head, and hell, maybe you're right. But when you've lived this way for the past five years, it's hard sometimes to separate the truth from the reality that lives within.

I know deep down I should apologize to her. Tell her it's alright, I'm not upset, and that we should just move on. I mean, that's what Wilks talked to her about earlier, right?

Clearly she's been moping about ever since, and Wilks was the first to have the balls to address it. He's always been good with the soppy stuff, whereas I have never been good at apologies—and right now, with these last few minutes of this game remaining, I don't intend to change that.

"It's looking good." Alf nudges me at my side as I come to realize I've been far too focused on this internal dialogue than the game at hand. "Don't you think?"

"It's not over yet," I tell him, knowing more than anyone else that you don't get your hopes up until you hear the final whistle blow.

"Alright, enough of your mood." Alf has no problem telling me off. "Try and be happy for once, will ya?" he looks down at the stopwatch in his hand. "We're forty-five seconds away from a special moment, and for some of the lads, their first win on Crawley. So, now you've got..." He looks down again. "Thirty seconds to shift your mood. Got it?"

"Yes, *Dad*," I mock, prompting him to swat my shoulder as I playfully roll my eyes.

Alf smirks, crossing his arms in front of his chest, and like I promised him I would, as the final whistle blows, I let out an overwhelming cheer, watching as the lads race off the field and towards my side.

"We did it! We fucking did it, boys!" they shout in unison as the crowd joins in on the excitement. There's nothing quite like a team embrace.

Your team is your family. Sure, you'll fight, have favorites, go through ups and downs, but at the end of the day, you accomplish things as one, and that's what family is all about.

"You know what this means, right?" Hart pulls back from the hug, prompting my stomach to drop as each of the boys' eyes light up in mutual delight.

"No!" I catch onto exactly what they're anticipating to do, stumbling back with my sore knee as they reach for their water bottles that line the bench.

"Stop him!" Wilks shouts. "Don't let him go!"

Alf places his hands on either side of my shoulders, halting me in place as the team douses me with what's left of their bottles by squeezing the water all over me—sending chills down my body.

"Sorry, Coach," Green chimes up with a false sense of an apology. "It's tradition!"

I shake my head, only prompting the water to splash out of my hair and onto everyone around me, now Delaney included, as I come to realize that she's worked her way over to the group and filmed the entire thing.

"Make sure you post that on the socials, Delaney!" the team shouts. "That will get some hits, for sure!"

She smiles over to them, tucking her phone into her back pocket as we meet each other's eyes once more. Only this time, the look we exchange is unlike the one we shared earlier. It's almost as if she's suppressing her own excitement at the expense of allowing me to feel my own. She's taking a back seat. I can see it all over her face.

"We're celebrating tonight, lads!" Alf declares, lifting his fist into the air as Delaney and I break our stares.

"Fuckin' right we are! We're getting absolutely smashed tonight, boys," Hart declares.

"Tenners at eleven, everyone, and don't be late!" Green smiles into the air. "That includes you too, Delaney." He points in her direction.

"Oh yeah, Delaney should definitely come with us," Wilks agrees. "After all, she's the mastermind behind this win today."

Their declarations prompt the other lads to join in on words of encouragement.

"I'm flattered," she speaks with a sense of solemnness in her voice, quieting them down. "But this was all you guys! You made this happen, not me. So enjoy your night. I don't need to be there."

"Delaney," they groan out one by one as she denies them for a second time, inadvertently looking over to me—a subliminal message the lads seem to pick up on as they drop their petitioning.

Now, all the lads glare at me as if I'm the villain when, in actuality, I'm the victim here. Was the water bottle frenzy really a tradition, or was it concealed payback for upsetting everyone's favorite public relations manager?

I knew I'd remember it eventually.

"Delaney's coming," I speak to her for the first time in days, scolding myself for my sharp tone since I didn't give myself a chance to consider a way to make those words more tender. "Right, Delaney?" I drop my voice as my request turns into a pressuring insistence that takes her by surprise.

"You want me to come?" Her voice is full of distrust and skepticism. "Are you sure?"

"Of course," I admit, as Alf hands me a towel, and I run it along my face. "Everyone wants you there. I want you there."

#Thirteen

DELANEY

IN AN EAGER STATE TO get to Tenners as quickly as possible, most of the players opt to shower and change at the stadium, which means that we're already on our way to the bar within less than an hour following the match's end.

Lucky for me, I never go anywhere without looking my best, nor without carrying my secret stash of beauty supplies for whenever a touch-up might be required. Therefore, by the time I managed to freshen up in my office, I was just in time to find myself amongst Wilks, Hart, Green, and another few players who had decided that walking to the pub was the best choice.

I know for a fact that I've walked more these past few weeks than I have my entire life.

As we guide our way down the narrow streets of Crawley, Wilks leads the group, skipping up the street before he turns to face the rest of us. "So, Delaney!" He catches my attention with a wide gesture of his arms. "Since this is your first time at Tenners, we're gonna need to give you the full run-down."

I look up at him, assessing his words. "Full run down?" I repeat back to him.

He nods eagerly before I playfully scoff in laughter. "Listen, guys, I've been to a pub before. This isn't my first rodeo. No pun intended."

The boys are clearly unaware of who they're talking to here. They have no idea of the party Delaney that used to exist not only in her upper years of high school but also throughout all of college. Sometimes, I miss her—but then again, I'm reminded that the highs of nightlife are no match for the hangover lows that follow.

"See?" Wilks shakes his head in disapproval, his floppy hair resting atop his forehead before he wraps an arm across my shoulder. "That's where you're wrong! Tenners isn't just some pub, Laney, and I can assure you there is no place like this in Nashville—"

"I'm from Houston," I correct him.

"Same thing." He shrugs with a playful curl of his lips. "Tenners is the best pub in all of England!" he declares, prompting the boys to join in on his claim as he releases me from his embrace.

The level of testosterone that surrounds me is unmatched. I feel like I'm walking with an entire posse of bodyguards—it's pretty relieving, I'll tell you that, but a part of me aches for one person whose emotion I can't wrap my head around, as much as I can hardly wrap my mind around Wilks claim.

Why did Warren want me to come to the pub? Did he really mean it when he wanted me to join? Or was it just the death glares from the group leaving him with no other choice?

I break free from my thoughts as I'm reminded of Wilks's playful nature as he waits patiently for my response. "And let me guess," I smirk as I fold my arms across my chest. "You were the one who granted them that title?"

"But of course." Wilks cockily puffs out his chest. "After all, I do have the best taste in the country!"

"Oh shut up, boyo," a few of the lads call him out, smacking him in the back of the head as they groan in disgust.

"Can you get on with the point here?" Hart speaks up from the back of the group. "You haven't even told her the rules yet!"

"Rules?" The word piques my interest as I meet Wilks' eyes with intent. "What do you mean, *rules*?"

We continue for another few strides until Wilks brings the group to a halt outside of Tenners. It's an old bar with a flickering light sign and what appears to be an already packed interior.

"The lads and I were chatting back in the changing room, and since this is your first time here, we thought we'd break down some rules."

"Which are?" I waste no time attempting to get straight to the point.

"Well, rule number one." Green appears from behind me. "Be careful who you're talking to."

Green's rule receives a universal head nod from everyone in the group but me. I hate being told what to do.

"What?" I can't help but dispute his request, a sense of annoyance in my voice. "Why?"

"Listen, babe." Hart leans in. "If the lads in here get one wind of your accent, they'll be all over you tonight."

"So what?" I'm beginning to lose my patience. "Do you expect me not to speak or, worse, put on a fake accent?"

"No, no!" Wilks raises his hands in defense. "Not at all, and good luck to us if we tried to stop you from speaking." He laughs, nudging my shoulder. "I suppose what we're trying to say is, stick with us. Don't want any randos coming after our girl."

I release a breath, softened by his words and their willingness to look out for me. "Fine," I stubbornly agree. "Is there anything else I need to know?"

"Oh, rule number two," I hear someone call out, "If Dodgy offers you a drink, don't take it."

"Yeah, yeah, that's a good one mate." Wilks nods his head, agreeing with the next rule. "I didn't even think about that one."

"Did you say *Dodgy*?" I question. I've come to learn that everyone around here is granted a nickname. But Dodgy? "Who the hell is Dodgy?"

"Hey! Quiet your voice, Delaney." Green places a calloused finger against my lips. "We don't want Dodgy to hear you—"

"What the hell are you lot on about?" Warren catches us all off guard with the sternness of his voice—myself included as I stumble backward, and can't help but notice that his eyes are fixated on Green's touch against my skin, an action he immediately revokes.

"Oh, just warning Laney about Dodgy, that's all, Coach." Green looks at me for assurance, his hands now behind his back. "Right?"

I nod, meeting Warren's gaze.

I'm reveled by the fact that, for once, he's dressed down a step. I hadn't realized Warren owned any articles of clothing that weren't button-downs, blazers, and dress pants. Yet, as I stare at him up and down, I realize that he's stood in a knit sweater and jeans paired with a jacket.

Seeing him this way feels intimate—like something I shouldn't have been privy to, but am so thankful I do, even despite how awkward this tension is between the two of us.

I'm silent. I don't even think I can hear myself breathing... maybe because I'm not. Being caught up in his burning gaze makes it virtually impossible to process a single thought.

A visibly unamused Warren rolls his eyes, looking me directly in the eyes as he speaks. "Dodgy is harmless," he admits. "He's a sixty-eight-year-old man who hardly knows what day it is."

The faintest bit of laughter from the group releases some pressure from the conversation.

"Then why do you call him Dodgy?" I direct my attention towards the rest of the boys, although it's Warren's response I want to hear the most.

"We call him Dodgy because we dodge him at all costs." Warren reaches for the front door, swinging it open. "But listen, you tell me if he, or anyone else is bothering you, alright?"

He carefully scans me up and down, waiting for my response.

I hadn't realized I'd be stuck in place as I try to swallow this lump in my throat.

"Go on." Warren gestures for me to take a step inside.

Somehow, I break free from not only my thoughts but my permanence on the concrete below as I shuffle past him. The second I make my way into the pub, it's as if everyone's attention falls on me. I stick out like a sore thumb. Seemingly, I've over-dressed for the occasion—no shocker there, but it certainly doesn't help that I'm only one of a measly few women here—and the only one under 40.

"Um...I thought you said this is where you go to meet all the pigeons?" I'm reminded of Wilks' claim a couple weeks ago, where he referred to Tenners as being the place to meet the "ladies."

Wilks bursts into laughter, as do the rest of the team. "It's birds, Delaney." He clutches onto his stomach. "Birds, not pigeons."

"Same difference." I stick my tongue out at him, giving him a taste of his own medicine.

"Right, lads, go get some tables," Warren instructs, prompting the boys to do just that. He always somehow finds a way to interrupt intimate moments—or awkwardly insert himself into a part of them.

This whole time, I'd always thought Alf brought the "Dad" energy to the group, and maybe that's true. Alf is the "Dad." The way he's diverted his time towards the bar and seamlessly remembers everyone's drink order tells me just that.

But Warren? Warren's the "big brother"—the one all the boys respect, look up to, admire, and most importantly, listen to. What Warren says goes, and as much as he asked me not long ago if I ever take "no" for an answer, I think the real person whom that question should've been directed to is himself.

With full transparency, Warren's array of mixed signals has been more exhausting than setting up today's events. He's got me on a flip-flop of emotions. One second, I feel like we're friends, and the next, we're avoiding each other for reasons I can't seem to understand. Now, here we are, standing side by side at the bar after he's outwardly back to being pleasant.

He's giving me whiplash—and not in the way I like.

Truthfully, I don't know what to expect from him anymore, and maybe that's just it. Maybe I should expect nothing and give him nothing in return. A perfectly devised plan, one I'm putting into action starting now, as Warren asks, "What do you want to drink?"

I break free from my internal thoughts as I mutter, "No." From just his eyes alone, I can see that this single word tortures him. They're darkened, narrowed, full of question and disbelief as his face drops in confusion.

"No?" He repeats back to me slowly, as if, just as I suspected, he's never heard it before. "What do you mean, *no*?" He bites his tongue between his teeth—a deviously calculated action that makes me want to question the longevity of this plan. I hadn't factored incredibly hot facial expressions as a crack point.

"I mean," I tear my attention away from his mouth before sucking in a deep breath. "No. I'll get my own drink." I flash him my signature sweet smile before smugly turning my attention away. Let's see how he likes the flip-flop game, shall we?

"Delaney." He clears his throat, and it takes everything in me to ignore him. "I insist. Let me buy you a—"

"No thanks," I cut him short, leaning up onto the bar counter, where I can't help but feel Warren's intimate stare on my body.

I brush it off, waving down the bartender, who, eventually, I seem to catch the attention of. Though the awkward stare he shoots at me as he walks over is nothing like the southern hospitality I'm used to back home.

"Can I help you, love?" His eyes first divert over to Warren before he looks back at me.

"Can I have a strawberry daiquiri, please?" I request, batting my eyelashes at him innocently. "Oh, and can you not rim the glass? I'm not a fan of salt. Double-blend it, too, please. Thanks!"

The bartender gives me a look that I'm not quite sure is that of confusion or concern. "Uh..." He throws a dishcloth over his shoulders. "This is not the establishment you think it is." His hands gesture to the run-down bar, which I've hardly taken any notice in examining. Frankly, there isn't much to see. "We only have one thing on the menu here, love. Beer. So, which kind will it be?"

Heat rises to my cheeks. I've never been a fan of beer, but now, it looks like I'm going to have to become one. "Well..." I stutter awkwardly, scanning the options on tap. "In that case, I'll have—"

"She'll have my usual," Warren butts in. "Actually, make that two, Roger."

"You got it, Park." Roger nods, completely disregarding my input as he turns away from the two of us and starts on our drink order.

"I said I'd get my own." I purse my lips as one, folding my arms in a huff as I turn to face Warren and straighten my back to size up against him. Although it hardly makes a difference, his frame is practically giant against mine.

He mimics my movement, crossing his own arms across his chest. He's far more intimidating and far more intoxicating as he fires back, "and I said I'd get it for you."

There's something oddly satisfying about saying "no" solely to prove a point and watching him groveling to get me to say "yes." He's falling right into my trap, and he hardly knows it, or maybe he does. Given the way he can hardly look away as Roger places two freshly poured glasses onto the countertop.

"That'll be eight pounds," he speaks, and before I can even reach for my purse by my side, it's Warren who's first to slam down the cash.

"Enjoy your drink, *Delaney*," Warren says with sincerity, saying my name for what feels like the first time in a lifetime. I hadn't realized just how much I missed it—though, buying me a drink is hardly enough to make up for his behavior this week.

I say nothing. Instead, I reach for the glass point-blankly, sucking in a firm breath as I reach his eyes one final time before walking away from his side and finding a table in the back corner.

"SO, when are you going to tell us what your square-off with Coach was about at the bar?" Wilks leans in, trying to whisper into my ear. It's a terrible attempt—I've never met someone who speaks louder than Wilks. In fact, he does such a terrible job that everyone at our table easily picks up on our topic of conversation, their eyes lighting up in delight.

If I've learned one thing here, it's that these boys are major gossips. Seriously, they're worse than my freshman-year roommate in college—Jessalyn, who I quickly learned would spill everything I'd share with her to our entire sorority.

Because of that, I started to make up lies somewhere along the way. Lies that, eventually, every girl in the house soon believed. I think the best one was when I told Jessalyn that Harry Styles and I had a whirlwind, forbidden romance on my summer break before college. Of course, it was a lie—but no one had to know, and hell, the fact that they even believed it really boosted my self-confidence.

I suppose I've always had a thing for British boys.

"Oh, it was nothing." I push our awkward...stressful...frustrating interaction to the back of my mind, slowly sipping on my drink, one that, if I'm being honest, isn't half bad. Though, the worst part was when Warren darted his attention over to me, seeing that I was already halfway done. I could've sworn I saw the faintest smile on his lips because of it—now, I'm refusing to finish, just as a way to combat his smug yet undeniably rich ability to rid me of all built-up resentment I have towards him right now.

"Yeah, right," Hart juts in, visibly un-impressed at my attempt to sweep what happened under the rug. "You two were definitely hashing it out. Has he not apologized for being a dick to you yet?"

I shoot him a glare that says, "What do you think?"

I don't think Warren is capable of saying the words "I'm sorry." I mean, if he were, he would've said it by now.

"You know what? You two just need to make up already." Green sips on what must be his fourth pint of the night—slurring slightly. He's the lightweight amongst the group.

"I'm not apologizing!" I protest much quicker than I wanted to, sinking into the booth to hide from the resulting stares of my outburst. "I already did that," my voice is now just above a direct whisper. "And it didn't go anywhere. Warren should apologize to me! I didn't do anything wrong. I was just trying to make sure he was okay."

Wilks places a reassuring hand on my arm. "Just make peace, Laney. Coach is stubborn, remember? We established that earlier. So, just bite the bullet and be the bigger man...*woman*," he immediately corrects himself, clearing his throat awkwardly as he rests back against the booth.

"Yeah, Wilks is right," Hart chimes back in. "I know what you two should do. Just shag and move on already. We can all see the way you look at him."

Everyone but me laughs slightly at his remark. Yet, before I can rebut his allegation, their expressions turn devious. It's as if they've all come to a unanimous decision without me.

"You know what, Hart?" A playful smirk washes over Green's face. "Great idea. That's exactly what you should do, Delaney. Go over to Coach, and tell him that the only way you think you'll be able to get past this drama is to shag and move on."

"Shag?" I'm unfamiliar with the language. "What does shag mean?"

"Stop, guys—"

"It means you want to let bygones be bygones," Green interjects Wilks' attempt at clarifying the word, leaning across the table.

"It does?" I ask, stupidly scanning the other drunken group, who nods confidently.

"Absolutely," Hart says with an undeniable confidence as he reaches for my hand, guiding me to stand up. "You should go and tell him. Actually, go do it right now!"

"Now?"

"You guys—" I hear Wilks' attempts once more, but not in time as Hart gives me a push in Warren's direction, and I unknowingly make my way over, swallowing my pride as I'm ready to move onwards and upwards from this silly melodrama.

"Um...Warren?" I murmur as he sits alongside Alf and a few of the other boys with his back turned to me.

My pitiful attempt to catch his attention doesn't work, leaving me awkwardly hovering over the table before I finally gather the courage to reach out to touch him.

Alf beats me to it before I can as he tilts his chin upwards, prompting Warren to turn around, his sharp gaze freezing me in place.

For a moment, I forget exactly what Hart told me to say, only remembering the keyword of "shag," which ends up being the only thing I blurt out to Warren when he says, "Yes?"

What is wrong with me?

"What did you just say?" Warren asks in disbelief.

I swallow the dryness in my throat. "I...uh...I wanted to say to you that I'm tired of things being awkward between us, and I think we should just shag and move on."

As the words fall out of my mouth, so do a series of snickers from behind me, prompting me to turn around, where I see everyone but Wilks beside themselves in laughter.

I close my eyes for a brief stint, my shoulders dropping.

What did I just do?

"Did they just tell you to say that?" My wide eyes shift back onto Warren, who gestures in the boys' direction. He's pissed. Beyond pissed. Clenching his jaw together so firmly, I'm afraid what he'll do if I say "yes."

"I, uh—"

"Delaney..." Alf now speaks up, my worried gaze meeting him. "You do realize you just asked to have sex with him, right?"

The apples of my cheeks turn into a ball of flames. "But they said...the boys said..." My anxiety-stricken words leave me with no other option than to stop talking altogether, staring back into Warren's intent stare. "I'm sorry...I...I need to go."

WARREN

"Delaney, wait!" She scurries out of the bar before I can stop her, her eyes watery and her face full of embarrassment—and most importantly—*betrayal*.

Though a part of me is dying to replay her proposition in my mind, I can't suppress the anger that builds inside me at the sight of her so overwhelmed.

I slam my hands down on the table as soon as she's out of sight, pushing myself up before I know it. "Oi!" My voice is loud, forcing the bar to go silent. I can't hold back the sheer frustration in my boys as I storm over to their table. "What the fuck was that?" I shout in annoyance.

Hart, still finding this situation amusing, tries testing the waters as he pats my shoulder playfully. "Oh, calm down, Coach." He's got a smug, proud look on his face. "It was just a joke."

"Just a joke?" I snap, causing him to retreat his hand and cower inwards as I suck in a breath, internally measuring up what's more important right now. Smacking some Goddamn sense into these boys, or going after Delaney, who's run off to Lord knows where. Mentally, I curse myself, opting for the latter, given that the only reason she came over to me was to right my wrongs. A task that should've never been hers, to begin with. I release a breath, lowering my tone as I stare back up at the boys.

"I hope you all like running," I tell them through clenched teeth, reaching for my jacket. "Because after that stunt, you're sure as hell in for a whole lot of it in the next practice."

"Coach!" Wilks protests, standing up from his chair, hands

flared up by his sides. "I tried to stop them. Don't include me in this!"

"I don't want to hear it." I place my arms into my jacket. "See that everyone gets home safe, will ya, Alf?"

Alf elicits a faint nod in response as I race my way out of the bar and into the cool breeze outside—knowing that nothing will be more chilling than if I don't find her and make this right.

#Fourteen

DELANEY

IF ANYONE HAD the expertise to write a guide on what *not* to say and do around Warren Park, it would be me.

In an effort to patch things over between the two of us, I've only managed to make things more awkward. Granted, it's not my fault that the boys told me to say something completely unhinged—though I was idiotic enough to believe them.

I'm sure it's not the first time someone has approached Warren with such a proposition, but I'm certain it's the first time he had such a hesitancy to respond.

Sometimes, I wish I could have the slightest glimpse into what goes on inside his head. I can't decipher if the piercing image that's ingrained in my mind was that of disgust, frustration, reluctance, or a mixture of all three.

My mind spins with thoughts as I exit the bar and step into the freezing outdoor air. Tenners is located in a rundown corner of the street, surrounded by giant, overflowing garbage bins and a looming stench of *I-should-never-have-come-here.*

I follow the streetlights toward the main road, wrapping my arms around myself to combat the wind when I collide with a frail frame leaning against the street post.

"Oops." I stumble back. "Sorry..." I attempt to press the

button to cross the street—one that his body restricts access to. "Would you mind clicking that for me?"

"Sure thing." He flashes a toothless grin. "But only if you tell me where you're headed."

I flinch at the sight of him—I'm used to getting hit on in public, but usually, the men that do it don't look like they're collecting their pension.

"Not interested," I mumble in response, keeping my eyes on the ground as I attempt to maneuver around him, mentally preparing to walk the long way home instead.

My sidestep is cut off by him stepping in front of me and blocking my path.

"Is that an American accent I hear?" He attempts once more. "You know, I've always had a thing for American girls."

He's brave enough to take another step toward me, reminding me of the exact words of advice Hart had shared earlier:

"If the lads in here get one wind of your accent, they'll be all over you tonight."

Dammit. I knew I should've spruced up on my fake English accent.

"Can you just let me get by? I'm trying to go home," I plead. I'm long past being patient at this point.

A gasp escapes my lips as he grabs onto my shoulders, leaning in far too close for my liking. "I'll take you home, don't you worry."

"Get your hands off of me." I attempt to pull back. "Let me go!"

"Oi!" A loud voice commands from a few feet behind us, causing the man to freeze in place.

I know that assertive tone. It's one that I've grown all too familiar with over the past few weeks.

Warren.

He came after me.

"Fuck off, Dodgy!"

This is Dodgy?

Warren storms towards us. Not only is his temper making itself visible on his face, but I can see it in the way both hands are clenched into a fist, his nostrils flare, and how his eyes fill with rage.

It only takes a few strides for Warren to reach my side, where suddenly, my panic is replaced with a strange sense of relief—despite his less-than-friendly appeal.

"She's with you?" Dodgy speaks back up, a hint of remorse in his tone as he releases his grasp. "Sorry, Park..." he stutters over his words. "I wouldn't have gone for her if I knew she was...*yours.*"

I can't help but notice the way Dodgy stumbled backward at the mere sight of Warren like a scolded puppy putting its tail between its legs. It feels as though everyone around here knows Warren respects him. Yet what catches me most off guard is Dodgy's use of the word "yours" and Warren's lack of hesitation to deny it.

"You listen when someone tells you "no," or you're going to get yourself into a whole lot of trouble. You hear me?"

I almost scoff as I'm reminded of our stand-off at the bar. It takes everything in me to bite my tongue and not tell Warren to take a piece of his own advice.

"Yes, Warren," Dodgy responds, his voice barely audible as he scurries away down the street.

I wait until he's out of sight before looking up at Warren, who's been visibly surveying my frame the entire time with a look I can't decipher for the life of me.

"Are you alright?" he asks. Concern breaking free from his stare.

I nod faintly. Though I'm not okay. I look pitiful—standing out here alone in a t-shirt and having to warm myself up with my bare arms. All the while having to deal with strangers, including the man who somehow still feels like one standing across from me.

"Right..." Warren mutters, taking off his jacket and placing it around my shoulders. Before I know it, I'm engulfed in the warmth that once radiated off of his body, not to mention the heavenly scent of...*him*. A scent I can hardly put my finger on but would recognize in a heartbeat...would be content to linger on my skin forever.

"Right, what?" I ask quietly, wrapping his jacket around me without thinking twice. My teeth are chattering, but now I'm not sure if it's from the cold or because I'm out here on an empty street alone with Warren—a tempting thought that makes my mind wander beyond belief.

"Let's go on a walk," he proposes, gesturing his head to the side as his hands find their way into his pockets. "We need to talk."

I'VE NEVER KNOWN someone to say, "We need to talk," but remain virtually silent.

We must have been walking for 15 minutes by now, and not a peep has left his mouth. I don't think I've ever heard silence so loud. Something is troubling yet soothing about having this quiet between the two of us—it almost feels as though we're having two separate conversations in our minds but are too afraid to vocalize them to one another.

"So..." I finally speak up, toying with the cuffs of his jacket sleeves to keep my hands busy. I hadn't realized just how much they draped over me until now. "Where exactly are we walking to?"

I hear him release a breath and, in my peripheral vision, stop a few feet ahead. "Take a look for yourself."

I peer up from my feet, only to be met with familiar surroundings—it's a place I come to every single day. We weren't just walking absent-mindedly. Warren knew where he was leading me.

"*The field*?" I question, tilting my head inquisitively—I don't know if I've ever seen it lit up at night like this. It's a magnificent sight, though it lessens the sky above us, making my heart wince. "What are we doing back here?"

Warren peers over at me for a brief moment—and the look in his eyes reminds me of the time we first met. He was so unsure, yet I could see him fighting it in his eyes. I never thought I could unsettle someone so much, yet Warren has managed to uncover one of my hidden talents. One that's working his wonders as I watch him fiddle for his keys in his back pocket and reach for the front gate. "Well, I said let's talk..." he responds point-blank, removing the lock. "So, what better of a place?"

He swings open the gate and steps through, gesturing for me to follow.

Despite his enticing offer, I remain glued in place.

Why did he want to talk here?

All at once, Warren picks up my hesitation, pausing thoughtfully. "What's wrong?" he narrows in his stare. "Nervous?"

"Nervous?" I lift my chin up in denial, releasing my hands from one another. "I'm not nervous."

I can tell he's having trouble accepting my truth, which frankly isn't much of a truth at all. Of course, I'm nervous. Everything about being with Warren is equally as settling as it is unsettling. I never know what to think, but I always know how to feel. And despite this tension between the two of us—my feelings are hardly taking a backseat.

The cold air visibly escapes his lips as he leans against the gate. "You're just quiet..." he responds, shrugging casually before walking up ahead. "Usually, I can't get you to stop talking."

I swallow, watching as he makes his way onto the grass. "You coming?" he prompts me once more.

Finally, I urge my legs to move forward, instinctively pacing my way back to his side. "You can't get me to stop?" I tuck a loose strand of hair behind my ear, watching as our feet brush over the dew on the grass, watering the baseline of my jeans. "I'm sorry, Warren, but you're the one who likes the sound of your own voice. I mean, just ask the *lads*!"

The word escapes my lips before I even realize it...rationalize it. This town is rubbing off on me. He is rubbing off on me—and not in the way I wish he would.

I see a hint of amusement in his eyes as he tucks his hands carefully into his pockets. "Lads, eh?"

We're walking side by side now, our arms so close to grazing one another that it causes me to flinch.

"You lot are friends now, are you?" he says in question. "Would've thought otherwise after that scene at the bar."

For a second, I'd almost completely forgotten about that fiasco. Warren does that to me—leaving me to draw a blank until the heat that rises to my cheeks reminds me that I did, unknowingly, ask this man to sleep with me only a mere hour ago.

The silence I omit somehow confirms the reality of his lingering question. "Hey, if that's what's making you nervous right now, then stop," he instructs, halting the two of us in place. "Half the lads don't know what it means to shag, anyway," he playfully scoffs, a subtle smile tugging at the edges of his lips.

I find myself staring for a second too long before I'm commanded to look back into his eyes. "Do you?"

I don't realize I've asked him such an intimate question before it's too late. Now, I can't help but suppress a smirk of my own, raising my eyebrows deviously and scanning his face for a reaction.

A flushness falls across his cheeks as he rubs his hand along his bottom lip—and that's when I see it.

Warren's nervous.

Warren's a projector.

Rather than recognizing his own faults, they somehow naturally fall onto others—a comfort mechanism, if you will.

"Nervous?" I bite my lower lip, strangely overjoyed at the notion of teasing him. I've never seen Warren falter, nor had I realized just how much of a serotonin boost it would give me.

His response comes through as an unimpressed scoff, only making me want to challenge him that much further.

"What?" I add on, shifting my weight from one leg to the

other as I fold my arms across my chest. "You said we should talk, so this is me talking."

He shakes his head ever so softly. "This is you prying," he responds, his blunt tone no match to the look of mischief in his eyes. He likes this. I know he is. "Our sex lives shouldn't be the topic of conversation right now, should they, Delaney?"

Seeing the word *sex* on his lips leaves an aching sensation inside of me. Warren and I are paradoxes to one another, entirely out of sync. At the same time as I release a breath, he inhales deeply—but still, that doesn't stop the overwhelming urge...the *desire* between the two of us. It's strong, intense, and unlike anything I've experienced with anyone before.

"Well..." I tear my eyes away from him, although I can still feel his searing into me. "What am I allowed to talk about, then? 'Cause it seems that every time I do something, it either rubs you the wrong way or I make a complete fool out of myself. Take tonight, for example. Just admit it, Warren, the two of us have been butting heads since the moment I arrived."

He disagrees with a simple shake of his head. "I wouldn't say so."

I hadn't realized that somewhere amidst this conversation, we'd continued walking. Now, we've lapped the field twice, and still, it feels like minimal progress has been made in this conversation.

"No?" I cock an eyebrow, debating whether or not to suppress the scoff in my voice. "You put me through a 'trial' before I could even start my job, Warren."

He tilts his head in thought, shrugging as he speaks. "I taught you what it means to earn your way onto a team."

I purse my lips. "Well, you haven't approved of a single one of my ideas."

"They're not bad when they don't involve a strip tease and an overplayed radio song." Again, he defends himself.

I roll my eyes. "Well, what about when you hurt yourself the other day, huh?!"

My outburst causes us both to stop abruptly in place...*again.*

Like a metaphor, now, as we're finally in the heat of the conversation, we reach the center of the pitch.

"What about it?" Warren chews on his bottom lip in concentration, causing a lump to form in my throat at the sight of it. He makes it insanely difficult to stay frustrated at times.

I hug myself in response, though as I do, I'm reminded of the fact that it's still Warren's jacket that engulfs me. Suddenly, there's a familiar scent in the fabric that tells me I shouldn't be feeling anything for this man.

I force the thought out of my mind. I have to before I say something else I regret tonight.

"I..." I stutter as he glances at me impatiently, waiting for me to finish my sentence. "I was just trying to help you, Warren, and you totally gave me the cold shoulder. I don't think I deserved that."

He runs his hand along his forehead in thought before he takes a seat on the field. For a second, I question his movement before he waves me over. "Come." He gestures, almost as if he's extending his hand to help me down. "Sit."

Normally, the thought of sitting on the ground would earn a grimace and a resounding "no" from me, but at Warren's request, I find myself kneeling before I know it.

We sit in silence for a moment until, finally, he speaks back up. "Listen, Delaney." His tone is sincere. "I didn't mean to be so short with you the other day." The words appear to get tangled in his mouth as he says them. "So...let's try and forget that happened. Alright?"

"Short?" I repeat, refusing to let this go so easily. "You were non-existent." I pull my knees up to my chest and rest my head on top of them. "Is this what you call an apology, *Coach*?"

For a split second, I see his eyes darken as he holds my gaze. All the while, the muscles in his jaw visibly tighten and then release. "Why do you keep calling me that?" he sucks in a controlled breath before I watch him deeply swallow.

Had I been? Oh...I hadn't noticed.

I slyly lift my head up despite the fluttering that erupts in my stomach from his glance. "Why do you ask?" I challenge. "Does it bother you?"

I can see the rise and fall of his chest as he contemplates his response. I know he wants to say something. It's like I can see it lingering on the tip of his tongue. Instead, it's what he really says that surprises me much more.

"*I'm sorry.*"

His voice is softer than normal—with a deep-rooted sense of remorse. Yet, I can't help but wonder if his simple response is a calculated way to avoid the answer to my original question.

I raise my eyebrows expectantly. "For?"

He shoots me a glare, evidently fed up with my games, as he leans back onto his hands. "I'm not gonna spell it out for you, Delaney. You know what I'm trying to say."

I mimic his motion, feeling the dampness of the grass stick to my hands. "Why?" My attitude seethes through my tone. "Can't spell?"

He subtly shakes his head, the faintest laughter breaking free from his usually stern lips. It's a beautiful sight. He's a beautiful sight. "You're cheeky. You know that?"

I chew on the inside of my cheek to suppress a smile. "And you're terrible at apologies. You know that?"

He looks at me softly, opening his mouth to speak when the stadium goes dark all at once—now, the only light source is the moonlight above us. Yet, even amidst the darkness, I can still see that blue gleam radiating from Warren's eyes.

"Shit." Warren attempts to stand up. "Sometimes that happens—I don't know why the generator didn't kick in. I'll go and re-boot—"

"It's fine," I cut him short. "Stay...*sit.*"

Somehow, he does at my request, comfying himself on the ground, and this time, I can't help but notice how he's sat down just that bit closer to me.

God. I've never had him all to myself for such an extended period of time. A part of me wishes I could reach out and *touch him*—actually feel the warmth of his skin for myself as it makes its way directly onto mine.

I'm sure there would be a lineup of people who'd be desperate for five minutes of his time. But here I am, occupying a whole lot more than that. It gives me an odd sense of satisfaction, arrogance, and pleasure. I'm all he's thought about tonight. He left the bar... his team to sit with me right now. I never imagined I'd like the idea of that so much.

He clears his throat before he looks back over at me with that intent gaze. One that tells me he could make me fold any second.

"I suppose we both have areas to improve then, don't we?" He speaks thoughtfully, jumping right back into where our conversation got cut short.

"I guess so," I pause, assessing his words as we hold each other's attention until, nervously, I start to pick the grass off of my palm, hardly contemplating my next question before it escapes my lips. "Why did you bring me here to talk?"

Warren starts to mimic my movements. Eyes down, pulling on the grass strand by strand before he peers back up at me—eyes full of query. "Tell me." He unconsciously glides his tongue along his lower lip. "Where do you feel the most safe?"

I expect the question to leave me stuck in my mind, with no which way out. But it doesn't.

Instead, I think back to Saturday mornings with Gramps. Sitting on the couch—watching this stadium through the screen. Little did I know that one day, I'd find myself being a part of it.

All at once, rather than answering Warren's question, my attention diverts to the photo of Gramps that had been placed above the tunnel entrance. I'd never commented on it, but that small yet impactful gesture completely rocked my world the first time I laid eyes on it.

I'd never seen the photo before, but Gramps' smile...God, it doesn't matter how much time goes by without him here. I'll always be able to remember that smile.

"Your grandfather made this a safe space for me." Warren seemingly catches onto my diverted gaze.

I swiftly turn my head back in his direction as he continues.

"He had that ability, you know..." he admits, toying with his fingers.

I swallow. "Ability to do what?"

This is the first time we've ever talked about my Gramps before. It always felt like an unopened wound between the two of us.

Warren smiles faintly before he's back to staring up at the sky. "To make the simplest of things feel like *home*." His words almost make me believe that they weren't for me but for someone else— someone watching over us.

He looks back at me for a final time. "That's why I brought you here," he reveals. "Not just to this stadium, but to the field. Because though it might be some simple grass with lines and two nets, this field is the only place I've ever truly felt like myself. I lost a part of me when I got hurt—and I never thought I'd find it again. Your *Gramps* was the only one who made me believe in second chances."

Hearing Warren call Gramps by my own nickname strikes me to my core. "I'm certain he loved you." The words break free from my lips without a second thought.

Warren's eyes widen as if he's never heard the word before. Though, it doesn't matter if he has or hasn't because being with him right now—seeing what he's done for Crawfield and knowing even just a slither of who he is...how could Gramps not have loved him?

He swallows. "I loved him too," He speaks back up. "Though," there's a somberness in his voice. "I don't think I ever told him."

I refuse to let another second go by allowing him to believe that. "He knew," I tell him wholeheartedly. "Trust me...he knew."

Unlike earlier, now, as Warren breathes in, I notice myself doing the same. It's incredible how such a simple action like breathing—an unconscious necessity to life, can hold such an ulterior message.

It feels as though we're breathing in a fresh start between us. The oxygen is new—the air has been cleared, and perhaps this is an opportunity to give this partnership another go.

As we exhale as one, I'm left wondering if the look on his face is telling me the same thing. What's he thinking as he meets my eyes? Are we on the same page?

I don't know.

Maybe Warren and I will never be on the same page...the same chapter...but I know for a fact that we're in the same book, and for now, that's all that matters.

#Fifteen

WARREN

38 MATCHES.

That's all we have each season to count on to showcase what we've got and who we are. It's eight consecutive months of hard work, travel, and dedication. Yet, it still hardly feels like enough.

It's all I've known my whole life—the routine of practice, play and repeat. It's not an easy lifestyle to maintain, and throughout my years of playing competitively, it took its toll on me in more ways than one.

Sometimes, I forgot that I'd gotten into football because it was my passion. I soon realized that sometimes, you must take a step back to propel yourself forward.

My injury proved that to me, along with the fact that other important things in life need to be prioritized, and for me...that's family.

I'd say I had quite a simplistic upbringing. Small town, supportive family, good education. I never went without. My mum made sure of that.

My dad was never in the picture much, and despite how you'd likely anticipate this story to go, I didn't spend the majority of my childhood pining after him.

Did it suck at times? Yeah, sure. But when I look back and

reflect on the past, I quite like that it was only Mum and me. She was the first person on my team before I even knew that I wanted to be on one. And with me being the only son...the only child, I took on a sense of responsibility and commitment that motivated me to take care of her, just like she had for me my whole life.

I'd say somewhere along the way, Ira filled the void of a lack of a male figure, but that wouldn't be the sole case. This team... this job has given me an opportunity to learn not what it means to be a Dad, a role that, who knows if I'll be lucky enough to get the opportunity to take on one day. But instead, it's taught me what it means to show up, care, support, *love*...and that's what any great man should do for the people in their life. Father or not.

I'm indebted to my family. That's what kept me going through the lows of my life—and knowing that each of the lads has one of their own, it's a valuable lesson I want to pass along.

The workaholic side of me propels me to take back my allowance of a couple of days off as a result of one of our away matches getting postponed until later this season.

Now would be a perfect opportunity to spend some additional time practicing and honing in on our gameplay. But then again, it's been a few weeks since I've visited my Mum. She's only an hour away, but finding time to break free from Crawley tends to be harder than it may appear. Especially when I've been managing a new member of the squad—one who would refuse to wear a uniform unless it was pink with rhinestones.

Since our heart-to-heart a few weeks ago, I'm inclined to say that Delaney and I have had a better start. I'll be the first to admit that working with her hasn't been as excruciatingly painful as I'd initially thought.

She's taken this whole PR role in stride. Now, I hardly need to go knocking on her door to question what insane "viral" idea she's come up with.

Part of me wishes, at times, I could. There's nothing quite like getting into a mid-day skat with her...especially when I see how flustered she gets any time I question an idea, I know she's got her heart set on.

I'd be lying if I said it hadn't been a breath of fresh air seeing her every morning these past few weeks. She adds a sense of relief to the group—an aura of positivity and light. Her "Good morning, everyone. Beautiful day, isn't it?" Even when it's absolutely rubbish weather outside, it is just a reminder that I've never met someone who looks on the bright side of things quite like her.

Nor have I appreciated women's fashion more than I do each day when I see what kind of outfit she opts to runway strut down the hallway in. She's an absolute work of art. She wears her clothes, her clothes don't wear her. And when I tell you, the sheer wear she put on me last week as she strode past my office in a sexy pair of high heels, I had to personally go to church on Sunday to rid my mind of all my thoughts.

"So..." I hear a gentle knock at my door, Delaney leaning against the doorway as she folds her arms across her chest. "What's the plan for this week? Anything I can get done while everyone's gone?"

I have to catch my breath, given that the air escaped my lungs at the sight of her standing in a sleek black dress with her hair in a slicked-back low bun. It was the last thing I thought I'd catch sight of going into this weekend.

"See you soon, Delaney." Hart beats me to a response as he surveys her up and down, followed by a few other players joining in on the goodbyes as they make their way past my office door.

"No goodbye for me?" I have to tease, considering the only other sentence about to come out of my mouth was, "Stop looking at her like that."

There's no denying that everyone on the team has feelings for her. It's been apparent since day one. But what's even more apparent is her ability to tune it all out—at first, she entertained the suggestive remarks, but now, her focus is redirected. She comes to me. She talks to me. She gives me all her attention.

Fuck, I love it.

"Yeah, yeah. See you in a few days, Coach," they half-ass a goodbye past my door before they're out of sight.

Delaney's playful laugh makes my lips curl into a smile, but as her attention falls onto me, I drop my face, carefully watching as she shifts her weight from one leg to the other. I won't pretend to question how she's walking in those shoes, but at the same time, I'm so happy she is.

I clear my throat, pushing back from my desk as I reach for my briefcase that lingers in the corner of the room. Sure, I may be "out of office" this week, but that doesn't mean I can't complete a few tasks to keep me on track, does it?

"Why are you still here?" I hardly peer up at her, knowing I've seen more than enough as she guides her way into my office.

She sinks into my spare desk chair, the one I never did build up the courage to get rid of. "I'm just chugging away at a few things, that's all," she remarks, dissecting her nails.

I shoot her a look that, hell, I can hardly make sense of myself. All I know is that she's torturing me with the way she now sits up in the chair, flashing me those wide eyes and tucking that same leg over top of the other.

"Don't act all surprised." She smirks, resting her hands on either side of her face, elbows pressed into her thighs. "Don't you know Americans live to work?"

I close my briefcase, hopeful that the sound of it slamming shut will *slam* some sense into my mind. But it doesn't. Instead, I plant myself in front of her and lean back against the desk.

There's something enticing about the way her eyes narrow in on my hands before they stare into mine with a doe-eyed gaze. She's got this innocence to her that I know is all a front—it has to be.

"You're in England, *love*," I say carefully, hardly realizing I've called her that until the way she subtly runs her tongue along her lower lip tells me she's heard it all right. She heard it loud and clear.

"And?" She now stands up, and this time, she doesn't even flinch to tug down on her dress that's inched up her thighs.

I swallow deeply. Even leaning back across the desk, I still have inches on her. She's a tall girl to begin with, but just not quite enough as I take the liberty to stand up straight and tower over her.

She peers up at me with a flutter of her lashes.

"Here we work to live." I have a hard time speaking. "Not the other way around."

A silence falls between us until I'm compelled to pull back, recognizing that I've been staring at her for a few seconds too long as I tuck my arms into the sleeves of my coat.

"Besides..." I carry out the thought. "I assumed you were going to use this time to see your family."

Now, she's the one who has trouble making eye contact as she toys with the bracelets on her wrist. "As if they'd have time for me..." she mumbles under her breath.

I pretend as though I haven't just heard her response, one that pangs my stomach with a sense of defeat. "What was that?" I probe.

"Nothing." She's back to looking me square in the face, unaffected. "Sorry to bug you." She tucks in the office chair, making her way towards the door. "Enjoy your time off, Warren. I'll be here if you need anything."

She's hardly a step out of the doorway when I'm urged to stop her. "Delaney." Her name escapes my lips like honey, so sweet, so slow.

But unlike the hundreds of times I've called out her name since she'd arrived, now it's followed by two words I can hardly rationalize. "*Join me.*"

She's silent, her inquisitive stare pausing on me as she places a delicate hand against the doorway.

She's intrigued.

I carry on. "I'm going to see my Mum up north for a few days. Would you like to come?"

"You..." She seems to have a hard time processing my invitation, biting down on her lower lip to hide an eager smile.

My breath catches in my throat.

"You want me to come with you to meet your whole family?" she asks, looking up at me with curious eyes.

"My whole family is just my mum," I tell her. "Besides..." I attempt to mitigate my desire for her to join me with a claim I know she'll believe. "She'd kill me if she knew I was leaving you all alone."

I flick off the light switch to my office as I reach the doorway, prompting her to rest along the wall.

"Well..." She pauses in thought once more. "I don't know. Maybe I shouldn't. What if she just wants to spend time with you and—"

"Meet me back here in an hour." I'm tired of hearing her attempts at rationalizing why she should or shouldn't come when her desire is evident across the apples of her cheeks. "We'll leave then. Okay?"

I watch as she straightens her spine, clasping her hands as one. "I'll see you then."

DELANEY

"So, where does your mom live?" I ask Warren while attempting to fiddle with the small dial of his car's radio.

I don't think I'll ever get over just how small everything seems to be here. I'm from Texas after all. Go big or go home.

I don't think I could name one guy that I dated who didn't have a Range Rover or a Jaguar. But all that's changed, and now, even though I'm cramped inside Warren's pathetic attempt at a car—somehow, I'm not mad.

"You're bringing all that?" Warren had questioned as he watched me drag my suitcases in toe through the stadium's parking lot.

I shrugged, unsure what the big fuss was about. It was only a suitcase, duffle bag, and two purses. I was underpacking, if anything. "You said a couple nights, right?"

He shook his head in a mixture of disapproval and what seemed to be awe, considering all he seemed to have packed was a measly briefcase and backpack. I don't think that would've even been enough for a fraction of my makeup.

Nonetheless, he shoved his stuff to the side and grasped my luggage from my hand. "I can't imagine how many suitcases you brought with you from home." He effortlessly lifted them up one by one before he flashed me another inquisitive look.

"Oh...you have no idea," I smirked, just like I do the second I find a channel that's not announcing some sort of football match as we begin our trek.

God, with Warren's radio history, I'm totally convinced he's never heard a pop song in his life.

He purses his lips together and presses his tongue against his cheek, a telltale sign that he's trying to suppress a smirk. As he clutches onto the steering wheel, my eyes are drawn to the vascular veins that start in his hands and disappear beneath the cuff of his sweater.

"What?" I fall back into the seat, exhausted by the look of him. "I'm just trying to find a song."

He peers over at me momentarily before his focus falls back onto the road. I've never hated road safety more in my life. "I'm not laughing about the radio," he responds, explaining nothing.

"Then what are you laughing about?"

"It's strange, that's all." He responds. "Hearing you call her *Mom*. I've never called her that once in my life."

I fall into slight laughter. "Well then, welcome to my life these past few months. Half the time, I have no idea what y'all are even saying. Ponse, chuffed, wanker, daft?" I rhyme off the list of sayings I've been delighted to add to my vocabulary. "I'm certain you guys have made half of these words up."

The rehashing of such statements actually forces a real laugh out of Warren. It's a noise I hadn't thought I'd ever have the privilege to hear—I mean, it's one I'm sure far, and few people have. Yet it's a sound I'd listen to over the radio any day.

To my surprise, these past few weeks with Warren have been a breath of fresh air. So much so that completing my job has hardly felt like work at all. I'm happy, and despite my earlier reservations, Crawley has grown on me more than I thought was possible. Yet, it's not just this town that's changed their tune—it's Warren as well.

I think he thinks I'm oblivious when it comes to the way he's been acting around me when in reality, I'm just really good at hiding my emotions.

Since our talk at the field, I've noticed him crack day by day. Want to know what's been the chisel to the ice?

Dresses—form-fitting dresses.

Heels—four to six inches at minimum.

Repetition—the way I'll knock in a pattern on his door, unallowing him to say "come in" before I take the liberty to do so myself.

Greetings—a cheerful hello as I carefully take my time to stroll past his office in the morning.

Changes—the occasional change of lipstick and perfume. All things I've noticed he takes an extra second to inspect, whether he consciously recognizes he's doing it or not.

Warren is intent towards me, and he has been from the moment we first met. He'll often emit a gaze of sheer wonder. I know this because it's a look that I recognize well—a look that I see reflected back to me in the mirror every day.

My whole life has been a journey of self-discovery, yet being here in Crawley has felt like a whole new awakening. I've never been one to fit in easily. Being here has been a true test of that. But for the first time, I've stuck this through...battled out the growing pains, and now I've found myself here.

Somehow, on my way to spend a couple of nights with Warren—I don't think we both expected this to happen.

"We'll be there in about an hour," he finally answers my question. "So sit back, relax, and enjoy the view."

I glance over at him as he speaks, and part of me doesn't believe what I'm seeing could possibly be real. The sun is setting across the horizon, causing honey-hued rays to filter through the windows and bathe Warren in golden-hour sunlight. His jawline is accentuated by the gentle shadows playing across his face, a dreamlike glow cast over his features.

He looks almost ethereal, like something from another world.

I'm well aware that the view he's referring to is the beautiful countryside we're driving along. Yet, little does he know, the real view isn't a mixture of cliff sides and fields.

It's *him*.

#Sixteen

DELANEY

WARREN'S MOM'S...*MUM'S* house is situated on a quaint street surrounded by abundant greenery. Flowers, shrubs, you name it, Ms. Park has got it. I've grown to love the architecture here. It's something we don't have back home—character in the most ordinary of things. England immerses you in its history, teaching you that sometimes, the most simplistic things have the greatest beauty.

The car rocks back and forth as Warren pulls into the gravel driveway, giving a slight wave of his hand to a few neighbors as we make our way down the street. The drive over was pleasant, not nearly as long as I'd anticipated. As we made our way through the town, I noticed a sign that read "London Borough of Enfield."

"Is this where you grew up?" I couldn't help but wonder, watching the familiarity in Warren's eyes as he scanned through the neighborhood. I could only imagine some of the fun he got up to around here, not to mention what memories were racing through his mind.

He shifts the gear into park, unbuckling his seat belt. "My whole life," he confirms, his voice smooth and assured before his attention darts forward—a sneaky face caught peeking through the blinds before they're gone in a flash.

Warren chuckles softly, playfully rolling his eyes. "Mum always waits by the window for me." He flashes a subtle smile, reaching for his door handle before he pauses. "Well, c'mon then." He gestures for me to step out. "Come say hello."

"Warren!" His mom rushes out of the house in a worn-out pair of slippers and a floured apron wrapped around her waist before he even has a chance to shut his door.

Without needing a second glance, I can already see the resemblance between the two of them. Warren's got so many of his mom's features—straight nose, wide eyes, narrowed jawline, though there's one feature that stands out amongst the rest. One that would lead me to spot her from a mile away.

The smile.

The cheeky expression.

The tenderness behind those cheeks.

The sincerity that follows.

I can't tell who's the first to pull who in, given that she's virtually disappeared now that Warren's accepted his mom into his embrace.

Their interaction with one another pangs my stomach, and not in a jealous way. No, it's a friendly reminder of just how special it is to have someone in your life who loves you with all of their heart. It's clear to see that between him and his mom. It's a feeling I longed for my whole life, yet a feeling only one person has ever been able to grant me.

Gramps.

"I missed you!" Warren's mom smooches him on the cheek. The obnoxious kissing noise and lipstick stain follow as she pulls back. "How are you, my love? How was the drive? Do you need me to put on some tea for you? I've got some mince tarts in the oven right now. I know they're your favorite—"

The sound of me closing my car door is enough to make Warren's mom stop mid-sentence. Now, her undivided attention falls onto me as she fluffs out her hair and wipes away some of the flour on her apron.

"Warren..." She looks back up at him in question, though not a single ounce of frustration washes over her flush cheeks. "You didn't say you were bringing a guest...or should I say girl—"

"It was last minute, Mum," he cuts her short, turning to look back at me over his shoulder. "She was going to work all week if I didn't drag her out here."

His mom seems to brush off his bothered expression as she nudges him playfully, heading straight over to me and embracing me into her arms.

It's exactly the bear hug you'd hope for.

"Hi, Ms. Park." I finally build up enough courage to speak. "I'm sorry to intrude on your time with Warren, but he's right. I probably would've worked all week. I'm Delaney."

She pulls back, her eyes wide with surprise. "Delaney?" she says my name as if she's heard it a million times before. "This is Delaney?" She whips back around to Warren.

"*Mum*..." Warren's got that impatient tone in his voice, one I'm used to, as he guides his way over to the trunk of the car. It's like he's a teenager again, scolding his mom for embarrassing him.

"You know who I am?" I half laugh, attempting to make eye contact with Warren, but he's too busy reaching for our suitcases, which in reality is an attempt to avoid my real question of "You told your mom about me?"

"Your name may have come up in conversation." She shoots me a wink as he's turned away.

I'm already obsessed with her. She's about to spill all the tea on Warren—over tea—and I'm here for it.

"Ms. Park, didn't you say you had some tea and mint pies ready?"

"*Mince*," Warren corrects me, slamming the trunk shut.

"Mince," I recoil sheepishly, heat rising to my cheeks. "Sorry. I'm still getting used to some new words here."

She pinches my cheek adoringly. "Ignore him," she whispers. "I swear that boy's got PMS."

I choke back a laugh when Warren whips his head in our direction. "What did you say, Mum?"

"Nothing, darling. Just how you'll see to the bags, right?" She shoots him a playful stare.

He nods, trudging forward as she interlaces our arms as one. "By the way..." She guides me inside. "It's Helen...call me Helen."

I'M beside myself laughing as Helen rehashes the shenanigans of her youth, leaving Warren to roll his eyes with each and every story. Ones that obviously aren't the first time he's heard.

I was hardly given a house tour, given that the second I walked inside, my nostrils guided me straight into the kitchen. Needless to say, two cups of tea and five minced tarts later, I'm hardly able to choke out what I'm about to say next. "If we were in college together, I would've called you raising hell, Helen."

"Oh, my gosh!" She folds forward, clutching her stomach with one hand. "You're too funny, Delaney," she remarks before her laughter subsides, and she smiles at me with delight. "Gosh..." She folds her hands as one and tucks them underneath her chin. "You're just like how Warren described you!"

Her revelation causes a silence to fall over the dining table, and now I'm not sure if that thudding I can hear is my heart or Warren's. Yet, the red of his cheeks as he hides behind a napkin tells me perhaps it's a bit of both.

Warren has been so quiet that at times, I forgot he was even here. Though his continual gaze and subtle smiles every now and again made his presence hard to forget.

"All good things, I can only hope..." I mimic his exact motion, watching to see any falter in his movements—any truth behind what exactly he's said about me.

He pulls the napkin back down, and before he can even muster up a response, Helen beats him to it. "Of course." Her smile is soft and sincere as she gently places a hand on my shoulder. "All wonderful things."

I believe her words to be true, but I want nothing more right now than a whole transcription of this telephone call with him and his mom. I need to know word for word what he said and how he described me...and I need it on loop for the rest of my life.

"Shoot, look at the time," Helen's voice inflates as she peers up at the grandfather clock that rests along the wall. "It's almost tea, and Delaney hasn't even been shown to her room yet." She stands up, shuffling to collect the plates from the table before disappearing into the kitchen.

I look over at Warren for assurance, confused by what she means, as I hear her frantically move about. "Tea?" I whisper. "Didn't we just have tea?"

Warren smirks, his breath short as he leans forward ever so softly. "She means supper," he clarifies before pulling back.

The word is yet another I'll add to my list of words in England that mean something completely different back home.

"Warren!" Helen's voice makes him rise to his feet. "Mind showing Delaney the guest room? You'll make sure she's comfortable, won't you?" She shoots him a mixed signal stare—yeah, that's raising hell, Helen, alright.

"Yes, Mum." He plants a kiss onto her cheek before he flashes me a faint tilt of his head, gesturing for me to follow.

I smile at her before tucking in my chair and walking in Warren's shadow.

The creak of each step as we make our way up the staircase reminds me of our family beach house out in South Carolina—a place we'd vacation to at the end of each summer.

The home was right along the coast—yet it clearly took thousands upon thousands of dollars and a whole team of interior designers to grant the place a rustic feel. Whereas, as I glance at the photos that hang on the wall up the stairs, I'm reminded that fancy decorations aren't what makes a house a home—it's the little things that matter.

I can't remember a single candid photo we had hung up in my house as a kid. Mom and Dad were always insistent on taking posed family portraits as if we were in some sort of elite club. I always hated the way the photos turned out. So stiff, stressed, forced—many words that described my life back home. A facade. It was all an act.

Yet, without needing to know anything about Warren's childhood firsthand, I can see that he was a happy kid. The way he beams from ear to ear, with a pair of dorky glasses and ears too big for his head in the photo in front of my eyes, proves that at one point in time, Warren wasn't this all work, no play, kind of guy. There's a fun side to him...it just needs to be forced out.

"The guest room is just at the end of the hallway." Warren waves for me to continue upstairs. I hadn't realized I'd been frozen in time, intricately assessing each photo on the wall. I could spend hours here—a part of me making a mental note to revisit this section of the house later.

"I'll go get your bags." Warren inches his way past me and falls out of sight.

I continue to walk ahead, my hand connecting with the cold metal of the door handle into the guest room before I'm halted in place, distracted yet again. This time, it's not by a photo. It's a slither into another room in the house, one I can already tell is special in and of itself. Yet, it's the sign that says "future football star" on the door that tells me everything I'm confident I'd already known.

I gulp slightly, seeing this as the perfect opportunity to take a peek in. I creep my way forward, careful not to make a sound until I reach the bedroom door, gently pushing inwards as I'm met with exactly what I'd anticipated.

Warren's childhood bedroom.

It's like I'm transported into the past—and at any second, Warren is going to run in here as a twelve-year-old boy and shout at me for being in his room.

The walls are blue, a darker shade of blue than you'd likely opt to paint a room, but it doesn't matter. You can hardly see the paint since memorabilia covers each wall from head to toe. Jerseys, medals, photos. Every square inch of drywall is scoured with something.

You'd think most teenage boys would have some sort of sultry photo on their wall of a Playboy or sports-illustrated model, but not Warren. No, Warren's got photos of David Beckham...a soccer player I only know 'cause I'm a massive Spice Girls fan.

My hand covers the massive smile I hadn't realized had washed over my lips, my eyes now drawn towards an old dresser along the wall, where I'm met with another picture. This time, it's Warren, maybe sixteen, seventeen at most, standing in that stereo-typical soccer pose, wearing a maroon jersey with one foot on the ball and his arms behind his back. His hair is floppy and falling in his face, and I can't help but smile at the sense of boyish mischief in his eyes.

"Delaney?" I hear Warren shout—the distance of his voice tells me that, thankfully, he's still downstairs.

Move.

I'm quick to drop the picture, fleeing from his room and back out onto the hallway. A sense of relief washes over my chest when I see that he's completely out of sight. "Yeah?" I call back down, suppressing the anxiety in my tone.

"Do you need all of these bags brought up?"

"Um...if you can..." I gently stretch my arm over to close the bedroom door to its original position, standing up tall as I watch him make his way up the staircase.

He pauses in a huff, meeting my eyes. "Is there a dead body in here or something? This weighs a ton."

I roll my eyes, placing my hands on either hips. "Gross, no. But the real question is, is there a 'future football star' in *there*?" I gesture towards his childhood bedroom.

He paces his way over, pulling the luggage in from behind him, staring at the sign before a faint smile falls along his cheeks. "The sign wasn't wrong."

Helen, yet again, has impeccable timing as she shouts up for us. "Warren, Delaney! I'm gonna order takeaway. What do you want?"

I rub behind my neck, craning it to the side. "Takeaway?" I repeat the word in question.

Warren runs his thumb along his lower lip. "You've still got a lot to learn, don't you?"

Oh...you have no idea.

#Seventeen

WARREN

"SO, TELL ME." I've hardly been able to sit down and take a few sips of my coffee before Mum's quick to jump into a series of questions. She couldn't care less that it's the first thing in the morning as she sits with her hands propped up against her face, eagerly waiting for my response. "How's the team?"

"Good," I respond, given that the team is doing well so far this season. Sure, we've lost some matches here and there, but our ratio to winning and losing has substantially been in our favor.

"How's the boys?" she opts for next.

"Great." I use yet another simple word that perfectly encompasses their well-being.

"Well, how are you?" She tilts her head in thought, that concerned Mum look in her eyes.

"Fine." I bring my coffee cup to my lips, taking a sip. It's hard to describe how I'm feeling these days—it changes each second.

She leans back in a huff, visibly fed up. "Are you going to respond to every question with one syllable?" she asks.

"Maybe," I smirk, realizing that I'm already due for a refill on my coffee as I push back from the table and stand up. "That was *two*."

I see her roll her eyes before I'm back in the kitchen, reaching for the coffee pot.

"What made you bring Delaney here?" I hear her call out from the dining room as I'm mid-pour.

I swallow at the mention of her, realizing that all night we achingly slept beside each other—a wall between us, mind you, but I hadn't realized just how tortuous that would feel.

The coffee that's overflowing from my mug and spilling all over the counter is the only thing that snaps me out of that thought as I jump back, rushing to grab a dishcloth. "Christ."

Mum beats me to it, handing me one from behind her as she leans up against the countertop. "Thought you wouldn't be able to answer that with one syllable." There's a glimmer of trouble in her eyes.

"What are you trying to get at here?" I'm hardly inclined to entertain the conversation, rubbing the counter spotless, regardless of the fact that there isn't a single drop of coffee left.

"She's beautiful, you know." Mum fiddles with her robe, folding it across her chest in a comforting motion. "She's exactly the kind of girl I hoped you would end up with."

"Mum—"

"Ah!" She's raising a finger ahead of me before I can even dispute the thought. Although, I can admit that there's nothing to debate here. Delaney is beautiful. More than beautiful. "You don't need to say a thing." Mum takes a final sip of her tea before placing her cup into the sink, taking slow strides in my direction and adjusting the neck of my sweater. "You're over thirty years old, and you've never brought a girl here, have you, Warren?" She meets my eyes. My lack of response seems to confirm her thoughts as she shoots me an affirming nod. "That tells me everything I need to know."

Mum's always been one to draw on the facts—it's what I love and dislike most about her. She says it how it is and doesn't hold back. My fear is that she'll say these things to the wrong person... the only one I don't want to hear them.

"I won't say a word." Mum pats my shoulder as if she can read my mind. She must be able to because Lord knows I haven't said a single thing in response to question it. Though my glazed eyes are giving it all away. "You can tell her yourself."

The tail end of her words is followed by the sound of pitter patters down the stairs. It's such a delicate and faint noise that you wouldn't have been able to hear it unless you were listening for it.

I suppose I hadn't realized that I'd been gripped on on the staircase all morning—waiting.

"Good morning!" Delaney sing-songs before I even get a chance to turn around. The sound of her voice fills me with a strange sensation. Warmth? Relief?

"Good morning, darling!" Mum breaks free from the kitchen, pulling her in for a warm embrace. There's something special about seeing the way Mum's already so inclined by her. Seeing them together causes a pang in my stomach, an aching of some sort.

Mum has always been the most important woman in my life. She raised me, took care of me, put up with me, and knows me like very few people do. I've always known that my mum's stamp of approval would be the most important variable when it came to my past relationships. And I suppose that's why I never brought anyone to meet her. It's as if I already knew what her answer would be. Yet, with Delaney, I didn't even need to think twice.

"Would you like some tea, Delaney?" Mum offers. "I'd be happy to pour you a cup."

"Oo, that would be *lovely*." Delaney smiles proudly, and I have to fight myself not to mirror it on my own lips. It's ridiculously cute hearing her adopt a new way of speaking.

God, I shouldn't be thinking like that.

"Let me grab that for you, then." Mum releases her, forcing all of Delaney to come into view.

Good heavens.

There she is, a light, bright, and early in the morning, only as she stands before me, she's not done up to the nines like usual. This time, she's simplistic. A side I'm even more enticed by. She's wearing a matching tank top and shorts set, and by the way, the material glistens against her soft skin with each and every movement, I'm inclined to say it's silk. Though, I didn't care what it was—all I know is that I like it.

A lot.

Her dark hair is loosely thrown into a high ponytail, drawing the features of her delicate face upwards. The light glistens off the high points of her cheeks. She must've put on some makeup. Surely, she had to. No one wakes up and looks like...*that*. It's not physically possible. I'm so confused right now. I'm convinced she has the power to make me question my right hand from my left at any given moment.

Mum abruptly nudges me, a calculated action given that her eyes dagger into my own as she mutters, "Stop staring and say good morning," before disappearing back into the kitchen.

Oblivious to Mum's not-so-subtle messages, Delaney plants herself into a dining chair that surrounds the table, reaching to admire the daisies Mum carefully laid out in a vase before she grants me her signature smile. It's a smile I've come to anticipate every single day. "Morning, Warren."

I take a breath in. I hadn't realized I'd stopped since she came into view. "Morning." The word comes out short and choppy— as if I hardly said it at all. It takes all of my strength to keep my eyes off of her as I walk back over to the table and pull up a chair across from her.

It must be nine in the morning, and despite Mum keeping us both up late last night as she opted to share an entire montage of my childhood, Delaney's fresher than ever.

"Sleep well?" I wonder, a simple question that Mum flashes me an encouraging nod as a result of, while she balances Delaney's cup of tea in her grasp, carefully resting it on a plate in front of her.

"Amazing." Delaney beams before mouthing a thanks to my

Mum. "The mattress was way more comfortable than the one I have at my place. I guess I just need to break mine in." She attempts to extend her body across the table to reach for something. "Mind passing me the sugar?"

I hardly hear her request that was evidently directed towards me. I'm too busy thinking about all the ways I'd like to break that mattress in for her—a part of me relieved that no one else has.

Wait.

Has she been with someone since she's been here?

The thought of it makes me tense up. Crawley's a small town. I would've known if she had. Wouldn't I?

"Warren!" Mum snaps me out of it, tilting her head in frustration.

"Hm?" I blink rapidly, attempting to break free from my thoughts. They're thoughts I'd never let escalate that far—especially not in front of my mum.

"Hand Delaney the sugar." She gestures to the dish resting beside me on the table. "Now, please."

I faintly nod, gulping down the embarrassment of being scolded by my mum in my thirties.

I hardly have to extend my arm to grasp exactly what Delaney was looking for when Mum nervously laughs to mitigate the tension. "Sorry, Delaney," she apologizes on my behalf. "He's not much of a morning person. Never has been."

Delaney nervously smiles, meeting my eyes before she brings the cup to her lips and takes a slow and controlled sip. "I suppose I've come to learn that about him, too," she admits, a truth that makes me frown.

There's much more to me than my wildering habits and poor mood swings. I just reserve that side of myself...I have to. My job isn't about being the most personable guy in the room. It's about being the guy that guarantees results.

Silence falls between the three of us. It's an awkward silence that's hardly suppressed by the sound of the clock behind me. Ticking with each second, like a pained lullaby, as I desperately fight the desire to fall back into another one of Delaney's unprovoked trances.

"Well, enough about Warren." Mum relieves the strain as she attempts to start up a conversation with Delaney. "I want to learn more about you. Warren said you're from Houston, is that right?"

She swallows the liquid in her mouth before nodding. "Born and raised," she declares. And for the first time in a while, I hear that sweet southern charm in her voice.

"Do you miss home at all?" Mum probes her.

Delaney ponders in thought for a moment—I suppose I continually forget that this isn't her home...her life. This is all temporary; she's got an expiration date, one I have no real idea of.

I'm unsure why that thought aches my core as she responds, "I do at times. I mainly miss my friends, and I'd be lying if I didn't say the weather, no offense, of course."

Mum playfully laughs. "No offense taken. I don't control the weather, dear. And if I did, it wouldn't be clouds and rainy skies every day."

Delaney joins in on the laughter, throwing an occasional stare in my direction as she continues in conversation.

"So, is this your first time in England?" Mum continues the question train.

Delaney rests back into her chair. "It's not. I've been here before, actually. Well, not here, *here*, specifically. But I've been to London."

"When?" Her revelation prompts me to sit up in interest. It's a single word—one syllable, but it's enough to see my Mum inflate with happiness, given that I've seemingly entered the conversation.

"I visited during my spring break of sophomore year," Delaney explains. "A couple of my friends and I explored the city together."

"That sounds fun!" Mum's voice inflates with interest. "What did you all get up to?"

Delaney tilts her head to look up in thought before revealing her hand, where she counts each attraction on her fingers. "We went to the London Eye, Buckingham Palace, saw Big Ben, went through to stores on Oxford and—"

"That's not London," I cut her spiel short as Mum shoots me an annoyed glance, prompting me to raise my hands in defense as I look over at Delaney. "I'm just saying, it's like you googled 'top ten things to do in London' and listed off the first four results."

Delaney's lips curl into a smile as she notices Mum shaking her head at me not-so-subtly. "Don't get too mad at him, Helen." She places a hand on her arm. "I did, in fact, do exactly that. But can you blame me? It's not like I had a tour guide or a local to take me around."

Her words light my Mum's eyes up like I've never seen them before.

No.

"You know what?" Mum stands up with enthusiasm. "I know just the person to help you out with that."

Delaney hasn't yet caught onto her referral as she eagerly joins in on the excitement, her voice practically a squeal. "You do? Who?"

Mum walks around the table, planting her arms on either side of my shoulder a little too abruptly as I remain seated. "Warren will show you around London," she proudly boasts. "After all, he only lived there for four years."

"You did?" Delaney is caught off guard by her revelation.

"He did!" Mum urges me to stand. "You'll take her around London, won't you, Warren?" She clutches my wrist, looking up at me hopefully. I can see the excitement behind her gleaming eyes, and I don't have the heart to snatch that away from her.

I release a breath before I'm met with Delaney's wondrous stare. A day in the city I love with the girl I...

"Sure," I speak before I have to carry out the remainder of that thought. "I'd be happy to."

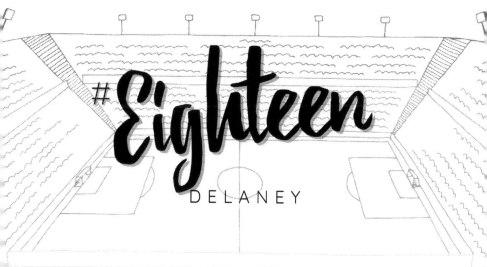

#Eighteen

DELANEY

I WAIT PATIENTLY OUTSIDE the front door, wrapped in a stylish coat and sunglasses. It's been weeks since I've seen the sun make an appearance in England, and I'm not about to pass up on it.

I pull my phone out of my pocket, and much to my disappointment, I'm met with one single notification waiting for me.

Mr. Cunningham.

I keep making a mental note to get back to him, but my attention always seems to get drawn elsewhere.

Like right now.

I watch as Warren attempts to break free from a conversation with his mom through the sheer curtains. I can only imagine she's giving him the rundown on what to say and how to act.

"Be nice."

"Stop being moody."

"You can tell her yourself."

I nearly tripped down the stairs when I overheard her say that to him—and my surprise was only heightened when he didn't deny the fact that he might have feelings towards me.

My legs had been trembling as I sat across from him at the dining table, foolish enough to think that he'd come outright and say it. I'm thankful I'm going to be out and about today. I need to walk off—or rather, run off this steam...the heat that he provokes between my—

"Ready to go?" Warren cuts my thoughts short as I see him step out of the front door.

I nod eagerly, assessing how a dark flannel falls along his chest, with each button carefully fastened in place, except for the top three, where the faintest layer of skin begs to escape from behind the fabric.

Warren is the only man I know whose attempt at dressing down only makes him look that much more put together.

"Have fun, you two!" Helen flashes a generous smile in my direction, forcing me to break away from the sight of Warren as he reaches into his back pocket and slips on a pair of dark sunglasses.

He nods in response to her, walking past me and opening my car door. Standing in place for a moment, I contemplate what to do. I don't think I've ever had a man open my car door for me—especially not one that looks remotely as good as he does.

I finally muster up a quiet "thanks," placing my hand next to his on the door as I climb inside and buckle up my seatbelt.

Unconsciously, we catch each other's stare. If you had told me two months ago that the man who'd made me "try out" for my job would be taking me into the city, I would've never believed you.

Warren clears his throat to break the exchange, firmly closing the door behind me as he gets in on the driver's side.

"So..." I push my oversized sunglasses up the bridge of my nose. "Know where you're taking me?"

A soft smile dances on his lips, ones that I've spent far too much of my time staring at lately—wondering exactly what they'd taste like. "Absolutely."

MUCH TO MY SURPRISE, we don't drive into the city. Instead, Warren parked outside the Enfield terminal station, where we got on what he called the "tube."

"The tune?"

"No." He laughs, grabbing onto the overhead handrails that line the cart. I can't help but notice a hint of a dimple that appears on his cheek, his eyes crinkling at the edges.

I think making Warren laugh might be my favorite thing in the world.

Sometimes I purposely mispronounce things just to hear him correct me. It's an odd kink, I know.

"The tube, Delaney. Like a tube of toothpaste," he continues with a shake of his head, looking down at me with a sparkle in his eye.

I think he likes teaching me—or, dare I say, *coaching* me—just as much as I love getting private lessons.

I bite down on my lip in disbelief, partly because of his statement and partly because of how much I hadn't realized what a terrible job I'd done suppressing my real thoughts about him today.

His gaze lingers on my lips for a brief moment before I speak up again. "You know, I've never been on a subway... *tube* before." I attempt to grab onto the handrail when the cart suddenly juts around a corner. "Woah!" I stumble slightly, barely able to recover and steady myself.

"I can tell," Warren cunningly remarks, though I think I might've I saw a hint of hesitation cross his face as I went unsteady. "You need to hold on properly," he tells me, his tone suddenly more direct. It almost sounds like he *cares*. "It moves fast."

I roll my eyes at his dad-like energy before releasing both of my hands and feigning shock. "Oh no!" I pull back from the rail, standing in the center of the aisle and mimicking his concerned expression. "Betcha, I can stay still with no hands," I playfully wiggle my fingers in front of him.

"Delaney," Warren says through clenched teeth. "Hold on." Despite his comment, he's already got his hand out, hovering just above my waist in the event I fall. A part of me now wants to, just to have him catch me.

"Look, Warren!" I theatrically move around, having way too much fun bringing the grumpy side of him out—and maybe having him scold me. "I don't need handrails! I'm perfectly balanced on my... *woah!*" I'm displaced as the cart rocks, prompting me to fall back.

"Delaney!" Warren rushes forward, a sense of panic in his eyes. Just my luck, the hand that was reached out to grab me was held in the opposite direction than where I fell.

"Are you alright?" He releases his own grasp from the handrail as he takes a step over to me. Thankfully, if it wasn't going to be his arms that I fell into, it was an empty seat instead.

"I'm okay." The faintest bit of laughter washes over me. "I'm alright."

His sense of worry is quickly replaced with a bothered expression as he shakes his head. "I told you to hold on."

"Oh, relax. I was just trying to have some fun."

"You could've hit your head, or worse—"

The cart abruptly comes to a stop at the next station, and now it's Warren who's the victim of not holding on. He loses his balance and falls forward, right next to me—far less gracefully.

I can't help but burst into laughter, a fit that only prompts judging stares from the passengers boarding the cart.

"Oh, my God!" I can hardly get the words out, tears brimming my eyes. "Are you...are you okay?"

Much to my surprise, rather than being met with the cold frown I received last time Warren made some sort of decline, the look in his eyes is brighter than I've ever seen before. He's smiling. He's laughing. He's himself.

"Okay," he responds through his laughter, holding up his hands. "I'm okay."

We both re-adjust ourselves, standing back up. "You know..."

I lean in close as we both hang onto the same handrail. "You should really hold on."

He stares down at me, and I could swear for a moment that he leans in the faintest bit, too. I'm almost close enough to rest my chin on his shoulder.

A pure sense of awe on his face reminds me of that childhood photo up the staircase of his mom's house. I knew it was true. Warren is a child at heart—one I'm going to spend all day trying to unleash.

"You're a total goof, you know that?" Despite a snarky smile on his lips, he shakes his head in displeasure.

"Now arriving at Camden Road." A voice falls over the P.A system before I can respond, the doors opening to our right.

"C'mon." He releases his grasp from the railing, gesturing his hand out for me to step ahead. "We've got a city to see."

"YOU'VE GOT TO TRY A 99!" Warren hands me a vanilla ice cream cone with a chocolate bar sticking out of the top. "And once you're done, we'll head over to this pub up the road. My mates and I always used to sneak out of the house to go without our mums finding out."

Warren has spent the last few hours taking me on a personal "Park Tour" of his side of London—his words, not mine. I've never eaten more English treats, heard him talk more, and frankly, showcase a side of himself I'd always suspected—but didn't realize had the ability to be quite so relaxed.

"I'm absolutely buzzin'. I haven't been around here in ages!" His eyes are as bright as the sun beating down on us. Despite a few clouds rolling in, it's the most beautiful day—and not just weather-wise.

We're in the heart of Camden Market, which is already one of the coolest shopping experiences I've ever had. I'll admit: London has proven to me that it's an unforgettable city filled with even more unforgettable people.

Here, I don't feel as much of a fish out of water as I do back in Crawley. The market is diverse, filled with so many interesting people and items you'd never find in a department store. I hate to give Warren the satisfaction that he was right when he told me that Oxford Street has nothing on Camden. But it's true—everything he's said about this city. It's magical, just like it is, being here with him right now.

"Oh, look!" I hand Warren my ice cream cone as I dart ahead, my gaze having landed on a shop with fancy bow slippers on display. Since I'd first noticed Helen's worn-out slippers, I'd been itching to buy her a brand new pair. These were perfect—a pretty pink color that perfectly matched her sweet energy.

I watch as Warren follows me in the reflection of the glass. "Those?" His voice is ridden with distaste as he eyes the pair I'm pointing out. "If I know anything about you, you probably already have a million pairs of those."

I roll my eyes at his response, staring up at him with the faintest bit of a smile.

"Well, I like them. Plus, a girl can *never* have too many pink slippers."

He nods, pretending to consider my response, although I'm convinced he's calling me ridiculous in his mind. He leans in to inspect the slippers for a moment before speaking. "They look like the same material as your pajamas this morning."

I whip my head in his direction, taken aback by his remark. The fact that he studied what I was wearing long enough to recognize the same print makes my stomach tighten up.

The ice cream starts to drip down his hand, my eyes gravitating forward and catching his attention. I attempt to reach out to brush it away, but he beats me to it, pulling back and saying, "I'm going to go get a napkin."

I gulp, nodding ever so slightly until he escapes from my line of view. Watching him walk away is as wrenching as it is endearing. Because being apart from Warren prompts an unforgiving reminder that a piece of me longs for him in a way I don't think I've longed for anyone before.

Yet, at the same time, I know that no matter how far he goes, he'll always come back.

I take this as my opportunity to slip into the small shop, heading straight to the slippers and grabbing a pair. I march over to the counter and get checked out by the clerk after she wraps the slippers in a small box topped with a matching bow.

I've just stepped outside when I spot Warren making his way back. His brows furrowed slightly as he glances around at the surrounding shops. It's only when his gaze lands on me that it softens, and a small smile appears on his lips.

I shoot him a smile back, skipping down the shop steps as we finally meet each other. Warren tilts his chin in the direction of the gift bag in my hands, clearly unimpressed. "I was gone for five minutes."

"And you're lucky I got slowed down by the line in there."

He smirks before reaching to take the bag out of my hand and returning the remainder of my ice cream cone to me.

"Careful," I instruct, hands raised in front of him as he recklessly slings the bag over his shoulder. "Those are special."

He pulls it back down, dropping it to his side as he flashes me a playful pout. "Better?"

"Much." I take a pleased final bite of my ice cream before tossing the napkin in the trash bin up ahead. "Where to next?" I wonder, clasping my purse in anticipation. I'm in a shopping mood, and now that I've gotten one thing, I've got the urge to keep going.

He's just opened his mouth to respond when thunder echoes through the sky, the sun no match for the English clouds that now float above us.

"Seriously?" I groan in disappointment.

"Welcome to England, *sunshine*. Let's get out of here."

I'm frozen in place by his choice of nickname for me.

That's the first time anyone has called me that since Gramps. I never thought I'd *want* to hear it come out of anyone else's mouth.

Until now.

It takes him being a few yards away to stop and notice. "What?" He turns back. "You alright?"

"Yeah..." I nod my head, gulping down the lump that's formed in my throat. "Let's go."

"HURRY UP!"

"I've got a bum knee, Delaney. Give a man a break."

"And I'm wearing heels, Warren! This is a fair fight."

He rolls his eyes playfully as he picks up his speed and easily catches up to me, much to my annoyance—and his amusement.

It hadn't taken long for the clouds to start pouring down, emptying the market within minutes. Warren had been quick enough to spot one last taxi parked at the end of the street, and we'd made a run for it.

"Oi!" I wave my arm theatrically until they roll down the window. "We need a ride."

"Oi? Why are you trying to act like a local?" Warren can't keep his laughter inside, which naturally causes a smile to form on my lips.

"Hop in!" The taxi driver nods in the direction of the backseat.

"Cause it works." I shoot him a wink as I climb inside first.

"Where to?" the driver requests, Warren dropping his head down to shield it from the rain as he rests his arms above the cab. His hair is damp, and a droplet of water now rests on his bottom lip.

"Islington," he calls out over the pattering of the rain above us.

"Right, get in."

Warren attempts to get inside, but his action is cut short. Good Lord, this must be the smallest cab in the world.

"Would you move over a bit?" He looks over at me, one leg in the cab while the other hovers outside the doorway.

I assess the room beside me.

There is none.

"I can't," I protest.

"Fuck," he mutters under his breath, pulling his other leg in and managing to squeeze inside before slamming the door shut.

Now, without anywhere else to go, his leg and the entire left side of his body are pressed up against mine. It's no secret that I've noticed how big he is compared to me—trust me, *I've noticed*—but being in this small space beside him makes it undeniable.

The weight of his body against mine is no match to the weight I feel in my chest—at the suffocating desire to have him pulled in even tighter.

"Sorry," he mumbles, readjusting himself to give me more space despite how badly I want to tell him not to. "Fancy us choosing the smallest cab in all of England."

I open my mouth to respond, but it's too dry to make a sound. Instead, I flash him what I know is a pathetic attempt at a smile. It's all I can do. He's inches from my face, the water from the rain dripping down his hair as he pushes a loose strand back. It's as if I can feel his breath on me.

It's driving me insane.

"Shouldn't be a long ride," he speaks up again, yet his eyes are diverted onto his hand resting on his thigh. I follow his gaze, noticing how my bare skin is inches from his touch, causing my breath to catch in my throat.

I want him to touch me.

There's this menacing tingling sensation rushing through my thigh as a result of his pinky finger barely grazing my skin.

I'm positive my imagination is making this microscopic movement a much bigger deal than it really is, but when I watch as his eyes hone in on my intent gaze, and his finger hardly brushes my skin for a split second before pulling away, I'm reminded that no sense of fiction can surmount this reality.

I have to rip my eyes away, but I don't make much progress as I stare up at him instead. His eyes. His jawline. His neck. He's never felt so...real.

"We're here." The two of us seemingly release a breath at the sound of the cab driver shouting out that we'd arrived.

"Right, let's go," Warren says, his voice quieter than it's been all day. He pulls away from me as soon as he opens his door, and I feel an aching urge to pull him back in.

Now, the rain has stopped, and the sun is fighting to break free from the clouds, in the same way I'm fighting to break free from the all-consuming desire that Warren makes me feel.

#Nineteen

WARREN

LIFE SPEAKS to me in subliminal messages—and right now, that message is "when it rains, it pours."

Although the weather has been on and off all day, the downpour of emotion between Delaney and me has flooded my mind.

I'm convinced that sitting in that cab next to her—feeling not only the warmth of her skin but watching as the droplets of rain glistened off her face and ran down the side of her neck into forbidden territory was "the nail that sealed the coffin shut."

The coffin being me.

Another fucking subliminal message.

Christ.

"What time is the final train?" Delaney laughs her way out of the pub as she waved goodbye to the bartender. Everywhere she goes, she seems to leave a lasting impression.

I'm in awe.

I have to peel my eyes away from her to glance down at my watch—time has escaped the two of us today. We'd spent hours in the city, with me showing her around my favorite spots and her dragging me along to every little store that caught her eye along the way. I'm surprised by just how much I enjoyed it.

"Shit." I realize the time. "The last train back to Enfield leaves in half an hour."

"That's plenty of time!" Delaney waves her hand to brush off my comment, refusing to see the urgency. "Delaney Matthews never misses a train, and that is not about to change."

"Well, there's a first time for everything."

My comment provokes a subtle smile to appear on her lips. It's a small gesture that represents the sole reason why I'm not completely stressed about missing this ride back.

"Then what are you waiting for?" I hadn't realized she'd strode on ahead, leaving me standing still as I watch her make her way. "You won't catch the train moving at that speed."

I roll my eyes at her comment, but she's gone before I know it, skipping around the corner at the end of the street. I'd just started to jog after her when I heard her scream out, "Oh my goodness!"

My heart drops at the sound of her shriek, and suddenly, my feet have picked up as I race after her.

"Delaney?!" I shout before I'm around the bend. "Delaney? Are you alright?"

As I round the corner, I'm met with the sight of her covering her mouth in what seems like shock.

"Oh my gosh, Warren!" She squeals excitedly, waving me over. "Can you believe it? I love stores like this!"

I let out a breath of relief at her tone, slowing my pace as I walk over to her. A part of me hadn't known exactly what I would've done if something had happened to her—despite the irking reminder that if anyone tried to harm her, it would be game over.

As I stand beside her, I finally take in what incited this outburst of excitement—only to realize we're standing in front of what must be the tackiest gift shop in the city.

You're kidding.

Is this the same girl who, hours earlier, had her credit card in hand while still standing outside of a luxury clothing boutique?

"Stores like *this*?" I clarify, trying to suppress the raging concern that feigns to break free from my voice.

She nods with an abundance of enthusiasm. Her eyes are sparkling bright as if she's looking at the most prized possession of all time—not a sign that says, "everything for a pound."

"Let's go in!" She urges me to follow. "I want to take a look."

"Delaney..." I try to shake my head to refute the thought, but I can't resist her pleading eyes drawing me in.

Fuck the train. I'd walk home if it meant she'd continue to look at me with those eyes all night.

"C'mon!" She steps inside the shop—the bell rings as she swings open the door. I'm quick to catch up, following her aimlessly as she weaves her way through the small aisles.

"All this stuff is made of shite plastic. Even a pound is over-pricing half of it."

"Oh, hush!" she scolds me—and for the first time in my life, I don't mind being told what to do. "It's the memories that matter, Warren."

I'm left silenced, watching as she carefully assesses each item, holding them so delicately between her fingers before her eyes catch a glimpse of something across the way, and she's off before I know it.

"You know, you really need to slow down—"

Delaney holds up a hand to cut me off before raising a bracelet up in my direction. Her eyes are like magic as I reach her.

"This is it," she announces. "We're getting these."

"*We're*?" I'm inclined to repeat a keyword in her statement.

She nods proudly, picking up a matching set.

The bracelet is the most obnoxious thing I've ever seen in my life. It's a boisterous blue color with splashes of red—*creative*—and the phrase "I love London" written in bolded white letters. To top it all off, in case you hadn't realized where London was, we've got a union jack, just to signify that we are, as if I could forget, in England.

Great.

"Thank you so much!" Delaney has already managed to cash out at the counter in the time span I've been standing here dumb-founded, dissecting how much I despise that bracelet. Yet, as she slips one on over her wrist as we make our way back down the shop steps, now it's suddenly the most beautiful piece of jewelry I've ever seen her wear.

"Perfect." She beams down at her wrist before raising it up to me. "Don't you think?"

I don't care to look at the bracelet. All I see is her. It's all I've seen all day long. No magnificent buildings, no architectural monuments, and no views that people would pay to see in their lifetime. It's just Delaney.

"Perfect," I repeat softly, my eyes not leaving hers as I speak.

Thankfully, she doesn't seem to catch onto my dazed state. "Here." She extends her hand out towards me. "Your turn."

I snap myself out of it and furrow my eyebrows in confusion. "My turn?"

"Yes." She narrows her eyes, revealing another bracelet from the shopping bag in her hand. She did end up purchasing that damn matching set. "You didn't think you were getting off that easy, did you?"

God, I could get off *so* easy if she kept talking to me like that.

Before I can open my mouth to respond, she's speaking again.

"You're going to be stubborn? Fine!" She shakes her head dramatically before reaching out and grabbing my wrist, a grasp that's as delicate as it is demanding. "You leave me with no other choice."

While holding onto my wrist in one hand, she slips the bracelet onto mine with the other, her fingertips grazing along my skin and forcing me to take a breath inwards. She struggles for a moment, the width of the bracelet being no match to extend over the breadth of my hand.

"Ugh, it's stuck." She frowns in concentration, attempting to tug on it. "I can't seem to—"

My spare hand connects with hers, halting her in place as I

help to pull the bracelet off my palm and onto my wrist. Her hand is small in mine, almost disappearing as I reach out to help her.

And just like that, this bracelet that I'd just been mentally ripping apart at the seams became the most precious thing I could possibly own.

Without pulling back, she looks up at me. We're inches away from one another. I'd been so focused on her hands that I hadn't realized she stepped closer to me.

She bites down on her lip as she keeps her gaze locked onto mine, an action that she has no idea holds the full power to ruin everything in me.

I want to pull her in. I want her closer. Fuck, I've wanted her closer for longer than I'd admit to. All it would take is a gentle tug in my direction.

But I can't. I have to step back. I have to pretend that what she's doing to me isn't about to derail the magic that was today completely.

We have to end this on a high note, though. I'm positive there would be no better way then closing out this day with her lips on mine. No better taste than her.

"Better catch that train." She's the first to break contact, her voice just barely above a whisper. My eyes are still scanning her face, which is slightly stunned as she pulls back, leaving me to release the breath I'd been holding that entire time.

Shoot.

Was she expecting something? Should I have made a move? Was her mind racing the way mine was in that brief moment?

"C'mon, slowpoke!" Her infamous smile teases her lips as she steps ahead again, seemingly shaking off that entire encounter as she shakes her curls out. "Delaney Matthews doesn't miss a train, remember?"

I peel my feet away from the ground they've become permanently embedded into. I would've stayed in this spot forever with her.

"I remember," I say so softly that I can barely hear it myself. "I remember."

"OH, DELANEY." Mum embraces her in her arms for what must've been the fourth time since we've attempted to say good-bye. "You come by any time you're free, you hear me? You're always welcome here. I hope you know that."

Delaney's smile is just as sincere as it is warm. "Aw, Helen." She goes in for a fifth hug. "That means so much to me. Thank you for everything."

"No, thank *you* for everything," Mum responds back to her, gesturing down to her feet.

Delaney had insisted that as I was packing up the car with our suitcases—or, more accurately—*her* suitcases, she couldn't forget to give Mum something.

I didn't know what she was talking about at the time, but now, as I follow her gesture, seeing those familiar pairs of slippers as they cozily rest on my mum's feet, I can't help but feel an over-whelming urge of tenderness flood my chest.

She got those for my mum.

"Have a safe drive back!" Mum waves Delaney off as she strides her way down the driveway. The gravel beneath her is no match for her high heels as she sinks into it with each step. "Take care of her, Warren," Mum instructs me as I'm quick to open Delaney's door, and she graciously steps inside.

"Oh, he will, Helen," Delaney smirks, her eyes catching mine for a split second before she's stepped inside and I have to remind myself to close the door.

"Warren!" Mum calls out before I can even make my way over to the driver's side. "Can I talk to you for a second...*inside*?"

I peer in through the windshield of the car, watching Delaney eagerly gesture for me to go ahead. I hadn't realized I was even looking at her for confirmation before it was too late.

I swallow deeply, afraid of what Mum is about to say—despite knowing exactly what the context of the discussion will be.

Thankfully, Mum was asleep as Delaney and I somehow managed to catch the train last night. We made it back to the house in the early hours of the morning.

I suppose she had been right with her claim—Delaney Matthews really doesn't miss a train.

Since then, despite loving my mum with all of my heart, avoiding her at all costs has been the only way to bypass this inevitable interrogation of "tell me all about London." In other words, "What happened between you and Delaney?"

I follow Mum into the house, inching slow steps until closing the door gently behind me and meeting her as she stands in the kitchen. Her lips are pursed in a playful pout as she patiently or dare I say *impatiently,* taps her foot against the tiles.

Mum's already got a new sense of Delaney's attitude since she's put on those slippers.

"Now, before you even say anything," I interject before she's even muttered a single word, "nothing happened in London."

"And that's where I'm going to stop you," Mum responds quickly, and before I know it, she's pulled me into her warm embrace as she rests her head against my chest. "Oh, Warren..." She releases a drawn-out breath. "You know how much I love you, right?"

I nod. How could I not?

"And you know how much I want you to find the right person for you, right?"

I nod again. I can't seem to find words, yet I'm persuaded that each one of these questions is rhetorical. A keen reminder of things I've always known.

"Then do me a favor." She pulls back, holding both of my hands into hers. "Allow yourself to accept that love, dear." She peers up at me with sincerity in her eyes before brushing along my cheek. "And do yourself a favor. Start to show it."

I have a hard time maintaining eye contact with her. Mum

always knows what to say and how to say it. She hadn't even needed to speak of Delaney's name for it to continue to loop through my mind. Instead, I gulp down, sending her the faintest nod with the most reluctant gaze before her attention is directed elsewhere.

"What's this?" Her eyes narrow in on my hand, forcing me to suppress my dread as she clutches onto my wrist. Her hand now rests over top of the bracelet that I laid awake most of the night, intricately memorizing each detail of, all in an attempt to forget the way Delaney's touch felt against my skin. The task proved to be virtually impossible.

Finally, I built up the courage to meet Mum's eyes. If I thought they were playful before, they're downright devious now. "Oh, Warren." She smirks with a shake of her head. "That's rather touristy, isn't it?"

I suck in a short breath, chewing the inside of my cheek to suppress a smile. "I couldn't help but notice Delaney had the same one, too, am I right?" She shoots me a suggestive stare. "Care to share more?"

Rather than opening a can of worms, I pull her in for a final hug, planting a kiss on her cheek. "Bye, Mum," I tell her as I release her from my embrace. "Thanks for having us. I'll talk to you soon."

I leave her standing in the kitchen as I guide my way out of the door and over to the car, watching as she now no longer secretly peers through the curtains but instead eagerly waves goodbye to Delaney and me as I buckle up my seatbelt and start up the ignition.

"God, I love your *Mum*." Delaney leans her head back against the seat, staring over at me with a bat of her eyelashes, as for the first time I hear her call her that. "I wish I had that more than anything."

A deafening silence falls between us until I can take it no longer and muster up enough courage to ask her the follow-up question irking my mind. "Had what?"

She reaches over to the car radio, her voice, and eyes more solemn than I've ever seen, paining me with each second. "A family that cares."

"I PROMISE YOU, Warren, it's *this* turn!" Delaney points ahead as we approach the third "I promise it's this way" so far. She's the only girl I'd allow to drive me in circles, both mentally and physically, without a complaint.

"Are you sure?" I have to look at her in denial. Our road trip back has almost been surmounted by the time it's taken us to find exactly where she lives. Something I've wondered for far too long.

"Yes, I swear!" she nods her head positively. This time it's her pout that makes me cave yet again as I flick on my indicator and turn at her request.

"Ah, yes!" she perks up, straightening her spine in her seat. "This is it. I recognize exactly where I am."

Little does she realize that I do, too. I might not have grown up in Crawley, but I've lived here long enough to know this place like the back of my hand. And the flat she just had me pull up outside of has to be located in one of the most troublesome neighborhoods in this town.

Isn't her family rich? Why is she living here and not at Ira's old place?

"Oi!" I hear a loud voice call out as Delaney takes the liberty of stepping out of the car and stretching her arms up into the air. It's an action that prompts her midriff to make a subtle reappearance in my line of view as I now realize I've gotten out of the car as well. "Looking good, Delaney."

"Hey!" my voice cuts through the darkness surrounding us. "Fuck off, and mind your own business," I snap, the words escaping my mouth in a sour tone before I can stop myself. My chest inflates with a strange feeling. Anger? Frustration?

Jealousy.

"Warren!" Delaney shoots her head in my direction, a sharpness mixed with a sense of dismay in her naturally angelic voice.

"What?" I hardly break my death stare that's locked on the young lads who just blatantly cat-called her from across the street. "I'm not going to let a bunch of tossers yell at you like that."

"Those tossers are my friends," she's quick to clarify. "That's James, and...oh..." She looks up in thought. "I guess I never asked the rest of them their names. But they're fine, and I'm fine!" She folds her arms in a huff, her face flushed as the death stare I had opted to give them reflects back in her eyes, aimed in my direction.

"Friends?" I'm stunned at the revelation as the lads work their way across the street.

"Who's this?" They assess my frame. "This your boyfriend or something, Delaney?"

Although Delaney isn't quick to dismiss the thought, I notice her face turns even redder as she shakes her head in response. I wish I could explain why I had eagerly turned my head to see her reaction. To see what she'd say. "No, this is—"

"Wait!" One of them slaps their friends across the chest in revelation. "I recognize you," he points right at me with wide eyes. "You're the Crawfield coach, aren't ya?"

"Yes, he is," Delaney proudly tilts her chin up in their direction to sing my praises. It's an amazing egotistical boost. "And he's great at his job."

I have to look away to hide the aching smile I'm suppressing as I take the liberty to unlock the trunk of my car. In the meantime, Delaney somehow manages to break into seamless conversation with the group.

"London...really?" I catch the tail end of their words of surprise as I pull each bag out and carefully place it on the curb, one by one.

"Yep." Delaney flashes me a tender smile. "We had the best time ever!"

"Need us to help you with the bags?" The group willingly offers as they step toward me. "We don't mind—"

"I've got it." I slam the trunk closed, causing Delaney to cock an eyebrow in my direction.

"You do?" I see her suppress a smirk by biting down on her lower lip.

"Mhm," is all I can speak as I grit my teeth at the sight, grab her bags, and try my best to ignore the fact that her "friends" are still lingering closely behind her, staring her up and down a little too much for my liking. "Let's go," I instruct, hoping it will be enough to pull her away.

"Bye, guys!" Delaney drops the lads without a second thought as she shuffles ahead, reaching the entryway of the flat and jogging up the stairs.

I'm not as quick to follow as I juggle her suitcases in my hands, still slightly short of breath as I reach her floor and watch as she patiently stands outside of her door. It's late, and the hallway is empty and quiet, but not even the overwhelming silence can overbear the unruly thoughts that plague my mind. The most important being that behind that door is a mattress that needs "breaking in."

Fuck me.

"Well, welcome to my home, Warren!" Delaney gestures theatrically as if she's on an episode of MTV Cribs before she starts to fiddle with her keychain to attempt to search for the right key. "Come on in. I'll give you a tour."

"I'm not staying." I'm quick to deny her request despite how badly I'd love to see everything that her place has to offer.

The smile disappears from her face and drops into a frown, causing a surprising pang in my chest. She puts me out of my misery not a second later as she glances back down at her keys, finally finding the right one as she awkwardly shifts in place.

"Oh...okay," she mumbles quietly, tucking a loose strand of curly hair behind her ear. I hadn't realized seeing her hair natural like this was by far my favorite. "Then, I guess all that's left to do is to thank you."

I stumble ever so slightly at her words. "The bags were nothing, Delaney. I didn't mind."

"I'm not talking about the bags," she protests, taking a step toward me as I freeze in place. "I'm talking about the past few days. For inviting me to your home. For letting me meet your mom. For taking me to London and putting up with me all day. I appreciate it more than you'll ever know."

I'm speechless. *Truly.* And despite the million and one ways I could say you're welcome, I have nothing. These past few days were nothing like what I'd imagined. Being with her. Seeing the city through her eyes. God, it was better than what I was expecting. She's better than anything I could've expected.

"I'm just happy you had a nice time." My words are as awkward as they are choppy, but at the same time, Delaney doesn't seem to care.

Instead, she's back to torturing me with that smile, letting out a soft sigh as she plays with the keys in her hands. "I did...." She sinks her hooks that much deeper into me as she again subtly bites down on her bottom lip. "With *you.*"

My. Heart. Stops.

All the oxygen leaves the hallway. I can't breathe. She's making it impossible.

I nod subtly—unsure of what else I can do. I need to leave. I have to. But I can't bring myself to move my feet away from her. I'll be glued to this spot forever.

"I guess we'd better call it a night then?" Her words are less than convincing as she looks up at me with her big eyes, the same look that I knew would drive me insane the moment I first saw her. "Mind passing me my bag?"

I hadn't realized her bags were still clutched beneath my grasp, holding on ever so tightly—just like I am to this conversation. I don't want it to end.

"Shit, yeah." I hand the first one over to her, my throat dry as I speak. She extends her hand out to reach for it, but her pitiful attempt to clutch onto the handle transpires into much more.

Now, her fingertips more than just brush over my skin, they fully encapsulate my hand.

As if we're working in sync, we both stare down at our hands before our eyes find each other yet again.

I'd always known it, but looking at her right now, there isn't a sliver of doubt. She is the most beautiful woman in the world. I'm certain of it as much as I'm certain I can't hold back from her a second longer.

"Allow yourself to accept that love, dear. And do yourself a favor. Start to show it."

I let go of my hesitation almost as quickly as I drop her bags to the ground, and before I can comprehend my actions, I pinned her up against the wall, clenching her wrists between my hands as my lips crash into hers.

Almost as if she anticipated it—*craved it*—she accepts my embrace and immediately pushes herself closer to me, pressing her body up against mine and causing me to let out a shaky breath against her lips.

God, I've needed this for so long. And now that I've had a taste of temptation, I can't comprehend how I've been able to hold out this whole time.

Now we start to move as one, a soft moan escaping her lips is all she needs to do in order to tell me she's wanted *this* just as badly as I've wanted her. "Warren," I hear her mumble softly, making little attempt to pull away from my lips as she speaks. My name is like heaven as it falls out of her mouth and into my own.

The sound of her whispering my name as she grinds herself into me is enough to push me over the edge. Finally, I lift her in the air, securing my grip around her tight waist as her firm hips press against my core, and she wraps her legs around me effortlessly. It's like she was made to cling against me.

"Fuck," is all I can force myself to say, biting down on her bottom lip ever so gently. That's all I can think to say. She's absolutely all-consuming.

"Come," she whispers breathlessly, yet it's enough to tell me

she wants to take this as far as I'm willing to go. She can hardly finish her words before I continue kissing her again with a heightened sense of anticipation. "C'mon..." Her tongue dances on mine, reaching for my belt, desperate to undress me. "Let's go inside."

And with that simple, formidable action, the reality of what caving into this temptation has gotten me into starts to sink in.

Fuck.

No.

No, no, no.

I can't do this. I refuse to do this. I have to stop. I need to stop.

I pull back harshly, causing her breath to hitch as her eyes meet mine—now electrified with a sense of sexual desire. It was a look I'd seen before, but one I hadn't realized I'd starved for so badly.

I gently place her down and take a reluctant step back, gliding the back of my hand along my mouth as if to rid myself of her taste, despite knowing it has the power to linger for a lifetime.

"Hey, are you okay?" She attempts to break the space I've created between the two of us as her hand cascades down my arm. "Why did you stop?"

"Delaney, I..." My voice trails off. The wrenching feeling of pulling away from her is almost as painful as it was resisting her. But as she peers into my eyes, I'm reminded of everything this girl stands for.

The reason why she's here in the first place.

The one person who I swore I'd never let down.

Ira.

The thought of hurting the one person Ira loved with his whole heart fills me with a pain I can't ignore. And like Ira, I know what Delaney deserves. This girl is sunshine personified. She's a lover at heart, and a part of me fears that I'll never be able to give that love back to her.

I've never known how to love someone like this. The only real love has always been between me and this sport that's consumed my life. There's never been room for more...I've never made room for more. Is there any room even left?

"Warren?" Delaney's eyes fill with disarray and a slight hint of disappointment as I snap back to reality. I can't tell if she's mad or confused. A part of me hopes it's the former. Her being mad at me is the simplest way to forget that this ever happened, part ways, and move forward.

"I'm sorry." I back down the hallway, leaving her dumbfounded. "I'm sorry."

#Twenty

DELANEY

48 HOURS.

It's been 48 hours, and the same word continues to loop in my mind.

Why?

Why did he just...stop?

No one has walked out on me. *Ever.* Little did I think that Warren would be the first one.

I mean, up until that spectacle the other night, I'd been convinced that Warren was sending me signals. That the way he was looking at me...the way he was kissing me meant...*something*.

Apparently, it hadn't, and those delusions had left me standing in my hallway alone, surrounded by materialistic things, as I watched the *one* real thing I've ever properly wanted walk away from me.

The season break is over today, which can only mean one thing: we're all meant to go back to business as usual. For the team, that's a simple ask—but they didn't just make out with Warren Park, did they?

God, nothing tasted quite like the way his lips did as they pressed against mine. Nothing excited me quite like the way he'd grabbed me and pulled me in against himself without an ounce of hesitation. Nothing felt quite like the way he'd effortlessly lifted me into his arms as his teeth sank into my lips.

Nothing will ever compare to Warren Park.

I'll be the first to admit that I'd been tempting him with all my might. Seriously, I was pulling out all the stops, and boy...was it worth it. I don't think I've ever been so desperate to get someone behind a closed door like I had been with—

I need to stop.

I've been torturing myself for days. I mean, even the sight of that spot outside my apartment makes my heart leap into my throat, which is why I've refused to leave ever since.

"Ugh," I audibly groan as I attempt to sit up on my bed, rubbing my head. My temples pound against my fingertips as I drag myself over to the mirror, examining every square inch of my face.

I'm almost unrecognizable. And it's not just from the visible bags under my eyes from the lack of sleep I've been getting as I've tossed and turned thinking about Warren. It's the fact that I know that this reflection isn't me. Delaney Matthews doesn't pine. But after Warren, this has to be a new personality trait.

In the past, Gramps said that my superpower was my ability to move onwards and upwards. If I'm being honest, I always thought that it was my superpower to get hot guys to chase after me effortlessly. But every now and then, when my abilities would falter, Gramps would speak his words of wisdom.

"When you want something, you chase it. You show people what they're missing out on."

As the words process through my mind, I notice that my hands comfortably rest above my dresser, and that's when it hits me.

With a devious curl of my lips, I stare back up into the mirror with a newfound sense of encouragement, breaking my gaze for a split second as I pull out my top drawer, exactly the bait I need to catch my prey.

Maybe I do recognize this Delaney after all.

I'M LATE. So late that I'm confident that at any second, practice is going to be called, and all this would've been for nothing.

Thankfully, Warren has no leg to stand on when it comes to my tardiness. What's he gonna do? Get mad at me for showing up late when he didn't show up for me at all? Yeah...that's what I thought.

I sneak in through the side entrance, doing my best to stay undercover as the team continues a play just ahead.

"Delaney! Is that you?" A voice calls out.

I'm not as secretive as I hoped, as Alf catches me off guard while I rush through the tunnel and onto the side of the field. Much to my dismay, his outburst causes all heads to turn in my direction, but it's Warren whose burning gaze I can feel the most —a gaze that refuses to allow me to look away.

Why does he always have to look so good? Like, can't a girl catch a break? Despite the whistle resting between his lips, I can almost sense his face shift as he sees me, his hardened eyes showing a hint of that softness I had begun to get familiar with. I swear I see a glimmer of shame cross his face before he turns away abruptly and blows the whistle, calling the group in to reconvene after their drill.

"So, how was your time off? Do anything exciting?" I almost forget that Alf is standing in front of me with a cheery expression on his face as I keep my gaze locked in on Warren. Desperate to get his attention for just a moment longer before I finally decide to glance away.

"Oh..." I meet Alf's wondrous eyes. "I definitely did some *exciting* things," I sarcastically remark, loud enough that I hope Warren can hear...and feel bad about it.

Unknowing of the *exciting* thing I'm referring to, Alf shoots me a delighted grin. "That's great, Laney! I can't wait to hear all about it."

Oh, I'm sure you'd much rather not.

I have to force a smile in response before searching for the time around the stadium. "Is, uh...practice almost over?" I ask him.

"Just about." Alf peers down at his watch. "Parker's been working these boys like there's no tomorrow. He's in one of those moods again."

"Is that so?" I can't help but act clueless despite knowing the cause of Warren's moodiness for once.

Alf's short with a nod as he meets my eyes. "Who knows with Warren?" He shrugs. "Maybe something happened during his break."

My throat tightens as he speaks. It's almost as if he's looking at me for assurance. I shrug, attempting to act unknowingly despite being all-knowing.

"Maybe," I offer, gulping down yet again as the raging desire to see Warren in his element again demands all of my thoughts.

"How about you go and talk to him?" Alf suggests, almost as if he's reading my mind. "You always seem to lighten the mood."

His request brightens my face for what feels like the first time in days as I take off my coat and rest it between my arms, revealing the loose satin dress I'd carefully opted to wear underneath.

You know what they say: oftentimes, the best things lie beneath the surface.

"That's a great idea, Alf," I announce with a cocky smirk. "I've actually been meaning to say a few things to him."

Alf raises an eyebrow in question, words lingering on the tip of his tongue as if he wants to speak—perhaps debate the scheming tone in my voice. But instead, he slowly nods his head and joins the boys on the field while I carefully stride my way over to Warren.

Yet, with each step his way, Warren conveniently opts to go the other. It doesn't matter though. There's no escaping. Warren can attempt to follow the boys on the field as much as he wants. I'll chase him down if I have to. I have a message to give him, and it's one I refuse to go unread.

"Hey, Coach!" I'm sharp with my tone, demanding his attention as I reach into the pocket of my jacket.

Somehow, he halts in place at the sound of my voice and looks over at me as his sharp eyes finally rest on mine. Thankfully, we're close enough so that no one else seems to catch wind of my outburst.

Warren's silent. I'm silent. It's awkward. He's awkward. This is off to a terrible start.

But realistically, nothing needs to be said here. I pull a paper out of my pocket and gently press it into his, watching his throat tighten up as his eyes linger on my touch.

"What is this?" He asks, his voice quiet and unsure as he pulls out the note, unbreaking of his gaze.

"Open it and find out." My face is stoic, but my voice is inviting as I head back through the tunnel, knowing damn well that this message will lead him right where I want him.

"Meet me in the change room."

WARREN

"Hey...um...Alf." I'm acting like a total incompetent fool after reading Delaney's note, desperately trying to concoct some sort of escape route straight down the tunnel and into the change room as quickly as possible.

"Yeah?" He hardly turns his head in my direction. It's a small thing to notice, but undoubtedly an action I've been guilty of omitting his way one too many times. I hadn't realized just how annoying it was until now.

I clear my throat, adjusting the collar of my shirt. It's gotten tighter after seeing Delaney again—though the image of her somber eyes as I left her high and dry in the hallway has refused to rid itself from my mind. Honestly, not a second has gone by where she hasn't consumed every ounce of my being. There's a reason why I'm still holding this practice—because it's the only thing stopping me from crawling back into bed and reminding myself of how much of a fool I'd been.

"I...uh...need to go and clear something off my desk." I foolishly opt for it as my excuse. "Mind taking over?" I gesture in the direction of the boys.

Alf eventually looks my way with a smug look on his face. "Sure thing," he speaks. "I'll stay here while you go talk to Delaney. Sounds like a *great* plan."

Heat rises to my cheeks, though Alf cuts my panic short as he places a reassuring hand on my shoulder. "Oh, relax, son." His voice drops so that the boys don't hear, or so I assume. "Do you think I don't already know?"

"Know what?" I stammer, deciding that playing "dumb" is the best course of action here. It's all I know how to do right now. Play dumb, act dumb. Make dumb choices.

Alf shakes his head, leaning in close. "I've not got the best eyesight, lad..." His voice is that of a whisper at this point. "But I can see that there's something between the two of you from a mile away."

I'm blinking rapidly, having to pause and push the realization that everything he's saying is true to the back of my mind. I can't confirm, but I also refuse to deny. Instead, I find the middle ground by saying, "Don't be ridiculous, Alf."

It's ambiguous enough that as I pat him on the back and mutter a simple "thank you," all I hear before I turn down the hallway is. "Good luck with that *paperwork*, Park. Sounds like you're going to need it."

Now that I'm finally out of sight, I can relax my face as I run my cool hands across my jaw. Each step towards the changing room feels like an aching reminder of the other night.

I slap myself ever so softly across the cheek as I wait outside the changing room. I need a pep talk. No, I need someone to pep talk some sense into me.

Go in there and tell Delaney that you made a mistake. *This* can't happen. *We* can't happen. That's easy enough. Say it and be done with it—

"Took you long enough."

God help me.

I'm frozen. Frozen in place at the sight that meets me as soon as I enter the changing room. I'd been charging my way forward with a confidence that has now completely dissipated from my body.

"What?" Delaney asks me innocently, slowly inching her way forward in nothing but lingerie.

A sheer black set—with lace. God, how I love lace.

God, how I love...

"You seem surprised," she remarks, cockily raising her eyebrows with her arms folded across her chest.

Fuckin' hell, I'm surprised.

What the hell is going on?

In processing that thought, she somehow finds her way in front of me, her fingertips dancing along my shoulder. "Why so tense?" she asks rhetorically. "Don't you like what you see?"

She rests a hand on my chest as she leans in closer. It's enough for me to catch the intoxicating scent of her whispering into my ear. The feeling of her breath against my skin sends shivers down my spine. "Oh, wait...you haven't seen it all."

She pulls back, striding her way back over to the benches that line the back of the change room while I'm left staring at the back of her.

It's a cynical sight. I'm going to hell for liking this so much.

"Delaney...what are you doing?" I finally choke out, forcing myself to come back to reality, even if it's a pathetic attempt that lasts a brief moment. "Put your clothes on, *now*." My demand lacks such a force that even I find it laughable.

She pouts with those lips—ones I know the taste of all too well.

"No," she responds simply, placing her hands on her hips, an action that used to frustrate me, but now...

Yeah, I'm definitely going to hell.

"Delaney..." I'm quick to look over my shoulder as I speak. "Someone could walk inside. Alf isn't going to hold the practice for much longer."

"So?" She remarks with a shrug. "Let them. Then they'll see exactly what *you* missed out on."

Her words infuriate me to my core. No one is seeing her like this. No one but me. *Fuck.*

"Delaney, I—"

"Save it." She cuts me off with a raise of her hand. "I don't want to hear you anymore, Warren." She's back to that cocky little attitude of hers, and it's only making me want her more. "You see, where I'm from...you don't start something unless you're going to *finish* it."

Her words flip something inside of me, my judgment clouding with pure desire at the sight of her as I lock my gaze in. She has no idea who she's playing against right now. Absolutely no fucking idea.

I remain silent, pursing my lips together as I press my tongue against the inside of my cheek, the sound of my footsteps echoing through the room as I step toward her.

For a moment, I partially allow my eyes to brush over her body, an action that doesn't make her cower in the slightest. A part of me wants her to, but the other part likes how she's not backing down without a fight.

It'll make this more fun.

Finally, I reach her, brushing a piece of her hair away from her face as I lean in to murmur against her lips. "You really think I won't, don't you?" I say with a kiss of my teeth.

She looks up at me with intrigue and submission in her eyes. "Won't what?"

This time, I can feel the vibration of my own voice as I speak these words to her. "Won't fuck you right here in this changing room, Delaney?"

Somehow, my voice comes out quiet, though part of me

wants people to hear. I want them to know what's mine. What is about to be mine. What has always been mine.

I can hear the breath hitch in the back of her throat as she bites down on her lower lip, her wide eyes looking up at me with innocence despite the sinful thoughts that I know are running through her mind.

"I don't know." She teases. "Will you?"

I carefully brush my thumb over her bottom lip, knowing I'd give up all rationality for one more taste of her. "Don't tempt me to start, Delaney." I force myself to pull back with a tilt of my head. "Because if I start, I *will* finish."

With a final bat of her lashes, her response sends me into orbit, and now I know I'm doomed.

"Prove it."

#Twenty-One

DELANEY

AS IF THEY were never apart, our lips are back together as one.

I push my hands into Warren's hair while he wraps me around his waist. Now we're chaotically dancing around the changing room, attempting for more.

Desperate for more.

Before I know it, I'm pulling off Warren's blazer, pushing it off his broad shoulders, grasping for his shirt next in an attempt to rid him of all his clothes.

God, I need to see him shirtless.

God, I need to see him naked.

I need to see him all over me.

"Take your clothes off," I attempt to speak through the short breaks we take in between kisses. An action that hardly lasts a second before our mouths guide their way back to each other time and time again.

"Shh..." He whispers against my lips, his touch tender in comparison to mine as he sinks his fingertips into my waist. "Stop talking."

I want to negate his request, but his soft yet raspy voice makes me believe that he could say anything to me right now, and I'd still refuse to break our lips apart. Regardless, the menacing part of my mind reminds me of logic as I mumble a quiet, "Why?"

We pull away with just enough time for me to peer up at him, seeing the tenseness of his face. The way his jaw is clenched, and his eyes have narrowed in on me. This isn't the same Warren that walked into this locker room, and I like it.

He doesn't respond. Instead, he grabs ahold of my waist, pulls me back in, and presses me against him. His lips hover millimeters away from mine, tempting me with his refusal to have them meet.

"I'm tired of that little mouth of yours, Delaney." His voice is full of a haunting impatience.

I tilt my head in confusion, biting down on my bottom lip to suppress my pout. I can always tell by the way his eyes follow my movements that this simple action puts him in the palm of my hand without fail.

"Stop that." He once again grazes his thumb along my lower lip before pulling it away from beneath my teeth. "Stop that right now."

I refuse to listen, attempting to pull back, but his grasp is so secure that I've got no chance of breaking free. Instead, I take the liberty of being this close to him to clasp onto the belt of his trousers, toying with each buckle before using it to tug him in closer.

"Maybe you'll change your mind when you see what this mouth is capable of." I look up at him temptingly, watching his chest rise and fall with each breath as I release the buckle from the loop. My hands now seamlessly glide along the waistband of his pants, slipping carefully into his underwear.

"Delaney," he speaks, his voice just above a whisper. So faint. So gentle. But it's not enough to mask the sheer desperation that's begging to push its way through.

"What?" I don't stop what I'm doing as I search for his zipper, one that's hardly a challenge to find given his protruding bulge.

Swiftly, I pull down on his zipper and release his pants from around his waist.

One layer to go.

"What's wrong, *Coach*?" I tempt him, leaning up and planting gentle kisses along his jawline as I speak, letting my breath brush against his skin. The word so effortlessly falls out of my lips, turning me on just as much as I can see it darken Warren's eyes above me. "Is there something else you'd like my mouth to be doing instead?"

Nothing. He says nothing.

Until he does.

"All I want is to see that pretty little mouth of yours wrapped around my cock."

I'm left speechless.

My mouth dropped open ever so slightly until he placed his hand below my chin, closing it for me.

"Get on your knees," he whispers, his voice now affirmative, strong. "*Now.*"

And I'm on my knees.

There's no other choice. There is nothing else I'd want to be doing than clinging onto his every last word right now. I've pulled down his final layer, and before I know it, I'm taking in his length in a slow and controlled motion.

Clutching onto my hair, Warren's hands get tangled within each strand as the faintest moans break free from his lips. I'm not sure who is being tortured more right now. Him, as his head falls back and eyes flutter between consciousness, or me, watching all of this happen.

This will be a mental picture I'll never be able to forget.

"Fuck, Delaney," I hear him mutter as I grasp ahold of either side of his hips, my fingernails digging into his skin. I want to be permanently embedded into him forever. Leave my mark.

I can feel him tense above me, his grasp on my hair tightening as his length twitches between my lips until suddenly, I'm brought back onto my feet, spun around, and pressed up against the wall.

"Oh, you're asking for it." His voice is hot against my ear. The feeling of him against me makes my legs tremble in anticipation. All at once this changing room has just gotten a million degrees hotter. "Are you hot, sunshine?" His hand runs up along my spine, sending shivers despite the scorch between my thighs until he meets the clasp of my bra. "How about we remove a few layers, shall we?"

Before I can respond, Warren effortlessly unclasps my bra and discards it to the side. Now, his hand slips ever so slightly inside the waistband of my panties, his fingertips inching to my core before he pulls the fabric down my thighs.

Without a pause, I'm spun around to watch as Warren takes all of me in, his eyes assessing me just the way they'd been doing since I first arrived. Except this time, he doesn't need to undress me with his eyes. His hands have already taken that liberty.

With a step backward he sucks in a breath and slowly undoes each button of his shirt one by one. My mouth goes dry at the sight until he pulls it off either shoulder and allows it to drop to the floor.

He's so hot, it's criminal.

"You, my love..." He walks back forward, leaning into my ear while caressing my breasts between the palms of his hands. "Have been extremely fuckable from the moment you walked in here. You know that?"

He pinches my nipples ever so slightly as he lowers his body down, dropping onto his knees. My heartbeat intensifies, pounding in my ear as I watch him.

"Because of that..." His mouth trails up my bare leg, his hands resting on my calves as he plants slow, tender, and controlled kisses along my skin before he stops along my right thigh. "I'm going to have to take matters into my own hands."

As I process his words, he lifts one leg so that it rests on top of his broad shoulder as he trails a few kisses along my inner thigh.

Feeling his breath practically against my core causes me to go limp with temptation, yet his large hands hold me still as his face disappears between my thighs.

"Warren..." I breathe in sharply at the sensation of his mouth against me, clutching handfuls of his hair between my fingertips and tugging not so gently. I don't care. "God...Warren."

He hardly pulls back, murmuring against my heat. "Coach," he whispers. "You call me *Coach*."

Holy fuck.

My head falls back in a trance as if I'm a parallel to him. I'm weak, I'm gone, I belong to him. I've always belonged to him.

"I'm close." I can hardly formulate the words. "I'm so close, Coach."

Just calling him that alone almost has the power to make me come undone at his touch, but as he pulls back and lifts me into the air, sure, the tension between my thighs may dissolve, but my urgency only heightens that much more.

"What are you doing?" I look at him helplessly. Yet asking questions is no use. Warrens made his mind up as he scoops me back in his arms and strides into the bathroom.

"I want to look at you." He drops me in front of the mirror that sits adjacent to the sink, towering behind me as he pulls my hair back and cranes my neck to the side.

There is nothing hotter than watching him as he takes control, and I willingly fall victim to his touch. He kisses my neck with such a hunger I know the remnants of him will linger long after this is over.

"Do you hear me?" He speaks as I stare in his eyes through the reflection of the mirror until he tilts my chin up, forcing me to hold his gaze. "I want you to look at the way I'm about to fuck you."

Without hesitation, he lifts me back up into his arms, wrapping my thighs around his waist as he follows through on his promise by lining himself up with my entrance, leaving me to watch in the mirror across the way.

"Tell me what you want." He's teasing me now, hardly inching his way inside me. "Tell me now."

"I want you," I say wholeheartedly. I don't think I've ever spoken a truth quite like it. "I want you, Warren."

He glares at me, and I swallow hard, realizing my mistake.

"I want you, *Coach*," I correct myself, and as the last syllable escapes my lips, a moan subsequently follows as Warren pushes himself inside of me, thrusting with a deep sense of urgency that leaves me trembling in his embrace.

"You're so fucking tight," he whispers against my skin, his lips trailing from my lips to my neck as he speaks in between kisses. "So fucking tight, Delaney."

His movements quicken as my eyes flutter shut in pleasure. My head leans back against the cool wall as I dig my fingernails into his back. I can't possibly get enough of him. I want him as close to me as possible.

"Look." He pulls out, causing a quiet moan to escape my lips before he hushes me by bending me over the sink in front of the mirror. I hardly have time to respond before he clutches my hips firmly and re-inserts his length. "Look what you made me do. Are you proud of yourself?"

I somehow manage to muster up a slight smirk, a look at that only heightens the darkness in his once-blue eyes. "Yes, Coach," I continue to call him at his request, meeting his gaze in the mirror and giving him that devious stare that I know drives him crazy— despite the fact that I'm about ten seconds away from going completely feral myself.

"You're a bad girl." He picks up his speed, and I'm about one more line away from falling to the floor. "But you're such a good girl *for me*."

I'm not sure how much more I can take. My hands clutch the edge of the porcelain sink.

Fuck, how can this get any better?

He pulls out a final time, and before I can even fathom why, he's pulled me into the changing room shower and turned on the showerhead. The warmth of the water that falls above us is no match for the warmth that re-emerges between my thighs as he finally re-inserts himself back into me and rests me against the shower wall.

Our faces now touch. Our lips can't seem to break from one another, and as he softly murmurs my name against my tongue, I know that he's about to come undone at any second.

"Fuck..." A loud groan falls from his mouth as he unloads inside of me. God, I want to hear that on repeat, over and over and over. "Delaney." The growl of his voice is now masked by the sound of the water making contact with the tiles beneath us...that, or the fact that I'm completely releasing myself.

"Fuck, Coach," I cry out, an action that prompts Warren's hand to fly over my mouth as I slowly moan into the palm of his hand.

"That's it," he murmurs, kissing away the beads of water that rest on my cheeks as I come undone, trembling against him until eventually I peer up to meet his eyes. "Such a good girl." He leans his forehead against mine before he eventually pulls out.

I bite my lip to suppress a smile before pulling him right back in. "Uh...didn't you forget to ask me something?" I shed light on the fact that things just went from zero to 60 in a matter of seconds, and not once was any sort of contraceptive mentioned. I'm on the pill—I have been for years, but still, wouldn't that have been something he wanted to know before he went in without any protection?

Warren furrows a brow, brushing some water out of his eyes. "Like?" he questions.

"'Like,'" I repeat back. "If I was on the pill or not? I mean... you just came inside of me without even knowing."

He smirks, and it only makes my ovaries do a 360 flip. "*Sunshine...*" He runs his tongue along his bottom lip before leaning in closer. "I've waited months to be inside of you...I don't care. Besides, I told you I would finish, and...I'm a man of my word."

WARREN

"Quickly!" I fasten my belt into place, doing up the buttons of my dress shirt shortly thereafter.

Our time together had been cut short by the sound of a whistle blowing out from the field, indicating that Alf had called practice and that the boys were moments away from barging into the changing room.

I can't help but pause to watch as Delaney pulls on her satin dress, the fabric falling effortlessly over her skin. Her beautiful, gentle skin that I'd just left kisses all over and frankly, already wanted to touch again.

"I'm going as fast as I can!" Her voice is full of urgency and the faintest bit of annoyance. It's so fucking hot.

I brush aside the smile on my lips until I can finally speak. "Listen, we don't have much time. I need to get back out there," I explain. "I'll watch out to make sure no one sees you leave, alright?"

Delaney agrees to my plan with a subtle nod of her head before reaching out to me pulls me back in for another long, drawn-out kiss. I'm breathless as she whispers, "Whatever you say, *Coach*."

I groan against her tongue. "Don't tempt me again," I have to murmur into the kiss, attempting to pull away but somehow still leaning into her, letting my lips stay on hers for as long as possible. "Because this time, we *will* get caught."

"And is that really so—"

Another sound of the whistle is enough to jolt us both back to reality as we finally break apart. The room silent as we match each other's blank stares.

"Just be quick!" I remind her before I walk out of the change room. The relief I feel as I see all of the players still out on the field is unmatched.

Well, all but one. And that one is who I somehow manage to walk right into as I make my way down the tunnel.

"Coach?"

Wilks.

Fuck.

"Hey, why's your hair wet?" His narrowed stare on the beads of water that drip down my forehead is diverted as Delaney makes her untimely escape from the change room and sprints in the other direction. Her own dripping wet hair is a clear indicator that causes Wilks to look back at me with a knowing smirk.

"Not a word." My voice is that of a demand. A threat before Wilks can mutter even as much as one syllable in response. "You hear me?" I repeat. "Not a word."

Despite the stupidly cocky grin on his face, Wilks nods his head, pretending to zip his lips as he makes his way down the tunnel.

"And oh hey, Coach?" he calls out one final time.

I halt in place, meeting his eyes as he gestures toward my button-down. "You may want to fix that."

I dart my attention downwards, noticing how I've completely buttoned up my shirt wrong. One side hangs longer than the other.

"Fuck." I attempt to fix it, yet an image in my peripheral vision demands my attention as my eyes gravitate upwards, meeting the photo of Ira that I was insistent on putting up just a few months ago. Now, it's one that tortures me as it stares back down.

"Don't look at me like that," I have to say, doing my best to hide a smile as I exit the tunnel.

#Twenty-Two

WARREN

"WE NEED to get the new away kits ordered by the end of the day. Then, that stack of papers that I dropped off on your desk needs to be in by Friday! Also, I forgot to mention we've got some special guests coming to watch our game tomorrow. So do you think we can reserve...*Warren!*"

I snap my head in Alf's direction.

I hadn't realized that despite him standing right in front of me, I'd been distracted beyond belief.

I can't help it. A devious face is peering down at me through the blinds, gesturing for me to join them with an obscure amount of nudity and hand gestures—leaving me stiff as a—

"Are you even listening to me?" Alf snaps again, his patience withering by the second.

I meet his narrowed eyes.

I'd heard everything that he'd said but couldn't tell you a single thing I'd retained. It's been this way since last week—distracted beyond my wildest dreams with a girl who makes reality feel like one.

"I'm listening," I lie through my clenched jaw, watching as Delaney slowly undoes her blouse.

Fuck, who gave her the office overlooking the field?

I have to suck in a breath, biting down on my lip to hide my smirk as I'm reminded that it was me. I did. Why? Because I wanted to be able to see her at all times.

"You're not," Alf's disgruntled voice remarks as he folds his grumpy arms across his chest. "What are you even looking at?"

Alf whips his head over his shoulder, and despite her top being undone, Delaney is quick to drop to the ground—making it stupidly obvious that it was, in fact, *her* who'd I'd been overcome with the entire time Alf was speaking.

He shakes his head, looking back up at me with a jut of his bottom lip. "Careful, Parker!" he speaks, that Dad tone now picking up in his voice. "You don't want to piss anyone off."

I furrow my brows at his statement. Piss anyone off? What's he on about? I shake my head. "I couldn't give a fuck who I piss off." I'm quick to throw back out at him. "Besides, what's going on between Delaney and I is no one's business. End of story."

Alf releases a drawn-out breath. I can see in his eyes he's about to embark on some words of wisdom. Advice, so to speak. But I don't need advice right now. Being with Delaney this past week has been euphoric bliss. I don't think I've ever smiled more in my entire life. Delaney makes me feel, and she makes me want to love. I've never felt that way before. No one has ever made me feel this way before. And I'll be damned if I let anything ruin that.

Sure, sneaking around is a mundane task, but it adds an element of thrill, excitement, and *risk*. There's nothing more exhilarating. I'm on a 24/7 adrenaline rush.

"You're right," Alf chimes back in, clutching onto the clipboard. "It is no one's business. But that doesn't mean it won't become someone's."

"Well, they can fuck off too," I retort, fed up with this conversation as Delaney peers back up from the ground. Her eyes are so bright that even despite the sun setting in the distance, nothing illuminates the stadium more than her.

"Maybe if you let me finish, Parker, then I can explain, and you'll know that the special guests coming are—"

"Listen." I'm fed up with the conversation by now. I don't need to be lectured. I'm a grown man. I make my own choices and Delaney? She's the best choice I've ever made. No one can convince me otherwise. "I've got to go. We'll catch up in a bit, alright, Alf?" I cut him short, striding my way past him before he could mutter so much as another syllable.

Once I'm out of sight, I find my pace quickening. I'm practically running up the staircase to reach Delaney's office. I feel like a teenage boy again—with these flutters in my stomach. It's that nervousness mixed with anticipation that floods your chest. It's a desire that keeps you up at night for the girl you know you'd risk it all for.

My knuckles hover above her office door, and as if she can sense my presence, Delaney swings open the door, clutching onto my wrist with a bite of her lip as she drags me in.

"Took you long enough," she coyly remarks, slamming the door shut and pinning me up against it. Though, *pinning* is a generous word. Her body is no match for my frame. I completely encapsulate her in my shadow.

"Miss me?" I murmur against her lips, feeling the way her cheeks tighten into a smile as I say it. Nothing feels better than knowing I'm the reason for that.

Nothing.

"Maybe a little," she deviously whispers into my ear, sending me over the edge as I scoop her into my arms and carry her over to her desk. I push everything that once rested on top onto the ground in a flash. I couldn't care less if I broke something. If I do, I'll buy it again. Everything is disposable but *her.*

"Seems like you're the one who missed me." She gasps for air as our lips hardly break contact from one another.

Of course, I missed her. I can hardly stand to be away from her for more than five minutes at a time without rushing back into this office. It's a vicious cycle.

"Maybe," I have to admit, watching as, yet again, my response forces a smile onto those perfectly soft lips. Lips that I'm desperate to spend the rest of my life memorizing, analyzing, and kissing.

"What was Alf saying to you?" she speaks, as my mouth finds refuge in the nape of her neck. She smells so good. I could suffocate in all that she is and die a happy man. "Warren?"

"Nothing," I grumble, tired of talking about anything that doesn't involve all of the things I plan to do to her against this desk. We broke the mattress in. Now, it's time to venture out.

"He doesn't know, does he?" The concern in her voice pangs me like a double-edged sword. Is she embarrassed to be with me? Or does she, too, fear for the looming repercussions that Alf alluded to?

I seek clarity in her face as I take a reluctant step backward, noticing the faintest ounce of concern breaking free from her dark brown eyes.

"No, love," I lie. "No one knows," I attempt to reassure her, despite knowing at least Alf *and* Wilks do.

Before today, Alf has been alright. It's been Wilks who has been practically busting my balls day in and day out. Hanging this secret over my head any chance he can get.

I'm pretty sure the lads are wondering why I've been so lenient on him lately, and it doesn't help that every time I do snap at Wilks, he shoots me a conniving smirk while zipping his hand over his mouth.

He's such a goddamn pain in my ass, but one I have to put up with for the time being.

"Are you sure?" She's hardly convinced as she slowly grazes her fingertips along the stubble of my face. Usually, I can't stand to go a day without a fresh shave, but when Delaney told me she likes how I look with facial hair, I threw away every razor I owned. "I just don't want people to look at you differently."

My voice inflates with confusion. "Look at *me* differently? Do you really think I care what people think?"

Her eyes are full of questions. So wide and curious. "I don't know." She can hardly look at me as she speaks. "Do you?"

"Sunshine..." I tilt her chin upwards, pulling her back in so my lips hover over hers. I can feel her body tense up as I place myself between her thighs, speaking these words against her lips. "I never have..." I speak slowly, forcing her to suck in a breath. "And I never will."

Our foreheads meet as I place a hand on either side of her thighs, sliding her toward the edge of the desk.

"In fact..." I crouch down, taking a careful amount of time to kiss along her chest and down her body until I reach her thighs. Those legs. Fuck, if I thought the way she crossed her legs was hot, the way she's spreading herself out of the desk is one for the spank bank. "Let me show you how much I don't give a fuck."

"Wait." Her one hand intertwines with my hair as the other steadies herself on the desk. "I didn't close the blinds."

I peer up at her with a devious smirk. "*Perfect.*"

It hardly takes a minute for her to squirm beneath my touch. "Oh God, Warren..." She's seconds away from unleashing against my tongue when a strong knock comes through the door.

I freeze in place—not from the knock, but from the voice that subsequently follows.

"Delaney?" I hear someone speak. "Are you in there?"

American.

Delaney is off the desk and buttoning back up her shirt before I even get the chance to stand back up.

"Mom...Dad?" Her voice is full of disbelief as I lock eyes with the two people standing in the doorway, staring down at me with a mutual sense of confusion and distaste. "What are you doing here?"

Fuck.

DELANEY

I've found myself at a loss for words very few times in my life. Most of them have been with Warren as he takes my breath away with the sheer weight of his touch.

But nothing, absolutely *nothing*, takes me by surprise, like seeing my parents as they impatiently march into my office, eyes glued to the fact that Warren is on the ground, and so is every single item on my desk.

"Are we...interrupting something?" Dad is quick to speak, a sharpness to his tone, one I can assure you I haven't missed these past couple of months.

"Not at all." I attempt to shuffle my way to Warren's side, reaching to collect the miscellaneous items off the ground. "I just dropped some things, and Warren here...well, he was helping me pick them up." I shoot him a stare that reads, "Go with it." "Isn't that right?"

Warren clears his throat, loosening the collar around his neck as he nods in agreement, collecting the items, recklessly tossing them on my desk, and standing up straight.

"That's right," he agrees, a nervous rattle allowing his usually strong voice to falter as he peers back over at me. "She can be a bit of a klutz."

Dad's less than impressed at this whole ordeal, while Mom's eyes are fixated on the way Warren's tie is off-centered, left astray. Shit.

"Oh, we know *our* Delaney!" Mom strides her way over to him and fixes it back in place before meeting his eyes dead on. "She's always been a bit of a mess."

Well, thanks.

The room is silent. The only sound is that of the ticking clock on the wall. Every second standing in this room feels like hell, whereas a minute ago, it was as if I was being transported to heaven.

"Nice to see you again, Warren." Dad breaks the exchange of awkward stares and questioning thoughts as he extends one hand out to him while the other rests in his suit pocket. "Hope Delaney hasn't caused too much trouble for you."

Warren straightens his spine. The sound of his hand connecting with my dad's is that of sheer force. I can almost see the tension Dad unleashes into his touch. "You too, *Hank*," Warren remarks.

Hank.

Wait.

Warren's already met my dad?

"This is my wife Shirley." Dad gestures toward my mom, who graciously leans in to plant a single kiss on Warren's cheek, an action he attempts to reciprocate as I realize that I'm still on the ground.

"Ahem," I clear my throat, catching everyone's attention. "What are you two doing here?"

"We...uh," Dad goes to speak but catches Warren's intense stare instead, looking at him in such a way that I can only tell means "get out."

It takes Warren a second to catch the message. So long that I have to shoot him a look myself for him to adjust his jacket and release a breath.

"I'll give you guys some privacy." He rubs a hand behind his neck, shooting me a pained and equally confused look before he's out of the door and out of sight.

I'm left looking down an empty hallway for far too long until my parent's voice commands my attention.

"Well, aren't you going to offer us to take a seat?" Mom scoffs. I shake myself out of it and gesture to the two desk chairs that linger in the room while I find refuge in my own.

"Don't look so happy to see us, Delaney," Dad sarcastically remarks. "It's only been almost three months."

Three months.

Where has the time gone?

At first, time moved achingly slow. But now...now, I only wish it would slow down as the realization of what the three-month mark really means slowly starts to creep in, turning my stomach inside out.

"I'm just surprised to see you." My eye contact remains inconsistent as I toy with my fingers. "That's all."

"I don't know why." Dad furrows his brows as one. "We told Alf we were flying in. We're going to watch the game tomorrow."

I bypass the fact that Alf knew they were coming. It doesn't matter now. They're here. I need to focus on that. "You...you're watching a game tomorrow?"

Mom nods eagerly in agreement. I've never seen her so excited to watch a sports game. The only sporting match I've ever seen her partake in is that of a shopping spree during the semi-annual sales at the mall.

"We had to see what all this fuss was going to be about, didn't we, Shirley?" Dad continued.

"But of course!" Mom enthusiastically shoots me a smile. "We hear you've done big things for the group!"

"Yes, lots of big things," Dad agrees.

I feel as though my head is on a swivel as I watch them both take turns finishing each other's sentences—leaving me with not a peep to say.

"Delaney, we're *so* proud of you! We really didn't think you'd be able to do it, did we?" Dad shakes his head in disbelief before looking at Mom.

"No, we did not," she agrees, clutching onto her designer bag that rests in her lap. "Frankly, I'm shocked."

Their doubt in me isn't a shock. The shock comes from the way the words "we're so proud of you" fell from their lips like it was nothing. I don't think I've ever heard them say that to me before. It's a foreign feeling I'm equally as desperate to have repeated as I am to disregard.

"Proud of me?" I opt for the earlier. "What do you mean you're proud of me?"

They both look at one another in unison as if they're confused by my obliviousness. "Well, you've done exactly what we sent you out here to do. Since you've started doing all the PR here, Delaney. We've had an overwhelming influx of interested buyers! I mean, we had to come down and see all of the magic you've created for ourselves."

"*Magic?*"

"Here's the great news!" Mom perks up in her chair, clutching the arms on either side whilst disregarding the sheer disbelief in my voice. "We're planning to put the team up for bidding!"

What?

"We're confident we're going to get far more than we expected for the team. Your work is done here, Delaney. You've made us proud."

#Twenty-Three

WARREN

"YOUR WORK IS DONE HERE, *Delaney. You've made us proud.*"

Mum always said it was rude to eavesdrop. She said if people don't want you earwigging on their conversation, then there must be a reason. I guess I finally know what she meant when she said that.

"I thought you said we'd keep the team if I did well. Not sell it!" Delaney protests, her voice full of betrayal and distrust. Two emotions fill me up as I find myself glued outside her door, over-hearing every word that has not only fallen out of her parents' mouths but hers too.

"Delaney," it's Hank who's first to speak up. God, his voice is the equivalent of nails on a chalkboard. How can someone look so much like Ira, have his DNA, for crying out loud, and be abso-lutely nothing like him? "We've been made offers we can't refuse. We're *not* keeping the team!"

"But you said if I could make them of value to us, things would be different," Delaney attempts once more, begging her parents to listen at this point.

"Well...plans change," Hank's voice is firm. It's as if I can see the smug look on his face myself, despite the wall holding me back from charging my way back in there. "Sometimes, you don't always get what you want. Things aren't always what they seem."

Things aren't always what they seem.

A statement. A truth. I allow myself to listen to the final line until I break free from the wall, charging my way down the hallway and toward the staircase.

My whole life, I've prided myself on being an honest man. Ira taught me that. He taught me that the good in people will always find a way to surmount the bad.

I believed it once.

But now, I don't know what to believe. I can accept a betrayal from Hank. He means nothing to me. But Delaney? She's been colluding with her parents this entire time.

I never questioned why she came here to Crawley. I just knew that Alf had told me it was the only way to appease both parties—a win-win. But now, it's all starting to make sense.

Delaney never cared about the team. About me. It was all about the money. The value. How many zeros can be added after our name on a check.

I'm so distraught that I hadn't even realized that my legs had guided me back into my office—though the way I've slammed my door shut and knocked my chair to the ground is a not-so-friendly reminder.

I run my hand through my hair, tugging through the knots at my roots before leaning in on my desk, slumping my head and shoulders down in defeat. And that's when I see it.

The bracelet.

The one that I'd hardly realized had become a part of me—just as she's become a part of me these past few months.

I stand up straight, toying with the material before I pull it off my wrist, snapping it in one quick motion and whipping it at the wall across the room.

DELANEY

Where the hell is he?

He's not on the field.

He's not in his office.

None of the guys have seen him.

He's gone.

"What the hell?" I impatiently tap my foot while raising my phone to my ear, attempting to call Warren for the fifth time—but the line cuts short yet again.

The cell reception inside the stadium is about as awful as the conversation I just had with my parents.

I was naive to think that they would change their minds. Stupid enough to trust that they'd see how important this team has become to me. And hopeful enough to think that, for once, they'd allow me to have one thing. One thing that's not materialistic. One thing I've worked for myself. One thing I'm truly passionate about.

One thing I refuse to put a dollar amount on. Because to me, this team has been invaluable in the lessons it has taught me and the person it has shaped me into.

With a frustrated huff, I make my way to the outside of the stadium in search for better service. As I reach the front gate, finally, more than a single bar illuminates my screen. I try my luck again, clicking re-dial—yet before I can lift my phone back up to my ear, I hear the sound of a ring just in front of me. I raise my head, and I'm met with the sight of Warren loading his things into his car and slamming his trunk closed.

"There you are!" I end the call, a sense of relief flooding my chest at the sight of him. I tuck my phone away and skip over to his side. "I've been looking all over for you," I say with a laugh, my mood instantly brightened. Seeing him has that effect on me. "Where have you been?"

Silent.

He remains silent with a face like thunder. Usually, he's quick to welcome me into his embrace. Wrap an arm around me, pull me in for a kiss, and whisper sweet nothings into my ear. But now, he's giving me nothing.

I can't help but furrow my eyebrows in confusion. This wasn't the same Warren I had just seen in my office, the one who'd come racing up the stairs to be by my side.

Something has happened. I just don't know what.

"Hey..." I place a delicate hand on his arm, leaning to plant a gentle kiss on his cheek—attempting to assess the situation. "Are you okay?"

He pulls back before my lips can touch his skin, shaking me free from his grasp as he looks away. I feel a pang in my chest, so painful that I almost flinch away. His eyes dwell on the concrete below us, refusing to meet mine.

"Warren?" I'm left dumbfounded by his inability to look at me. Usually, I have to tell him to stop staring. "What's wrong? Did something happen?"

A long, drawn-out pause is surmounted as his brows crease together, and finally, he meets me with a cold stare—those icy blue eyes chilling me to my core, freezing me in place. "I don't know, Delaney." His voice is sharp, full of impatience. "You tell me."

I take a step back. I can't remember the last time he spoke to me with that tone.

"I..." I attempt to speak, trying to make sense of his behavior, but I'm cut short. My eyes draw me to his wrist.

It's bare.

He took off his bracelet.

"You...took the bracelet off?" My focus is now drawn towards that detail in a pathetic attempt to distract myself from his earlier remark as I reach for his wrist. "Why would you take it off, babe?"

"Why would you lie to me all this time?" He snaps in response, yanking his arm out of my reach before I can even grasp a hold of him. His eyes cut into me like daggers, and I can feel myself bleeding from the wounds.

Both literally and verbally, I start to stumble. "Lie to you?" I can't help but repeat his words, stupefied. "Warren, what are you talking about?"

He cranes his head to the side, creases appearing around his eyes as he folds his arms. "It's all starting to make sense now," he speaks.

"What is?" My voice becomes frantic. I'm so confused, and his half-answers aren't easing my anxiety in the slightest. "What are you so angry about right now? I have no idea what you're talking about."

He releases a breath, maintaining his steady, intense stare at me while I feel like I'm about to crumble. "The real reason why you really came here. What you've been doing this whole time. You lot are clever, I'll give you that."

"Warren..." I'm reluctant to take a step forward, terrified by just how much I know it will wreck me if he takes another step back in response. "What do you mean, 'you lot'? You know why I came here."

"Don't play me a fool, Delaney," he speaks sharply. The way he says my name is nothing like the way he's ever said it before. Instead of gentle, loving, nurturing...it's angry. Condescending. It forces my body to flinch at the sound. "I heard what your parents said to you," he continues, nodding and staring straight at me as he speaks. "I heard what you said to them. Your plan all along. It wasn't to help us. It was never about that, and you know it. It was to fulfill Daddy's checkbook. Wasn't it?"

He's evidently waiting for a response, but I'm at a loss for words. I had no idea he was listening in on our conversation. I can't imagine how much it must have hurt him to hear what my parents had to say, and I know how terrible it all must have sounded, but I need to make it right. The only thing that matters now is telling him how I feel.

"No," I tread lightly with my words, my voice soft, afraid that at any second he'll be gone and I won't be able to explain myself. "You're misunderstanding. It's not like that at all—"

"Did you ever really care?" He shows no remorse in raising his tone. "Hm? Did you?"

I feel my chest rising and falling rapidly, my throat closing up as I stare back at him, speechless. I'm not sure what he's referring to. Is he alluding to the team, or is he talking about the way I feel about him?

Regardless, the answer is yes. A million times, yes. Of course, I cared. From the moment I first locked gazes with this hardened man with a heart of gold, how could I not? This team has become a part of me. *He* has become a part of me.

Sure, at first, this entire venture was all about proving my parents wrong. Proving to them that I could do something on my own and keep Gramps' legacy alive.

But since coming to Crawley, all of that had changed.

Suddenly, it was no longer about proving a point to my parents. It wasn't about impressing the people back home. It was about making memories with the people I had met here, the people who had become my new home.

I'd left behind the past, finally started to live in the present, and, for the first time in my life, was hopeful for the future.

A future with the man who stands in front of me—the man who's now staring at me as if we hadn't just spent the last three months going through the trials and tribulations of our relationship, to throw it all away over a misunderstanding.

"You didn't, did you?" Warren drags me out of my head, hardly allowing me time to process his words before he speaks again.

My heart sinks with the brutal realization that, at this moment, it doesn't matter what I say. He doesn't want to hear it. He's convinced himself of this narrative, one that perhaps I believed in the beginning but abandoned along the way. Surely, he can see that.

"Of course, I cared, Warren," I respond quietly while relentlessly shaking my head, as if that alone would convince him of my words. As much as I try to calm myself down, I physically can't stop. "Just please let me speak. Let me explain."

"I've heard enough." His voice is direct as he steps away from me. I instinctively take a step forward, desperate to be close to him, to keep him near me. "I think the best thing for you to do right now is go. It's clear that you weren't a part of this team. And you *never* will be."

I freeze in place.

I can't tell what hurts more. His words stabbing me like a knife in my back, or the way he looks at me as if I'm a complete stranger, as if an hour before, we both weren't entirely under each other's spell—entranced, infatuated, in *love*. I'd hardly known it was true, but now, feeling my one chance at it slip from my grasp, I've never been more certain of anything.

I've fallen in love with Warren.

And I'd thought he'd fallen in love with me.

It's insane how much can happen in the span of 60 minutes.

Tears threaten to pool from my eyes as I look up at him. "You don't mean that." My voice starts to crack, and I can hardly keep it above a whisper. A single tear runs down my cheek as I attempt to reach my arms out for him, wanting him to pull me in the way he always does, but instead, he swiftly dodges my embrace by putting his hand up.

I breathe in shakily and meet his eyes. I can't help but notice the way he, too, pauses, carefully watching the tear run down my cheek until I use the back of my palm to wipe it away. I could've sworn I saw *my* Warren attempt to break free from whatever version of him this is, but I can hardly blink before his face hardens once again, and he looks away from me.

"Warren." His name is that of a whimper as it escapes my lips for what feels like the hundredth time in this conversation. "Please..."

He assesses me—just like he did the day we first met. I mean, we're standing inches away from that exact spot. That first day, where we stood on either side of the gate. He'd been unknowing of anything about me, but to me, his presence had already consumed every part of my being before we'd even said hello.

"You should go." His voice is quiet, too, as he reaches for his keys in his hand, unlocking his car door. "Your work here is done."

"Warren!" I'm not quick enough to stop him as he opens his car door and steps inside. "Warren, stop!" I plead against the glass, tapping on the window and clutching onto the door handle he's since locked as he starts the car.

With one last glance at me through the window, he shifts the car into drive, and through my blurred vision, he's out of the parking lot, out of sight, and out of reach before I even know it.

I feel my legs go limp underneath me as I stand in the parking lot alone, the cool wind whipping against me—but nothing could possibly sting as much as the way Warren had looked at me as if he wanted nothing to do with me again.

Was this the last conversation I would ever have with him?

I feel sick at the thought of it.

"Delaney?" A confused voice from behind prompts me to whip my head over my shoulder in surprise, clutching my stomach as I attempt to steady my sobs.

It's the boys. The team. It's Wilks who's the first to free himself from the group that stands at the front gates, seemingly having just watched everything unfold.

"Are you alright?" His face is full of concern as he watches me shaking in place.

"I..." I assess each of their faces. Some are that of worry, most are mainly confusion, but beneath it all, I can't help but assume that each one of them hates me for what I've done. "I'm so sorry..." I pace my way through the parking lot, attempting to brush past them, but Wilks stops me in my tracks, placing his hands delicately on either side of my shoulders to steady me in place.

"Delaney!" He peers down at me with concern in his gentle

brown eyes. "Stop, it's alright. Talk to us. What just happened with Coach?"

I can hardly maintain eye contact with him, nor can I think of a response to any of his questions. All I can think to do is reach for the bracelet on my wrist, my hands trembling so heavily that I can barely pull it off. "Here!" I finally yank it free, resting it in my palm and squeezing it tightly—as if clutching it will transport me back to that night in London with Warren. "Take it." I have to peel my grasp back as I finally drop it into Wilks' hand.

"What's this?" The confusion is all over his face as the tears continue to stream down my own, and at this moment, I'm reminded of one of the first thoughts I had the night I first walked up to this stadium:

"Crawley is a small town that becomes a big part of your heart."

But now, my heart breaks by the second. It's a heart that no longer beats like it had before, and it's a heart I know will never beat the same way again.

I escape from Wilks' grasp, knowing that this is no longer the place it used to be.

"I'm sorry I let you guys down," I whisper through my tears. "It's time for me to go home."

Twenty-Four

WARREN

"WHERE THE FUCK IS MY PEN?!" I shout belligerently, tossing some stray papers off my desk. "I swear to fucking God, if someone took my pen, start digging your grave now."

"What the fuck are you going on about over there?" Alf quickly matches my irate tone as he yells at me from his office, making me release a huff of frustration.

"Where. Is. My. Pen?!" I shout, watching as he stands up from his desk chair across the hallway and snatches a pen from his own desk.

"Maybe it's where you left your manners," he grumbles, marching into my office and slapping it down onto my desk. "Here!"

"Oi, watch it." I shoot him a glare as he turns on his heel and leaves my office. "You didn't need to be such a prick about it."

Alf stops dead in his tracks. "*I'm* the prick? You're hilarious, Parker. An absolute comedian, you know that? Maybe you should stop being so worried about a pen and focus on the fact that Delaney's gone. Have you gotten that through your thick skull yet? She's gone."

His words stop me in place, my pen hovering above the paper as I clench my jaw tightly at the sound of her name.

"Good," I mumble in response, although the word feels like it doesn't belong on my tongue at all. "She never belonged here."

Alf rolls his eyes at my attempt to brush her off. "How can you sit there and say that?" he protests. I heave out a sigh before leaning back in my chair and looking at him. The gray is creeping through his hair, and given the hell I've put this team through these past few days, I'm not surprised. "She was a part of our team, Warren. She *helped* us. How can't you see that?"

That's it.

I slam my hands down on my desk and stand up, Alf now looking up at me.

"Holy fuck. How about we just focus back on what this is all about—playing football! Have we all just forgotten that?" My voice is full of annoyance.

Alf is silent, yet he shakes his head. He's tried to get through to me for days, but each time has proved to be more unsuccessful than the last.

"The lads are waiting for you," he finally says, peering down at the watch on his wrist. "Go focus on what this is 'all about' Park. I'll be in my office."

I brush past him without another word, my shoulder pushing into him as I walk onto the field.

To my surprise, the lads aren't out on the pitch kicking the ball around in their usual pre-practice warm-up. The grass is empty, and as I scan the area, I catch a glimpse of all of them sitting on the bench together.

"What the hell is going on?" is the first thing I say as I take them all in. "Get your asses on the field, now."

They remain un-wavered by my sharp tone. Hell, some of them don't even have their cleats on. They're just sitting there barefoot as if they're lying on the beach on holiday. They've chosen the wrong day to piss me off. As the saying goes, I've woken up on the wrong side of the bed this morning. I have been ever since I've been forced to wake up without Delaney lying by my side.

"We need to talk, Coach." It's Wilks who speaks on behalf of the group, standing up. I shoot him a look to tell him he's treading on thin ice. The last thing I need right now is to play his childish little games.

"Talking isn't what we need to be doing!" I snap in response. "Get on the field. This is your last warning."

"Not until you make up with Delaney."

His words hit me like a slap across the face. Sure, Alf has been on my case, given that Delaney left the keys to her office and all of her things on his desk, but the lads—they've remained radio silent until now.

I hold Wilks' gaze, both of us refusing to back away from the other's glare.

"I'm telling you all right now. Stay out of it. You have no idea what you're talking about," I speak through clenched teeth.

"And maybe you're right." Wilks strides his way in my direction, hands in either pocket as he shrugs nonchalantly. "But what we do know is that that girl completely changed our team. She made us better. She made *you* better, Coach."

As the boys nod along and murmur their agreement, I can't help but feel scorned by the fact that they legitimately believe that she made me better in their eyes. I've put my heart on the line for these boys time and time again. I didn't need anyone to make me better for them. I was already giving them everything I had. "You should hear yourself right now." I have to shake my head in disbelief. "You lot sound downright foolish. Stick to the football plays, lads, not the poetry. Delaney meant nothing to this team. Nothing to me."

I'm about ready to storm off the field, toss my playbook to Alf, and have him run practice. I can't handle this pettiness. I'm already a few yards away from the group when Wilks continues to egg me on from a few feet behind.

"Oh yeah?" he shouts out over to me. "Then you won't mind if I throw this away, will ya?"

I halt in my tracks, sucking in a breath before I'm inclined to turn on my heels and follow my eyes to his hand, where not one but two bracelets rest.

Mine, which is evident given that it's snapped in half. That bastard must've snuck into my office.

But what takes me even more by surprise is the other. One that's perfectly round, just the way it was the day it was purchased.

I'd never thought that a silly little one-pound bracelet could evoke anything meaningful in me. I'd wanted to burn it the moment I first set eyes on it. But seeing how Delaney has left it behind almost forces me to choke back some emotion I can feel well up in my throat. Clenching my chest with each breath I take in.

"That's what I thought." Wilks takes my silence as confirmation. I almost want to knock that cocky look right off of his face. "But you know what, Coach? You said you're done with her, right? She meant nothing to you? I guess that means I can just throw them away." He casually walks towards the bin that rests ahead of the tunnel, and before I can even stop myself, I'm blocking his path.

"What?" Wilks challenges me with a confident step forward. "What are you gonna do?"

"Back up, Wilks." My voice comes out as a low growl.

Yet, being the prat he can be at times, he remains unwavered. "Not until you agree to talk to Delaney."

"Seriously, *Gary*, back up right now."

Very rarely do I opt to use any of the lads' first names when addressing them. In fact, I can hardly recall how many times I've done it in the years I've known them. But right now, there's no friendliness between us.

"You know, Coach," he responds, playing with the bracelets in his hands as he speaks. "Maybe it *is* a good thing Delaney left. Because you've been nothing but a dick ever since. I'm glad she's not here to deal with it."

I can hardly contain the anger anymore as I shove him away

from me, causing him to stumble backward before he regains his balance and immediately pushes me in return.

The field erupts in a series of "woah, woah, woah" and "stop" as the rest of the lads rush forward, pulling us apart from each other. I feel a few of them grab me by the arms and pull me back before I'm seconds away from lunging at him and wrapping my hands around his throat.

"Enough, Warren!" It's Alf who emerges from the tunnel and reaches me, grabbing onto my shoulders and shaking me back to reality. "You need to stop. You're taking this way too far!"

"*You* lot are taking this too far." My voice is seething as I stare at them all one by one in the eyes, seeing nothing but fear and concern reflected back at me. Little do they know the amount of suffering I've endured these past few days. They couldn't even begin to imagine the half of it.

"We know, Coach," Wilks, slightly out of breath from our sprawl, speaks gently again as he looks at me. He can't hold himself back from wanting to reassure me despite his anger. "We're upset, too."

"No!" I shake my head in disagreement. He's just talking to talk. These boys don't know anything. "It's easy for you all to tell me to just 'makeup with her,' isn't it? But you didn't get to know her the way I did…I…I fell in love with this girl."

The moment the words leave my mouth, I feel a shift in the energy within me and surrounding me. For the first time, I'm honest with myself. I did fall in love with her. I *am* still in love with her.

It's just as electrifying as it is terrifying.

I pull myself out of my inner trance and continue speaking, desperate to shake the horrifying reality that is my emotions. "Not only that, I trusted her. I trusted her with you guys." I watch as their eyes falter, a sense of sadness washing across their faces. Seeing defeat in their eyes is by far one of the worst feelings in the world, surmounted only by the pain I felt as I had to see Delaney disappear in my rearview mirror while I drove away.

"She didn't care about us, lads; she never did," I tell them softly, my heart aching at the thought of it. I'd tried so hard these past few days to push that realization to the back of my mind, to convince myself that there was some otherworldly reason that we weren't meant to be together, but this was the reality. She hadn't cared about us, and regardless of how much I loved her, sometimes love isn't enough. "You know that nothing is more important to me than this team," I pause to clear my throat as I speak, shaking off the emotions that threaten to break through. "And I won't tolerate anyone coming in between what we've set out to do here. It's you and me, guys. No one else cares about you the way I do. No one."

It's silent for a moment, a few of the boys nodding appreciatively before Wilks puts a hand out to stop them, shaking his head in blatant disagreement. "What don't you understand? It wasn't just you that connected with her. Sure, you had a different relationship with her. Hell, we all did. But Delaney was a part of our team...and you just sent her away. Who's to say you won't just do that to one of us?"

I'm bewildered by his words, shaking my head profusely. "Of course not. I would never turn my back on you. My job is to be here for you guys, no matter the cost. You know that. You all know that..." I meet each one of their eyes in sincerity.

Green stands up, joining Wilks as they stand side by side. "Coach," his voice is shallow, but I can tell just from his tone that what he's about to say has depth. "You've done everything for us. You've been a part of our lives in more ways than we can count. Isn't that right, lads?"

"It's true," Hart agrees, joining in this cluster of outbursts. "Coach, you're the one who's at the field at the crack of dawn preparing us for practice."

It's Green who's next to join in. "You're the person behind every single win we've enjoyed and the person who reassures us after every single loss."

"You're the one who looks out for us day in and day out,"

Wilks finishes singing my praises. "You've always been here for us, Coach, but now..." He places a hand on my shoulder. "It's time for us to be here for you."

I look down at the ground and bite down on the inside of my cheek, alarmed by the sudden emotion that's overcome me. These past few days, I'd been doing everything possible to put up a front —to act as if losing Delaney hadn't left a gaping hole in my heart. I'd been lashing out left and right, and the whole time, all the boys wanted to do was make me realize that it was okay to *feel*.

It was okay to accept that I loved that girl.

That energetic, adorable, bubbly girl who had bounded in on her first day and encapsulated every ounce of my attention ever since.

"You need to talk to her, Coach," Green says, his voice gentle as he places a hand on my shoulder. "She was devastated. And we know that you are as well."

"It's too late," I speak after a moment, shaking my head. "She's gone back to the US. There's nothing I can do."

For once, I find the silence amongst the group highly unsettling before Wilks shoots the guys a devious grin in delight before placing the bracelets back into my hand.

"Well, Coach..." He smirks, and for once, his cocky smile brings a sense of reassurance to my soul. "Looks like you're the one who's going to end up going south after all."

#Twenty-Five

DELANEY

THERE IS something oddly comforting yet utterly heart-wrenching about listening to the same breakup playlist on repeat for a week.

On the one hand, it's a relief to hear that I'm not the only one to have experienced their heart being torn into a million pieces. But is it really helping that this playlist only consists of one song? *All Too Well (Taylor's Version)* 10 minute version. No. No, it's not.

Not even Miss Swift can take away the ache in my heart—and the worst part? The one person who I know can is 4,854 miles away.

Yes, I googled it.

Several times, actually.

The past seven days have felt like a total blur. Everything happened so quickly—from fleeing the field, clearing out my place, jumping on a flight back home. Yet now, as I watch the clock, day in and day out, time achingly ticks by the second.

It shouldn't be this way.

I should be back in Crawley...back with Crawfield...back with...

No.

I can't keep doing this to myself.

It's a vicious merry-go-round that's only making me more nauseous the more I think about it.

Warren left me.

He left me standing there without a chance to explain myself. A chance to make things right. And now, I can't help but wonder if he's also feeling these same levels of intense emotions. Or have I totally missed the mark, and he's thanking the heavens that I'm gone?

I don't know.

I feel like I don't know anything anymore.

Without him, nothing makes sense.

Warren was the answer to every problem—the end to every question. The clarity to every uncertainty and the one person I thought saw me, for *me*.

Maybe Gramps was wrong when he said I'd find someone. Maybe there isn't one perfect "someone" out there for me. Maybe I'm doomed to loneliness for the rest of eternity.

Stop it, Delaney.

I have to scold myself.

What am I doing?

Sitting up on the bed, I pull down on the skin on either side of my cheeks, blinking my swollen eyes a few times to help them re-open. I hadn't realized they'd been closed for hours, all in an attempt to stop staring at the clock.

I reach over to my phone on my nightstand, turning off my music before falling right back onto the bed, this time, nose-diving straight into another deep, dark place—social media.

The best thing about having a chronically offline ex is that you can't stalk them.

God. Am I already calling him that?

Ex.

I exhale deeply, but not before I stumble across Crawfield's social media page. I couldn't bear to log out of the account.

Why?

Because although Warren never allowed me to post him directly on the page, that didn't stop me from saving what must be over 50 posts of him in my drafts.

I never would've shared them...especially not after what happened. But now, as I torture myself by looking through them, I can't help but choke back some tears.

Nothing hurts more than seeing that smile on his face—looking into those eyes—remembering how those lips felt against my own.

I once thought nothing could be more pure than being someone's happiness, but now I know that's not the case. Because nothing is more pure than someone else being your happiness, and believing that it will last forever.

"Delaney, I told you not to film me!"

Warren playfully backed away from behind his desk, reaching to snatch the camera out of my hand in a video that plays on a loop.

"You said not to film you on the field," I remarked, giggling at his attempts to rip the camera out of my grasp. *"Baby, you look so cute when you're working."*

I hear him scoff between his own laughter. *"Please don't call me cute again."*

"Why not?" I pestered, yet he continued to reach for the phone, somehow managing to wrap me up in his embrace in the process. The camera didn't need to pick that up for me to remind myself. *"I want to remember this picture of you, Warren!"*

All at once, the camera fumbled out of my hands and fell straight to the floor, capturing the exact moment when Warren wrapped his arms around my waist, nestled his forehead against mine, and leaned in to hover over my lips.

"How about instead..." I heard him start to whisper. *"You take a mental image of what I'm about to do to you—"*

I lock my phone screen, slamming it into my chest.

I take back what I said earlier. Maybe it would've been easier if he had social media—stalking simple images of him would've been much less painful than re-living these memories all over again.

I pull my phone back up, refusing to look at the page as I swipe away, already diverting my attention back onto my playlist. I need to go into my *Reputation* era—no more *Red*.

My thumb gravitates towards my next playlist before my comeback era is cut short by an incoming call, causing my heart to skip a beat as I sit up straight in bed.

As pathetic and cliche as it sounds, in that moment, I dare to hope.

I dare to hope that it's Warren. Calling to apologize, to talk, to say he misses me.

And then my heart sinks like a stone.

I let out a dramatic groan as "Mr. Cunningham" appears at the top of my screen, forcing me to either stare at it until the ringing ends or decline it and let him know I'm trying to ignore him.

Why the hell does he keep calling me?

Curiosity overtakes my annoyance as I finally answer the call, putting the phone on speaker.

"Hello?" My voice is as dry as it is somber.

"Delaney." There's an urgency in the way Mr. Cunningham speaks, one I don't think I've ever heard before. "I'm going to need you to come down to the office as soon as possible, please."

"I'm in no position to go anywhere, Mr. Cunningham. I'm going through the biggest heartbreak of my life. I've been in my *Red* era for days."

"Your *what*?"

"You wouldn't get it."

Now I feel like I'm turning into my parents. God, I don't know which is worse: that or the pang of anger and resentment I'm feeling at his voice, solely because it's not the voice I wanted to hear.

"Delaney, I'm sorry I've been bugging you. I've been trying to get through to you for weeks. Your share of your Grandfather's estate—it's ready now. I want to discuss it with you. It's quite a substantial amount. Far more than most of your family got."

"I don't care!" I raise my tone, the annoyance finally getting the best of me. "Give it to someone else. I'm sure my parents would happily volunteer as takers. Besides, I don't even know what I'd do with that money. "

"Delaney." He attempts once more to calm me down, his cool tone only angering me more. "Please just listen to me."

"No. I'm done listening," I snap in response. "You know what? Someone needs to listen to *me* for once. Do you know how upsetting it is not to have someone hear you out? Explain? Even speak? Like, do you know how rude that is?"

There's a drawn-out silence.

"I might."

I close my mouth, scorned by his slight dig at me. Another silence passes between us before I respond. "Touche."

"Delaney." He's speaking gently now, causing me to sigh in defeat finally. "Your parents told me that they're planning to sell Crawfield."

I suck in a breath.

I thought that maybe, by some miracle, they would've changed their minds this week. But no. My parents are harder to crack than Warren was to convince to let me even start my job.

None of that matters anymore. It's not my problem.

"I don't work for the team anymore, Mr. Cunningham," I try to explain. "Everything is out of my hands."

I hear him sigh on the other line. "The silent bidding on the team is happening at five PM tonight. You know that, right?"

How could I forget?

"Yes," I mumble, hardly audible. "I know."

"And are you going?" he questions.

"No."

I've resorted to one-syllable responses at this point. I don't think I have the energy to do much more.

"Is that all, Mr. Cunningham?" I'm exhausted as the words escape my lips.

"Your parents have gone down to your Grandfather's place and cleared out most of his belongings. They thought that you might want to see what was left before they donate the rest."

Gramps' place.

I haven't been there in ages.

"You don't have to say anything else. Just remember what I told you about your share, okay?" He speaks once more, that hint of urgency back in his voice—almost as if he's trying to tell me something that I'm not catching onto yet. "5 PM, Delaney. Call me if you change your mind."

I TOYED with the idea back and forth in my mind like a mental game of ping pong.

It didn't matter, though, because even when my brain swayed me away, my heart still somehow guided me back to the one place I never thought I'd come back to.

Gramps' house.

The key on my keychain securely fits into the lock, allowing me to easily twist the handle open with a faint creek as I make my way inside.

It's just like I remember it.

Except now, it's empty.

But if Gramps taught me one thing, nothing makes a house a home like the memories you spend there. And that—*that* can never be taken.

I have to push aside the feeling of sadness that engulfs me as my legs guide me down the hallways. I can't help but look up at the photos that line the walls. I'm not surprised my parents have left these for last.

I place my hand overtop of a few dusted images set in their frames, smiling softly as I see Gramps throughout all decades of his life—knowing just how much he lived every moment to the fullest.

There's not much else left for me to go through in this place. My family has cleared it out, leaving little for me besides a few knick-knacks and miscellaneous decor items throughout the room.

It doesn't matter though. I don't want a single thing—I came here with one motivator in mind. To go right back to the one place I know my parents have left untouched.

Gramps' sports room. Or, dare I say, Gramps' Crawfield room.

I make my way down the hall and to the right, peering through the sliver in the door before I have to brace myself to walk inside.

This is the room of my childhood.

This is my safe space.

I push open the door, instantly greeted by the familiar aroma of Gramps' cologne, mixed with the lingering scent of wood, a gentle reminder of the vacancy that has settled into this once-bustling room.

It's all too overwhelming, and before I know it, I've fallen onto Gramps' couch. Right back into my seat. I sink in the same way I always used to, almost as if this couch had been made just for me. Growing up, I was convinced that Gramps had the comfiest couch in the world.

I was right.

My head falls back into the cushion, and for the first time, it feels as though I'm really seeing this room for all of its glory.

The various Crawfield uniforms over the years. The memorabilia. The footballs are carefully tucked into protective cases. And the TV. The TV projected it all.

Before I know it, I'm leaning across the couch, reaching for the remote and flicking it on.

I insisted to Gramps that I'd buy him a brand-spanking new TV. The biggest he'd ever seen in his life. But he was never one to be overtly extravagant. He said if it's not broken, don't fix it. Therefore, the TV he bought in the early 2000s lives to see another day.

And like a jab to the stomach, the first channel that comes on is right where it was left off: a football match.

Mom and Dad said Gramps passed peacefully in his home—and now, sitting here, I can't help but wonder if this was where his peace was.

Suddenly, the air in here feels tighter. It's so hard to breathe. So hard knowing that for the first time in my life, I'm here alone. Gramps isn't going to bound into the room with an arm full of snacks and eyes that light up my own.

He's gone.

It's a reality that is as hard to swallow as it is to live.

Before I know it, a single tear falls down my cheek, and that's when I speak. My voice is a whisper, but I know he hears it. "I miss you, Gramps," I admit wholeheartedly. "I don't know what to do. Tell me what to do."

The tears are flowing down my cheeks at this point, prompting me to lift my arms up to wipe them away as my sobs escape my mouth quietly. I keep repeating those six words over and over.

Tell me what to do, Gramps.

Beams of sunlight start to burst through the window that lines the back wall of the room, cascading rays of light over my eyes. I have to squeeze them shut, eventually opting to move from where I'm seated.

I shift my weight, sniffling as I work my way down the couch and find refuge on Gramps' side.

I've never sat on this end of the couch before, and now that I am, I guess I understand why Gramps always called me sunshine.

I was always in the light.

I was his light.

The thought only breaks my heart more as I dart my gaze in

the other direction, looking down at the coffee table that rests beside the couch.

On it is a simple empty glass—sweet tea.

A lamp—Gramps never liked to sit in the dark.

An album.

I freeze.

I wipe away the rest of my tears, for I can hardly trust the words I just read on the front are true.

"My time in Crawley."

My shaky hands grab the album and flip it open to the first page. And right off the bat, I see Alf.

I can't help but giggle at the thought that...there he is. Two decades younger, with at least 90% less gray hairs than he has now.

He's standing with Gramps, yet the two of them aren't looking at the camera. Instead, they're sitting in the stands and appear to be looking out onto the field. There's a sense of overwhelming joy in Gramps' eyes—one that I always saw when he was watching his beloved football team.

I flip the page.

The next photo is a series of images. Now, Gramps is in action. He's on the field, playing with the team, laughing as he falls down during one of the drills—*must be a Matthews thing*, I can't help but think.

I don't recognize a single player. These photos are old...none of these guys are on the team anymore. Most probably don't even play.

And that's how it is for the majority of the album as I flip through. Smiling at the photos just because I recognize every single location in there. They're now places where I've been able to make my own memories during my own time in Crawley.

Only a few pages remain, but this time, as I flip to the next, my breath gets caught in my throat.

Warren.

There he is. Fifteen...sixteen years old, maybe. I can't tell. All I know is that he's young. A bright-eyed teenager, standing beside Gramps.

There's not been a single photo where I've seen Gramps show affection to these players, but in this photo with Warren, there he is. Arm wrapped around his shoulder, with a proud look in his eyes.

I gently brush my fingertips over Gramps' face in the photo before instinctively moving them over to Warren. It's strange seeing them both together as if two of my most important worlds are colliding—two men that I loved. Two men who loved each other.

I wish so badly I could have spent time with them together.

The tears threaten to prickle my eyes again before I gulp them down and continue to flip through. I can't get enough. There's dozens of pictures of Warren, all joined by special hand-written notes by Gramps.

"An up-and-coming Crawfield star."

As I continue to flip through, he slowly becomes more than just "another star" to Gramps. Suddenly, he's *Warren.*

"Warren's first signing."

"Warren's first match."

"Meeting Warren's Mum."

The story is a beautiful one, showcasing the relationship that Gramps built with Warren over the years they knew each other. Seeing the love on Gramps' face grow with each year that passed and Warren stayed by his side—watching them grow together.

The narrative changes again, and now the words on the page no longer belong to a name—they belong to "my boy."

"My boy's first professional game."

"My boy's first goal."

"My boy's first time in the paper."

All at once, there seems to be a gap. Gramps appeared to date each image over the years, but now, there is nothing. There's a period in time where not a single picture is documented, and as I flip the page, I see why.

220

"When one journey ends, it can only mean another is about to begin."

There, Warren lies in the hospital, hardly giving a thumbs up to the camera as his knee is bandaged and slung in front of him.

Compared to the other pictures, in this one, there's no hope lighting up his eyes. My heart sinks as my memories take me back to the article I'd read back in Crawley.

Warren Park—Game-winning goal, career-ending shot.

The sight of this picture breaks my heart. Because despite the pitiful attempt at a lighthearted smile Warren is giving to the camera, I know just how broken he must have been in this moment.

I force myself to flip the page, and that hope in his eyes is one that takes several more page turns for me to see again.

Finally, there's a natural progression from Warren standing on the sidelines of the pitch to being right back on the field, falling into his role.

"My boy. Coach of Crawfield."

My heart softens at the photo. There he is.

The Warren that I stumbled into on my first day, the Warren that I've come to know as my own.

An emptiness follows that aching nostalgia as I reach the last page in the book—where, finally, it's as if the two of them have replicated the first picture they took together. The only difference is that now, instead of smiling at the camera, as their arms are slung around one another, they're smiling at each other.

I feel like my heart is about to burst.

"I know you'll find someone, sunshine. But when you do...I have one condition."

I look up at him curiously. "And that is?"

"They need to be a Crawfield fan."

I close the book shut. It's as if the answer suddenly makes itself clear in my mind—just like it did the day I stood up to my parents and began this Crawfield journey.

I've always been a fan of sequels.

"Thank you, Gramps." I place the album back on the table, turning off the TV as I march my way over to the door. I pause in the doorway, glancing over my shoulder at the room for one final moment before I finally close it behind me.

The second I make my way out of the house, I pull my phone from my back pocket and start to dial.

It only takes a couple of rings before a familiar voice picks up. "Hello?"

"Mr. Cunningham." My voice is determined and willed. "I know what I'm going to do with the money."

#Twenty-Six

WARREN

SHOES.

Underwear.

Socks.

Pants.

Shirts.

What more do I need?

"Are you missing anything?" Mum's on the other line of the phone—heckling me to check over my bags for yet another time.

God. Times were much easier when she used to do all the packing for me. I mean, times were much easier when I didn't drive Delaney out of the country.

"Yes, Mum." My voice is that of a low hum as I zip up my suitcase, refusing to open it again until I get to Houston.

There's a silence through the phone as I place it by my door, waiting for her voice to return to the line. "So..." she begins. "When does your flight leave again?"

Things have been stressful between Mum and me since she completely snapped my head off after I confided in her about what happened with Delaney.

I don't blame her, though.

I needed someone to yell at me—hell, the only reason I've

mustered up enough courage to actually go to the U.S. is because of the boys' so-called intervention. I knew I had to, but I needed someone to push me over the edge completely...kick my ass in gear.

"Nine tonight," I answer. She's asked this several times before and I know she's just using this simple question as a way to make conversation. "I should land around seven AM your time. It's a long flight," I explain as I scour my bedroom in search of my passport.

It's only four o'clock right now. I'm extremely early, given the airline said I can't check in until three hours before. But it doesn't matter. I refuse to miss this flight.

It's already been a few days longer than I'd hoped, considering getting a last-minute flight is almost virtually impossible. Besides, it doesn't help that I can feel my heart breaking that much more as each second goes by without saying, "I'm sorry."

"Things will be okay, Warren." Mum's voice is full of reassurance. It's like she can feel my hurt despite the distance. "I promise you, alright?"

"But what if they aren't?" I'm quick to put a damper on the conversation. A pessimist drowning in a pool of optimism. "What if this is all for nothing, huh?" My voice turns erratic now as I'm shuffling through the junk on my nightstand in a mad search for my passport. "What if she wants nothing to do with Crawfield anymore, Mum?"

I hear Mum suck in a breath. We've had this conversation far more times than I'd admit to—but it's only because she's the one person I can confide in to tell me how it is. The one person who, despite only seeing a slither of how I felt about Delaney, heard it all.

Mum wasn't lying when she told Delaney that her name may have come up in conversation because it had several times.

Sure, at first, Mum got tired of me moaning about her "PR tactics," but somewhere along the way, all that complaining turned into explaining. Explaining just how much this girl stumbled into my life (literally speaking), and completely flipped my world upside down—or maybe, just maybe, made it finally the right side up.

"Nothing to do with Crawfield." She breaks me free from the thought. "Or nothing to do with *you?*"

There's that truth I was looking for. One that, no matter how blunt, possesses the power to cut me to my core.

Mum seemingly takes my silence as the only answer she needs. "Listen, Warren." She speaks back up. "Even though I'm your mum, I don't know the answers to everything. But I do know that you need to tell her how you feel. How you care about her. How much you *love her.* And my darling, sometimes love is the only answer you need."

I fall back onto my bed, giving up on my search for my passport for the time being and re-focusing my energy on this conversation. "I don't know how to do that," I admit sheepishly. "I don't know how to tell someone that I love them."

My first thought goes back to Ira. Back to that conversation Delaney and I had on the field. She told me he loved me. I told her I loved him. But still, it doesn't matter because a part of me still beats myself up for saying it too late.

"Of course you do!" Mum wastes no time rebutting the thought. "You tell me you love me all the time, Warren."

I shake my head, running my hand across my face. "It's not the same! You're my mum," I explain. "It's easy for me to tell you I love you...but for some reason, it's impossible for anyone else."

As if she's bringing my thoughts to life, she speaks back up. "This is about Ira, isn't it, Warren?"

Again, silence.

She releases a sigh. "Son, I don't know what to tell you. Maybe you missed your opportunity with Ira, but now, you have another chance. You have another *Matthews* you can say it to. And this one..." her speech lingers. "This is *the one.*"

A knock falling over my door saves me from having to respond to the scary reality her words possess. I know Delaney is the one—I'm just praying she stays that way and doesn't become the one that I let slip through my grasp.

A few more knocks come through my door, a sense of urgency in the way I can hear the fists colliding.

"I've got to go, Mum." I sit up on my bed, swapping the phone from one ear to the other. "I'll call you when I land, okay?"

"Okay," she says somberly, a sniffle in her voice. "Have a good flight—I'll talk to you soon. I love you, Warren." This time, she really enunciates when she speaks.

I stifle a faint laugh, making my way towards the door. "I *love* you too."

I end the call, shoving my phone into my back pocket as I swing open the door, without peering through the peephole, as I'm greeted by the last face I thought I'd see:

Alf.

"Warren..." He's out of breath as he speaks, clutching onto the doorframe. "I've got to talk to you!"

"You alright, Alf?" His flushed face and heaving breaths remind me of the moment he raced over to tell me about Delaney coming to Crawfield.

Now, despite the deja vu, the roles are reversed. I'm racing to her.

"Yeah." He wipes along his brow. "There were too many people waiting for the lift. I had to take the stairs."

"I only live on the second floor."

He shoots me a glare.

One that I reciprocate with a playful smirk, backing away from the door and gesturing for him to come inside. "Why are you here, Alf?" I question, continuing my quest for my passport. "You know I'm leaving today."

"I know." He closes the door behind him. "But I had to come and see you first."

"Miss me already?"

"No, you pompous bastard." He sinks himself into one of the

chairs that lingers in the corner of the room, continuing to catch his breath. "I'm here to tell you some news."

"Are we really doing this again, Alf?" I shoot him an impatient stare, waiting for him to get to the point.

He straightens his spine before resting his elbows on his knees, perching forward. "The deal just went through," he reveals. "We have a new owner of Crawfield."

I swallow deeply. I knew that any day now the team was going up for sale—why do you think I've been on the phone with my Mum for hours—desperate to get out of here so quickly?

"I don't care about that, Alf." Even I have a hard time accepting my words for truth as I speak. "I have to leave for the airport." I continue shuffling around the room. "Where is my bloody passport?" I mutter under my breath, lifting up my sheets and tossing them to the side. "We'll deal with this when I'm back, okay?"

"No," Alf cuts me off, his voice firm and demanding. "We're talking about this now, Park!"

I purse my lips, clenching my jaw as I see the urgency in his eyes.

"Sit down," he tells me. "Now."

I grumble under my breath before I take a seat across from him, caving as I speak. "Two minutes," I instruct him firmly. "Not a second longer."

Alf settles back into the armchair. "It's gonna take you longer than that to read this." He pulls a folded piece of paper out of his back pocket, opening it up at a tauntingly slow pace before he gestures it in my direction. "Here you go."

I make no attempt to reach for it, instead staring down at it in question. "What is this?" I ask, my patience withering.

"Find out for yourself," he says, pushing it that much closer in my direction. "It's addressed to you. It just got faxed over from Houston—"

I snatch the letter from his hand, assessing it with a quick scan of my eyes before the name above the address line forces my breath to hitch in the back of my throat.

I dart my attention forward—Alf's eyes full of that infuriating *I told you so* look. "Still only want two minutes?" he asks.

I narrow in my stare before pulling the letter in closer, eyes fixating back onto that same name, the name I'll never forget for the rest of my life.

Delaney Matthews.

DEAR WARREN,

Is that even the way people start letters anymore?

I don't know.

If I'm being honest, I've never written one, nor did I think I would under such strenuous circumstances.

A phone call would've been much easier, I recognize that, but my lawyer, Mr. Cunningham, tells me I have to put everything I want to say into writing—it's an impossible task, really. There are so many things I want to say to you. So much truth that's left to be spoken, but for now, I need to start somewhere.

I couldn't help but notice as I started to write this letter that it's almost exactly three months to the date that I landed at Heathrow—skipping out of the airport with this refined sense of pride in myself, given that for once, I was excited about what lay ahead.

You see, a part of me always knew that Crawfield was special—I suppose it was because Gramps was so special to me and that some of the happiest moments in my life were spent with him, watching you all play.

That's why, when it got announced that my parents were taking ownership of the team and that they wanted to sell them, claiming that they were of "no value," I fought. Sure, it took some tears and a whole lot of convincing, but somehow I did it.

Now, I have to admit I had my own selfish reservations at the start. Coming to Crawley was only supposed to be a three-month mission to make the team worth more and prove to my parent's that keeping this team in the family meant something.

In the cab ride over to Crawley, I optimistically told the driver that things with Crawfield were all about to change—that with me joining your team, everything was going to shape up.

He'd asked if I was a "miracle worker." I hadn't quite known what he meant at the time, yet despite that, I'd told him the one truth I'd held onto my whole life.

"No, I'm not. But I believe in them."

I told him that because it was true. I did believe in miracles because, at that moment, I was living in one.

Everything about coming to Crawley felt otherworldly—especially you.

I know you're likely mad at me, Warren. Deep down, I'm still upset with myself. But the girl that showed up on that first day of practice is not the same girl that is writing this letter now.

It's the girl who fell in love with the early morning practices—admiring you from afar until slowly but surely, she worked her way to your side.

It's the girl who fell in love with Wilk's pre-game pep talks (despite how painful they can be).

It's the girl that fell in love with football just by the way she saw that love reflected in your eyes.

But most of all, it's the girl who found a piece of herself in Crawley. A piece she never knew existed until she fell in love with you in it.

You are Crawley, Warren. You're everything that made me love it there and more.

I can see why my Gramps always believed in you...because from the moment I first met you, I did, too.

So, sure, I was foolish to think that the value of legacy would've ever surmounted that of money to my parents, but they were foolish to think I wouldn't give up without a final fight.

Remember how I told you about persistence, Warren? Well...as you likely know, my parents put Crawfield up for silent bidding—

lucky for me, around that same time, not only did I have a revelation, but I came to learn that my Gramps had given me the means to make this right.

I'm writing this letter to tell you that I'm the new owner of Crawfield, Warren. God. It feels weird even writing that, but...I don't want to be. I'd like you to take over my ownership instead.

And before you drop this page and roll your eyes, please hear me out.

This is your dream...your team, Warren. You told me that night under the stars just how much this meant to you—how the lines within the field were the only safe space you'd ever known.

How my Gramps gave you a second chance.

It makes me smile knowing that he was just as important to you as he has always been to me, and I know in my heart, Warren, that the bond you two shared can never be taken...just like how I refuse to have this team taken from you now.

You don't have to forgive me. All I'm asking you to do right now is believe.

Believe in yourself, and if that's not enough, then believe that this is what my Gramps wanted for you.

I hope you make the right choice...Coach.

Yours,

Delaney.

I CAN HARDLY LIFT my eyes up from the page—by now, I must've read Delaney's letter so many times that I no longer have any concept of it.

It's Alf's voice that snaps me back into reality. "Twenty minutes." He peers down at his watch. "Took me thirty to process it."

I meet him with a blank, vacant stare. It's all I can do at this point as he stands up from his chair and places a firm hand on my shoulder.

"Here." He shell shocks me as he hands me an exact replica of the bracelet I'd snapped off and had been desperate to try and repair ever since.

"Where did you...when did you..."

"You have Wilks to thank for that." Alf flashes a faint smile before he removes his hand from my shoulder. "Go catch your flight, Park," he speaks, tossing my passport into my lap—one he'd seemingly found while I was reading the letter. "Bring our girl home."

Twenty-Seven

DELANEY

"DELANEY, be a doll and hand me the mashed potatoes."

Mom eagerly commands my attention—given that I've been sitting in a complete and total daze since the second I arrived at my parents for our annual Matthew's Thanksgiving.

I lean across the table—one that's filled with enough food to feed an army and reach for the bowl of mashed potatoes, handing it over to my mom.

"Oh, and don't forget the stuffing." She gestures once more, taking the bowl from my grasp without muttering so much as a "thank you."

I suppress the urge to suck in a breath of annoyance and do as she asks, handing her the stuffing and resettling in my armchair. I have no appetite—not just when it comes to the food, but to be here a second longer.

"Isn't this great?" Dad asks rhetorically as he eagerly sits at the head of the table, gesturing theatrically with his arms. "What a perfect way to finish up the week—Grandpa's house is cleared, the team is sold, and we're all together again." He counts on his fingers. "What more could we ask for on Thanksgiving? Am I right?"

This time, it almost pains me not to roll my eyes as I make

note of the order in which he described this "perfect week." Of course, referring to our family's *delightful* togetherness as last because, in his mind, it is.

I'm only here because I have to be—not because I want to be. Besides, I'm exhausted. I hardly got any sleep last night, given that I stayed up for most of it staring at both my laptop and phone screen with such intensity that I'm positive I've burned my cornea.

I couldn't help it.

After Mr. Cunningham faxed over the letter to Crawfield, I've been desperately praying that Warren would respond or (at the bare minimum) acknowledge it. Except now, it's been almost 24 hours of complete radio silence.

It's killing me.

It came as a massive shock when Mr. Cunningham revealed the truth behind my share of Gramps' inheritance: since the day I was born, Gramps had set aside allocated funds for me each and every year.

Yet, unlike how he supposedly did for my cousins, placing their accounts under their legal birth name, the confusion with processing my account was the name in which Gramps placed it under:

The Sunshine Fund.

Apparently, it took the lawyers some deep digging, but they were able to come to the conclusion that not only was "sunshine" a code name for me—but that this account had significantly more than any other relative.

After 25 years of fruitful deposits, at the time of his passing, the account had a net worth of over ten million dollars, all set aside for me.

Yet, the part that's still the hardest to digest—the note that Gramps left behind with it.

Bring the sunshine into others' lives like you always did for me.
Love, Gramps.

. . .

I WAS FLOORED.

Beside myself.

I hardly had time to process the news before I had Mr. Cunningham put in a formal bid on my behalf for the team—one that I knew would surmount any prospective buyer.

Four hours later, I got the news.

Delaney Matthews—official owner of Crawfield Football Club.

I could've sworn I saw Mr. Cunningham smiling when I started to jump for joy. But my excitement was short-lived.

Granting myself ownership of the team was only the first of many steps in my plan. The next being the hardest, and now the most stagnant in my operation forward—Warren agreeing to take over.

"Can you believe we got almost 500,000 dollars more than we were expecting?!" Mom cries out, mouth full of mash, yet the aching smile still manages to break through her eyes.

"I can." Dad stands up from the table with a wine glass in his hand and raises it into the air.

Oh no.

"What a great segway into our annual Thanksgiving thankful speeches, shall we?"

Please, no.

For as long as I can remember, every Thanksgiving, my family has initiated a round table sharing of what we're "most thankful for." One might say, what an appropriate gesture, given the season. I say it's the subliminal way my family likes to one-up each other's accomplishments year in and year out.

No one talks about health, happiness, and family.

They talk about investments, major deals, and how their stocks are through the roof.

It's pitiful. Usually, I try to escape to the washroom when I sense it's coming, but I suppose this year, my mind's been preoccupied with more important matters.

"Anyone want to go first?" Dad scans the eyes that line the table, prompting me to dart mine to the floor. Opting for that overused tactic of if I don't look at you, maybe you won't see me.

"Anyone?" He probes.

Don't pick me.

Don't pick me.

"Delaney!" Dad's voice inflates with joy as I deflate into my chair.

Shit.

"How about you go first?" he proposes, with a raise of his glass.

I awkwardly sink into my chair. "I'd rather not—"

Mom nudges her arm into me softly at my rebuttal. "Stand up," she instructs, forcing me to meet not only her unimpressed stare but everyone's that now zeros in on me.

I release a long, drawn-out sigh, slowly pushing my way back as I place the napkin that once lined my lap onto the table just ahead.

With my rise, Dad takes a seat, seemingly pleased with himself. "So," he begins. "Tell us all what you're thankful for."

Others might say it's hard standing in front of your entire family with a lurking secret in the back of your mind, but for me, it's easy.

My whole life, I've held back on my true feelings towards my family—my distaste for how they do things and the way they act.

So, realistically, there's always been a secret between us. Therefore, holding this one back about Crawfield just a bit longer doesn't hurt. Besides, it's none of their business anyway. There's a reason why they opted for a silent bid—my parents didn't care who took over the team; all they cared about was the money they got in return, and based on what I've heard so far—they're very satisfied.

"Anytime now." My cousin Mabel snickers under her breath, turning to face her sister Connie in laughter.

My cheeks flush a faint shade of red as I clear my throat,

meeting not only the impatient eyes of my family members, but that of the serving staff Mom and Dad have in the house.

I have 360 judgments all around me.

Great.

"Well," I attempt to speak up, yet my voice is hoarse. "I suppose what I'm thankful for this year is..." I look up in thought before the words come to me. "New beginnings..."

My voice trails off, not because I don't know how to elaborate on that, but because I know once I start talking about everything that has happened to me these past few months, I'm not going to be able to stop.

Going to Crawley completely changed my life.

It completely changed me.

It allowed me to see the world from an entirely new perspective.

There's no hand-outs. Life of luxury. Serving staff surrounding what's supposed to be an intimate family meal. *No.* Being in Crawley was simplified happiness, point-blank.

I learned what it takes to put in the work, day in and day out. I learned to be selfless, and rather than obsessing over my own accomplishments, I grew to learn to sing the praises of others—cheer them on and encourage them with all of your heart. Why? Because you believe in them, and no matter what differences you might possess, none of that seems to matter anymore because when you're on a team...you're a part of a family.

Family.

I'd never understood the word more than I do now as I stand in front of a group of people with whom I share a bloodline, but feel as though I hardly know a single thing about.

I look at my cousins Mabel and Connie—and as I do, I couldn't even tell you what their favorite colors are. Favorite stores? Sure. But beyond that, not a chance. Everything about them is superficial. But do you want to know who isn't?

Alf.

Alf's got a heart of gold, and I could recite an endless stream

of details about him—his children's names, their interests, how he
met his wife, his story leading up to Crawley...*God*. I learned all of
that in the first week.

Next, I look at my aunts and uncles—people who have
known me my whole life, yet a part of me feels like we've hardly
had a heart-to-heart once, a thought that makes me think about
the boys.

The boys—Wilks, Green, and Hart.

Sure, that's only three amongst a team of sixteen, but a part of
me knows that those three boys will be in my life forever. Let's not
forget that it's been Wilks who's checked in on me on behalf of
the group since the moment I left. Calling to see how I am—
making sure *I'm okay*.

Talking to Wilks makes me feel like I'm back in Crawley. He
always has a way of bringing a sense of peace to one's heart with a
little bit of that Crawfield chaos. I mean, he randomly asked me
the other day where I got the bracelet that I left him with. Why?
Who knows. Maybe he wanted one for himself?

He's a character that one, but one that's going to make
someone extremely happy one day—I just know it.

Finally, I look at my parents. The two people that I should
know more than anyone and should know me better than I know
myself, but instead, have hardly taken a chance to. It's a sad reality.
It's a painful truth, yet it's one that when I think about, I think
about the one person I know I shouldn't.

Warren.

I bared my soul to him in that letter. Hell, I even told him I
loved him. I don't know if I've ever told anyone that before, and if
I had, I know I didn't actually mean it. Because if Warren taught
me one thing, it's that you don't have to force love. It happens
naturally, and it happens sometimes when you least expect it.

I always thought the concept of love was so outwardly
complex. Yet, being with him, it felt so simple. The real complexities are what surrounds the way we left things, hardly easing my
mind at this moment.

A part of me is still hurt. A part of me wishes things didn't end the way they did. So sure, I love him, I think I always will, but frankly, I have nothing left in me to give.

"Is that all?" My cousins strike again, given that this entire time, I hadn't realized I was deep in the trenches with my thoughts. A blistering silence that's left everyone less amused.

"Like, c'mon, Delaney," Connie cocks a brow, folding her arms across her chest. "Didn't Gramps at least leave you with something to be thankful for?"

Mabel leans in, murmuring under her breath but loud enough so that everyone else can hear. "That is if he left you anything at all..."

I bite down on my lower lip in annoyance as now the whole table erupts into the faintest of laughter—my parents included.

Each of their mocking gazes and pitiful looks is enough to light a fire out from under me as I straighten my spine and furrow my brows.

"I'll have you all know that there is something I'm grateful for! Something that none of you would probably ever understand."

"Oh yeah? And what's that?"

I narrow my stare—realizing that Dad's the one who threw the comment back in my direction.

It unsettles me for a moment until I find my confidence again. "That I'm the new owner of—"

A loud knock comes through the door. One that causes everyone's attention to shift away from me and in the direction of the entrance.

"Are we expecting someone else?" Mom speaks up, a look of confusion washed all over her face.

Dad shakes his head in response, pursuing his lips before he gestures to one of the serving staff. "See who it is, will ya?" He demands impatiently.

My eyes follow the man as he exits the dining room and makes his way over to the entrance until he's out of sight.

"Go on, Delaney," Dad instructs. "Please, tell us all what we wouldn't understand."

The abrupt halt in conversation completely diminishes my confidence, as now, I start to toy with my hands in front of me, regretting my outburst to begin with.

This was a bad idea.

Time for some damage control.

"What I was trying to say was—"

"Delaney!" An erratic voice commands my attention as I shift my head in the direction it came from.

"Warren?"

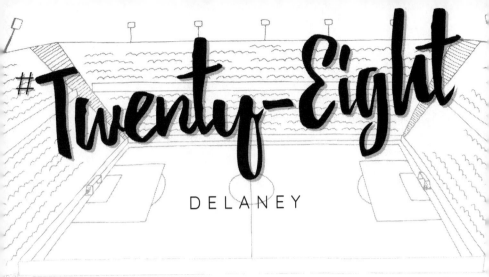

Twenty-Eight

DELANEY

"WARREN!" My mom claps her hands excitedly as I stand frozen in shock. "What are you doing here?" She asks the question I'm dying to know the answer to myself.

What is he doing here?

"Delaney?" I can feel Dad's burning gaze in my direction, considering I can hardly break my eyes away from the scene in front of me. "We didn't know Warren was going to be joining us."

I'm speechless.

Neither did I.

Warren is here.

He's standing in front of me.

Our eyes are locked as one, and suddenly, I can't breathe.

I have to literally pinch myself to make sure this isn't another one of the aching dreams I've been having since the night he drove away.

"Well, don't just stand there." Dad gestures towards the table, glancing at my diverting gaze through his peripheral vision. "Take a seat."

Warren clears his throat ever so slightly, the faint bags under his eyes telling me he's been awake for far too long on a flight I had no idea he was taking.

240

His hair's astray, made messier by his hands absentmindedly running through it. Unlike every other instance I've seen him, he doesn't appear perfectly polished and untouchable. He's standing with his shoulders slightly slouched as if he's carrying the weight of the world on them.

Lord knows I've been doing the same since the moment we hardly said goodbye.

It's a bittersweet feeling—having your wish finally come true. I've hoped for days that he'd come groveling back into my life, telling me he's sorry. Telling me how he's made a mistake and wishes things could go back to how they were. But now that he's here, standing just a few feet away from me, I don't know how to feel.

It's hardly comforting to know that that feeling remains—his ability to wash any and all rationality from my mind with just a simple look.

"I.." He's the one stumbling over his words now, unable to look away from me either. He seems like he has something that he wants to say, taking a step in my direction before pausing back on his heels. Finally, after a brief moment, he opts for a simple "Sure."

He starts to walk towards the table as I tear my gaze away and hyper fixate on the glass in front of me. Thankfully, the only other vacant chair is a few seats down from my own.

All the while, I can hear my cousins' hushed giggles, undoubtedly accompanied by a few stares of Warren up and down as he takes a seat—rewarding them with an icy glare from me.

"Benji!" Mom calls over to one of the serving staff. "Please get Warren a plate."

"That won't be necessary," Warren interjects, swallowing deeply. "I'm not here for dinner."

Mom and Dad exchange a confused glance towards one another before briefly shifting their gaze in my direction, considering Warren refuses to break eye contact.

"Well, I'm assuming then you're here to speak about the new owner?" Dad leans back in his chair expectantly.

Warren's demanding gaze continues to pierce into me—he's always had such an intensity in his eyes, but I don't think it's ever been stronger than now. It's as if we're speaking to one another without having to say anything at all.

Though, I imagine we're having two very different conversations.

"That's exactly why I'm here," he reveals assuredly.

I gulp down a sip of my drink, trying desperately to hide the heat rising to my face behind the glass. Does he know I haven't told them yet?

Now, the rest of the room is exchanging confused glances, murmuring to one another. "You realize we don't own the team anymore, right, son?" Dad questions, the topic piquing his interest. "Our family has washed our hands clean with Crawfield."

Finally, Warren pulls his gaze away from mine, looking at my dad with a raise of his eyebrows. "Not *everyone* in the family has."

I shoot up out of my seat in an attempt to distract away from Warren's untimely reveal—so abruptly that I almost knock my chair over in the process, prompting Benji to race over and steady it.

"You alright there, Delaney?" Dad furrows a concerned brow.

"Yeah." I twiddle with my thumbs awkwardly. "I just...I just realized I wasn't finished saying what I was thankful for."

"What a little klutz." My cousins snicker under their breath, and now, it's Warren shooting them an icy stare, instantly quieting them down. I brush their comment off with a shake of my head before clearing my throat and continuing my speech.

"This year, I'm most thankful for one thing." I scan the room, my heart pounding in my throat as I glaze past Warren. "*Crawley.*"

A silence falls amongst the space, as not one person is receptive to my words—besides Warren, whose face drops ever so slightly.

"Crawley?" Mom repeats in disbelief. "Seriously? You dragged yourself through three months there, Delaney, and *that's* what you're most thankful for?"

I fold my arms across my chest. "And those three months have been the most transformative time in my life," I throw back at her, trying everything in my power to muster up the courage to stand up for myself. I've been ridiculed long enough.

"At first, I didn't think Crawley would be the place for me," I admit. "The second I arrived, doubt started to creep in. I thought I'd made a mistake...but that wasn't true at all."

I allow a quick glance down at my hands before I look Warren directly in the eyes, preparing to speak my own truth. Somehow, even amidst all the uncertainty between us—he makes me feel assured. Understood.

"Crawley changed me. And in those three months, I learned so many things. Sure, it wasn't all sunshine and rainbows. I mean, some days were literally nothing but rain." I let out a half-smile, one that's reflected on Warren's face as I'm sure we're both recalling the same thing—that rainy day in London. The day I knew that Crawley wasn't the only thing I'd fallen in love with.

"Some days, it was really hard. Sometimes, I practically had to drag myself out of bed to keep going, but do you know why I loved it?"

The question is rhetorical, considering hardly anybody in my family seems to be following along with my rant anyway.

"Because it made me whole. It taught me who I really am."

Dad looks at me with a sense of disbelief—but not the type that leaves one in awe. The type that gives me the sense he's trying not to burst out into laughter.

"Don't be so ridiculous, Delaney." He scrunches his nose skeptically. "As if you didn't already know who you are. You're a city girl, for God's sake. What the hell exists in Crawley that somehow magically changed you, huh? What?"

I have to bite back the obvious answer to his question that threatens to escape my lips, given that he's sitting right across from him. Instead, I opt for a simple shake of my head.

"That's where you're wrong, Dad." I straighten my spine. "Because maybe that's who I was, but that's not who I *am*."

I watch as he scoffs, waving that dismissive hand in my direction the way he's done so many times before.

Little does he know, this will be the last.

"And who exactly *are* you then?" He mimics my action, straightening his own spine and placing both forearms on the table.

His mocking tone prompts Warren's head to whirl in his direction, his fist clenching tightly.

I hadn't thought Warren was a fan of my dad, but after seeing the way he's looking at him now, I can confirm my suspicion was true.

God, the way he absentmindedly makes me want to drop not only this rant, but my feelings of hurt towards him needs to be clinically studied.

A part of me wants him to look at me again, to give me the reassurance I so desperately need to keep going.

But before he can, I find it in myself.

"I'm the new owner of Crawfield."

Silence.

The room is silent. So silent that you could hear a pin drop.

Until suddenly, a deafening burst of laughter ensues.

"Oh, Delaney..." Not only are my parents in hysterics but so are my cousins, my aunts, my uncle—and damn, even Benji hurdles over in laughter.

But despite the boisterous noise, I can't hear a thing. Nothing demands my attention quite like the way I notice how Warren ignores it all—reminding me that all along, no matter where we are, who we're around, *he sees me.*

He's always seen me.

"Delaney, I think your little toast is over." My mom giggles. "That was definitely one we'll never forget. But let's move on, shall we? Who's next?"

"No," I cut off her attempt to bypass me like she has my

whole life. "I'm the one who bought the team! What don't you understand about that?"

"Warren, my boy." Dad now stands up from the table, brushing some moisture away from his eyes.

My heart drops into my stomach at my dad's poor choice of words. And judging by the way Warren sucks in a breath and tightens his chest, I can tell he's noticed it, too. His still-clenched fists have now turned his knuckles white.

"I'm impressed that you've been able to put up with this for three whole months," Dad continues obliviously. "Aren't you happy she's home?"

Now, Warren stands up, and seeing how he towers over my dad and silences the room makes my jaw drop.

He's about to snap.

But before he can speak, I interject a final time. If anyone is having the last word here, it's me.

"You know what? I don't care if you don't believe me." I toss my dinner cloth onto the table in frustration. "Frankly, it doesn't matter. Because at this moment, I know one thing for certain." I press a finger into the table in front of me, urging myself to continue. "Gramps is proud of me. He's proud of what I've done, and I'm proud of the decisions I've made."

I begin to back away from the table, my footing guiding me out of the room, but not before I look at them all once more, meeting and holding each of their gazes.

"I don't think you can say the same for yourselves."

#Twenty-Nine

WARREN

I'VE CHASED after many things in my life.

My hopes.

My dreams.

My goals.

But absolutely none of that is comparable to the chase that is going after *her*.

It's a marathon. One I never thought I'd partake in, but one I'd run for the rest of my life if I had to.

"Delaney!" I'm desperate to try and catch up to her. She made it so easy in London, but the truth is, I think she wanted me to catch up back then. Now, her long legs are putting me to the test as I pick up my pace. "Delaney!"

She stops dead in her tracks, turning swiftly on her heel as her hair whips over her shoulder. "What are you doing here?" Her eyes narrow in on me. "Why are you here?"

I freeze.

I pause.

I stutter.

It's a simple question, one with such a complex answer.

There are so many reasons why I'm here. So many things I want to say. But the challenge is, where do I start?

"Delaney." I seem only to be capable of repeating her name at this point. A comfort to the chaos in my mind. "I needed to talk to you. I want to talk to you."

A few pavement stones separate the two of us, and despite how much I want to break the distance, I know it's the one thing we need between us to have any sort of productivity in this conversation.

She folds her arms across her chest. Impatience is plastered all over her face—although she's also found refuge in the pavement, I know she wants to listen.

I nervously clear my throat, and right before I'm about to speak, she juts in. "I thought you said you wanted nothing to do with me, huh?" She steps forward. "I tried explaining everything to you, Warren. I *begged* you to listen to me. And you didn't bother to hear me out. So, why should I give you that chance now?"

She leaves me at a loss—a feeling I hardly find comfort in. I'd rehearsed what I wanted to say on the plane the best I could. Hell, I had 10 hours to do just that. But now that I'm here, now that she's standing in front of me, I'm drawing a blank. I can't process a single thought.

"You know what?" She shakes her head and throws her arms up in frustration, visibly fed up with my silence. "I'm over this. I'm done."

It takes her turning on her heel, ready to make another run for it for finally my sense to kick back in. Instinctively, I take a step forward and clutch onto her wrist, spinning her back around and pulling her in.

"No," I speak, peering down at her—into those perfect brown eyes that could get me to do absolutely anything she wanted. Ones that now kill me as I realize that I'm the reason for the tears escaping them and falling down her cheeks. "Please, Delaney...I just..."

It's a pitiful attempt at conveying my feelings, but as the water starts to well up in my own eyes, it's as if hers turn dry—a deep-rooted sense of anger, betrayal festering beneath. "Now you show emotion, Warren?" She roughly pulls back from my grasp, leaving my arm hovering. "Now you shed a tear for me? Save it," she scoffs. "You didn't need to come all the way here to put on this show."

"Show?" I have to shake my head to even remotely process the word. "Delaney...no. Is that why you think I'm here? Because you bought the team?"

"That's what you said at dinner, isn't it? So, you tell me."

"Well, I'm assuming then you're here to speak about the new owner."

"That's exactly why I'm here."

I'm reminded of Hank and I's less than amicable exchange at the dinner table, where my words, yet again, hardly encapsulated their true meaning.

"Delaney." My voice comes out tired and weak. I can hardly think straight any longer. "What I said was true. I'm here to speak to the owner...but not because I want to talk about the team. Fuck, Delaney, I just left them all behind because the only thing I can think about is you."

"Convenient timing." She stares at me with her brows raised. "You can't stop thinking about me and come running when you get the letter, is that it? Oh, and thanks for responding, by the way."

"I was already packing my things to come see you before I knew about any of this...before I even read your letter." I sigh softly, holding her gaze. "I was about to leave for the airport when Alf came barging at my door. I swear."

She swallows faintly, her brows softening ever so slightly as she hugs herself. Unlike the last time we had a heart-to-heart outside, this time, she's not hugging herself for warmth. It's for comfort.

"You were already coming?" Her voice is full of reluctance. "Why? Why now?"

I can't help but reach for both of her wrists, trying to ignore the pit that rises in my stomach as I notice they're bare, and that bracelet she once loved enough to wear every single day is nowhere to be seen.

She pulls her arms away ever so slightly, and I instinctively reach for her face instead. Her sweet face was the one I could kiss all day if she only gave me the chance.

"Delaney." I can't help but brush my thumb along her soft cheek before running my hand through her hair.

God, how did I fumble this so hard?

I hate myself right now.

Own up.

Tell her truth.

This is your chance, Warren.

This is your *dream.*

"You have two minutes." Her voice is a whisper, and she's refusing to look at me anymore as she rapidly blinks away the emotion welling up in her eyes.

I'm grateful she's given me that because all I need is three seconds to utter three simple words.

"I love you," I admit, and as the words escape my mouth, I start to question how I had such a hard time saying them before.

Maybe, and just maybe, it's because these words never made sense before her. Delaney is the one person who taught me what these three words mean. And now that I'm here, saying them, I'm assured that they've only ever been meant to leave my lips for her.

"I'm so in love with you, Delaney. Hell, I love you more than I ever thought was possible."

Her eyes widen as she looks up at me. Those magnificent doe eyes I knew would occupy their own space in my mind from the day I met her.

Tell her, Warren. A voice haunts my thoughts. *Don't hold back.*

"I loved you from the day I met you, Delaney. When you stumbled onto the field and fell to the floor, it felt like my world came crashing down with you."

I can feel my lips turn up at the corners as I speak, and hers mirror my own, her cheeks turning that adorable rosy shade of pink.

Keep going.

"I loved you even when you thought I hated you when in reality, the only thing I hated was how badly you had your claws into me. You consumed my world. My thoughts. My space. Literally..." I shake my head with a soft grin, pushing a loose curl out of her face. "I couldn't stand to be away from you."

"You can't just do this, Warren..." She closes herself off, shaking her head. She's so quiet that I have to lean my own head down to hear her. "I don't know what you want me to say...what do I say to all of this?"

"You say nothing, love. You let me explain. You let me tell you all of the things you deserve to hear."

"Like what?"

"Like the real reason why I invited you to my mum's. It wasn't just to stop you from working." *Sure, that was partially a factor.* "But it was because I wanted you close. I *needed* you close."

She sucks in a faint breath, ready to speak, but I cut her short.

"Or how about the choice to have your office overlook the field, huh? Do you think that was a coincidence? Or the way I turned down so many of your ideas, time after time? It was all on purpose. I needed reasons, Delaney. Reasons."

Her voice is soft when she speaks. "Reasons for what?"

I rest a finger under her chin and gently tilt her head up to look at me, my eyes grazing over her lips for a brief moment. "Reasons to rationalize why I couldn't fall anymore in love with you."

She nervously pauses, still holding her arms across her chest, refusing to give me anything. "And did you find any?"

"Not a damn one."

For a split second, I see a hint of my Delaney. My heart. My *sunshine*. She's in there. She's coming back to me, and I refuse to stop now.

"But I continued fighting it. I had to. I needed to find a

reason, an easy excuse, but then...London happened. And after that, I knew the fight was over."

I confidently run both of my hands alongside her face, leaning in ever so slightly. I wish I could kiss her. I want it more than anything.

"I didn't think it was possible to fall more in love with the city until I fell in love with you in it."

I let my eyes linger on her lips for a moment longer before reluctantly pulling back. I have to. I need to look her right in the eyes as I tell her the rest of what's on my chest.

"So, you can be mad at me, Delaney. Hell, I deserve it. I was a complete twat. But you need to know one thing to be true. You weren't the only one who found a piece of themselves in Crawley. Because Crawley...led me to you. So, I found a piece of myself, too." I let out a shaky breath. I hadn't realized my hands were quivering ever so slightly as they brush over her skin.

"And now that you're gone, it's not the same. So, no, I didn't just come here to tell you I love you. I came here to ask you to come back with me. All those things you said made Crawley special in your letter, well, they're not special without you. You are the magic. You are *our* missing piece, Delaney. I couldn't care less about your offer. All I care about is what your answer is to mine."

I pause.

"Come back with me, baby. Not just for me...but for the team. We need you. We miss you. We love—"

Delaney is quick to launch herself forward, wrapping her arms around my neck and planting her lips against mine. And just like that, I'm convinced there's no greater feeling than the one I feel right now.

The feeling of having her back in my arms.

I instantly embrace her kiss, wrapping my arms around her waist and pulling her in as close as possible.

"And I thought you were terrible at apologies," she whispers into the kiss. There's an abundantly devious yet irresistible smirk on her face as she pulls back and rests her nose against mine. "I guess I was wrong."

"Wait." I break away from her despite how much it's killing me. "There's more."

She shoots me a playful look of impatience. "What more do you have to say, Warren?" That sparkle in her eye just about makes me melt. "Haven't you said it all?"

I flash her a faint smile, toying with my back pocket. "It's not what I have to say..." I reach for the items that I've kept safely in my possession since I left Crawley. "It's what I have to give you."

Reaching for her wrist and bringing it up to my chest, I reveal the "I love London" bracelet from my pocket—the one that matches the bracelet on my own wrist as I pull up my sleeves to reveal it.

Her mouth drops, before her eyes shoot up and find clarity in mine. "You..."

"Can I?" I don't allow her to finish, gesturing to slip it over her wrist.

She bites down on her lower lip, suppressing a smile before nodding and holding her hand out to me.

Now, I'm the one placing this rubber bracelet onto her dainty wrist, bringing her hand up my lips the second it's secure in place.

"Promise me we'll never take them off again?" She grins softly before pulling me in tight.

"I promise, *sunshine*." I plant a kiss on the side of her head before wrapping my own arms around her again.

And just like that, we fall right back into where we left off. Kissing on the sidewalks. Entangled in each other's arms. Happy.

In love.

But before I can allow myself to bask in the bliss for a second longer, I can't help but seek clarity in the uncertainty that remains.

"Does this mean you'll come back?" I rest my lips against the top of her head before pulling back just enough to look down at her.

Now, she gently runs her hand along my face. "I'm coming home, Warren."

A full grin spreads across my lips at her use of the word *home*. I can't help but lift her into the air, prompting her to burst into giggles as her legs wrap around my waist. "I don't think I've ever seen you this happy," she teases, brushing her nose against mine.

"If you think I'm thrilled right now, the lads are going to lose it."

"Really?" She laughs. "They've missed me?"

"Of course, they have," I roll my eyes. "They were boycotting practice because of you. They were about ready to quit because of how much of an arse I was being."

She throws her head back in laughter, making my heart swell at the sound of it before she securely plants her feet back into the ground. "You've always been a bit of an arse, Coach." A wink escapes her sweet eyes. "But the fact that I'm in love with you, too, makes up for it."

#Thirty

DELANEY

"BLUE WITH GREEN HUES, or green with blue hues?" I intricately assess Warren's eyes as I rest on top of his desk, blocking him from getting through any of his paperwork. I lean back on the palms of my hands, tilting my head in thought. "Now, *that* is the question."

He smirks, shooting me a devious stare before he grabs my waist, slides me off the desk, and firmly places me in his lap. "Beautiful and curious, or curious and beautiful?" He murmurs into my ear, nibbling against my skin gently, sending shivers down my spine. "Now, *that*..." He kisses down my neck, reaching my collarbone. "Is the question."

This is how it's been. For days on end. Finding silly excuses to get close to one another and stall our way back into reality.

We'd caught the first flight back to London as soon as I'd packed up my things. My parents hadn't tried to stop me—and frankly, I'm not surprised. After my outburst at Thanksgiving, it'd become clear to them that I wouldn't keep squeezing into the mold they'd created for me. I was starting my own journey—one that belonged in the place I was always meant to be my home, with the people who I'll always call family.

Warren opted to keep our arrival back a secret, leaving ample opportunity for one-on-one time as we gear up for today.

The big day.

The day when we can finally stop hiding in the shadows and, for once, just be us.

"You're stalling." I lean my head back as Warren's lips find their way to my chest, tugging away at the fabric with his teeth.

"And do you have a problem with that?" He looks up at me inquisitively—and that's when I realize it.

It's not blue with green hues or green with blue hues.

It's sheer mischief in those eyes.

I'm in love.

He leans up and kisses my lips before I can respond, tugging on my bottom lip slightly.

"The boys are waiting." It's so hard to break away from his embrace. "I want to see them."

"Oh, so I'm not enough?" He coyly remarks, though there's a hint of playfulness in his tone.

"You've had me all to yourself for days, Coach." I push against his chest with a wink before hopping off his lap. "Now it's time to share."

"Fuck that." He stands up, wrapping his arms around my waist from behind and pulling me back into him. "I'm not sharing. You're all mine, Delaney."

"And you can remind me of that later." I turn around and plant a kiss on the tip of his nose, my hand brushing over the midriff of his trousers before I pull away and walk towards the door. "You coming?"

He sucks in a breath. "I will be tonight."

WARREN

"And then I said to her, how would you like a tour of my down under?"

The team's laughter echoes all the way down the tunnel as Delaney and I make our way onto the field.

"Get it? Down under? 'Cause she was Australian!"

"The jokes are subpar as always, Green." Delaney is the first to speak as we step over to them, causing the boys to whirl their heads around at the sound of her voice. "Glad to know I haven't missed out on much."

The lads freeze in place for a moment as they take in the sight in front of them. I can't blame them—Delaney has a way of demanding every ounce of your attention.

"*Miss me?*"

With those two words, they burst into a round of cheers and hollers. "Delaney!" They excitedly push their way past me and rush over to her side. "You're back! You came back!"

Now, it's Delaney's laugh that fills the room. "I came back." Her words soften my heart. I still can't believe they're true. "Of course, I came back."

"But why?" Their eyes are full of query, assessing her frame as if they're having a hard time comprehending that she's here. That she's with us again.

"Because." She shrugs with a grin, seemingly assessing her response before responding. "This is my home. This is my team. I mean...if you'll still allow me to be a part of it."

"You were always a part of it, Laney," Wilks smiles, pulling her into a hug.

I can see the moisture well up in her eyes as she hugs him back and then extends her arms out for the rest of them. "Oh, you guys...bring it in."

They do just that as they collectively embrace her into their arms and lift her into the air, spinning her around rather recklessly.

"Ah, I'm gonna get dizzy, you guys!" She squeals as her hair flies about.

"Oi, put her down," I shout over the chaos. "*Now.*"

At my request, the boys seem to take in my presence, releasing

Delaney from their embrace as I take the liberty to secure her wobbling state into my side.

"Well, would you look at that?" Wilks slaps Hart on the chest, gesturing ahead as Delaney now leans her head on my shoulder. "Told you Coach wanted her for himself all along."

Hart smirks. "Who would've thought?"

"So, you two friends again?" Alf now sneaks up from behind us, placing a hand on my shoulder before pulling Delaney in for a hug.

"Alf!" she cries out, wrapping her arms around him.

"Welcome home, Delaney." I hear him whisper, a proud smile lighting up his face. "We're so happy you're back."

I look across the space, seeing nothing but pure joy fixated on everyone's face, their arms wrapped around one another. And that's when the word comes to mind.

Family.

It's a term I use sparingly, for it holds so many meanings. But as I scan the room, it's never felt so simple.

This is my family. These are my boys, and this is the girl I'm going to spend the rest of my life with.

Simple.

I wouldn't have it any other way.

"Right, no more fawning about," I pull my whistle out of my pocket and raise it to my lips. "Let's get this show back on the road, shall we?"

"Ahem." Delaney shoots me a look and pulls the whistle out of my grasp. "Don't we have something important to share, Warren?"

I furrow my brows before it dawns on me. "Right." I look down at her with a gentle smile. "We do have some good news to share with you all."

I can't help but notice the wandering eyes in front of me—all of which hone in on Delaney's stomach before they peer back up into our eyes with sheer excitement.

Oh no.

Here it comes.

"Coach!" Wilks is the first to speak with a look of pure shock, a hand dramatically placed over his chest. "You dirty devil! We didn't think you had it in you."

And there it is.

Some things never change.

I look down at Delaney, watching as the realization comes over her. She frantically shakes her head, waving her hands in front of her face. "Um, excuse me? I'm not pregnant! Don't you all know not to ever to assume that?"

Their smiles fade into sheepish nods, forcing me to suppress a laugh as I squeeze her waist proudly.

"Never mind the news now." She blows the whistle herself. "You've all earned yourself some drills. Get on with it!"

The lads jolt up in surprise, dispersing themselves onto the field as they begin their warm-up drills. It's evident Delaney is proud of herself, too, as she meets my eyes.

"What are you smirking about over there?" She places her hands on her hips expectantly.

I lean down, whispering into her ear. "Just that I can't wait to change that one day."

Her cheeks turn bright red as she playfully smacks my chest, rolling her eyes until she redirects her attention back onto the field.

A moment of silence passes between us as we observe the team before she speaks up. "So..." She peers up at me. "How does it feel?"

I raise a brow in question. "How does what feel?"

"Being the owner of Crawfield Football Club."

The revelation still hasn't sunk in. I wanted to deny her offer. Her *very* generous offer. It didn't feel right, taking something so grand from her. Especially when I knew just how much this team means to her, as it does to me.

So, despite her insistence and, most of all, persistence, we found a compromise.

50/50.

Delaney Matthews and Warren Park—co-owners of Crawfield Football Club.

From the moment I first walked into this stadium, I've thought of this team as being mine. But now, as I look at her by my side, I know it was always meant to be *ours*.

I nudge her playfully. "I could ask you the same thing.

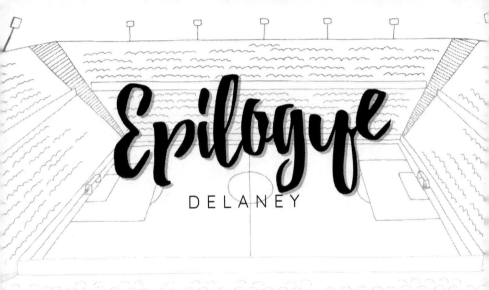

Epilogue

DELANEY

EIGHTEEN MONTHS LATER

"GET STUCK IN THERE, lads! C'mon! We've got two minutes left. You can do this."

"Take it easy, Parker." Alf places a hand on Warren's shoulder. "We've got this in the bag."

Warren starts to bite along the tips of his nails, watching the field intently—the nerves of the final game of the season are visibly eating away at him despite the fact that this has been Crawfield's best season to date. The team has held their own in the top three, fighting against some of the best in the league.

"See that, girls?" I peer over at the PR interns to my right. "*That* is perfect social media content. Crawfield Football Club..." I raise my hands theatrically into the air. "We'll leave you biting your nails for ninety minutes of high-intensity football fun."

They chuckle, flashing a few pictures of Warren until he flashes me an unamused stare.

"What?" I grin, striding my way over to his side. "Haven't you learned to put up with this by now?"

He kisses my cheek tenderly—the only time he'll ever pull his eyes away from a game. "You're not someone that has to get 'put up' with." He smirks. "Take all the pictures you want. I want to look back on them. I want to add them to the scrapbook."

My heart softens at the thought. After discovering Gramps' scrapbook back in Houston, Warren and I decided to start making one of our own.

Over the past eighteen months, we've filled the album with Crawfield's accomplishments and all the milestones Warren and I have reached together.

Officially signing for joint ownership of Crawfield.

Moving in together.

Expanding not only the team...but *our family*.

Warren gently places a careful hand on my swollen bump, brushing his thumb over it. I'm 32 weeks pregnant now—he followed through on his word, that's for sure.

I smile down at his hand and place mine on top of it before he brushes a loose strand of hair out of my face, prompting me to peer up into his eyes.

"I love you—"

The whistle blows, signifying that the game is over, and he releases his careful touch.

He plants a final kiss on my cheek before racing out onto the field, engulfing the team in his embrace as they all jump into the air and cheer ecstatically. And just like that, he's back to being wrapped up in his favorite world. There's nothing quite like seeing him this happy—he's a kid at heart, and these are his boys.

Like the chaos on the field, the entire stadium has erupted in roars and cheers. Yup, we've had a full house tonight—and every night this season.

I rest my hand on my stomach as I look out at the PR team I've built myself, who, one by one, are snapping pictures of the celebration and capturing all angles, just like I'd trained them to.

"C'mon over, Delaney!" It's Wilks that prompts me to join them. "This is baby Parks' first season high!"

I jog my way over—as fast as someone in their third trimester can—and join in on their embrace. The boys were beyond enthused when Warren and I broke the news. They've got their bets placed on a girl, but despite leaving the gender a secret until the baby is born, I've got a heck of a feeling they've got a future teammate coming.

They carefully engulf me in their arms as soon as I reach them, patting me on the back or wrapping me into hugs until Wilks reaches over and places a hand on my pregnant belly. "Hey, the baby gave us good luck."

Warren glares in his direction, prompting Wilks to retract his hand almost immediately. "Get your own girl, Wilks." His voice is serious, quieting the boys for a brief moment until he flashes a playful smirk. "I'm kidding."

The team bursts back into shouts and celebrations, laughing, smiling, jumping up and down together, yet right before they're about to disperse down the tunnel, I stop them.

"Wait!" I call out, halting them in place. "I want to take a group picture." I glance over at Warren with a smile. "For the scrapbook."

The boys all agreed to my request, nodding as they stood in formation in the middle of the field.

"Make sure you're standing in front of the tunnel," I direct them. "There's someone I need to get in the shot."

My eyes gravitate towards the photo of Gramps that still remains above the tunnel.

But now, I've added a slight addition. A saying. One that reads:

"Ira Matthews: Always believed in The Underdog."

I flash the picture to capture their smiling faces, and right before I'm about to put my camera away, Warren reaches an arm out towards me and calls out.

"Hey! You're on this team, too. Remember?"

The boys chime in agreement. "Yeah, join us, Delaney!" Green shouts out excitedly.

"Unless you're too cool for us now," Hart adds, prompting me to shake my head in laughter.

I hand my camera over to one of my PR interns. "Mind if you take this?"

She smiles, nodding agreeably.

I join the photo, standing right beside Warren as he tucks me into his arm.

"Happy?" I smile up at him.

"I don't think I could be any more."

ACKNOWLEDGMENTS

Writing this book felt like an extension of me, and my roots. As a first generation Canadian, not only was I raised in a British household obsessed with football, but I ended up playing it competitively myself for most of my youth. Because of that, I always knew that when I opted to write a sports romance, nothing would quite compare to the sport that consumed a major portion of my life.

Writing 'The Underdog' was incredibly special to me. Not only did it transport me back into my sports days, but it reminded me of my family. Ira Matthews, although a fictional character in nature, is real in my heart. Why? Because he's inspired by one of the most amazing men in my life, my grandfather.

I've been entirely blessed to have experienced a love like Delaney did in this novel, and I'm thankful to have been given the opportunity to share that kind of love with you. You are somebody's sunshine—whether you realize it or not, never forget that.

Welcome to the journey that is the Crawfield Football Club Series. Are you ready for what's next?

Also By...

KATE LAUREN

To You, Iyla

A Recipe FOR Disaster

a novel

ABOUT THE AUTHOR

Kate Lauren is a "certified fangirl" whose passions include writing contemporary romance novels, using suggestive innuendos any chance she can, and subliminally tying Taylor Swift song titles into her books.

Based out of Toronto, Canada, when Kate's not daydreaming about which fictional character she'll create next, you'll find her with her friends, family and husband—or nose-deep in her next novel.

Printed in Great Britain
by Amazon